MARIA FRANKLAND

Left Hanging

What price would you pay to save your marriage?

AUTONOMY

PRESS

Dedicated to those who strive to keep up appearances.

Join my 'Keep in Touch' list!

If you'd like to be kept in the loop about new books and special offers, join my 'keep in touch list' by visiting www.autonomypress.co.uk.

You will receive a free book as a thank you for joining!

Prologue

Russ looks behind to make sure his 'friend' is still following. They tread silently along the thick carpet towards the room he booked that morning.

They only met an hour ago – but it's long enough to be certain about what will soon take place. They've been planning it for over a week. Building tension. Creating anticipation. Russ slides the key card into the lock and smiles as he glances back at his companion again.

The door closes softly behind them. It's the other man's turn to smile as Russell empties the contents of his holdall onto the bed.

Chapter 1

Kerry

"Ed. Put the BBC on. Listen to this!" I stare at the TV as I call to my husband, who is in the next room. The front of Parkside, half a mile away, flashes onto the screen. The beautiful hotel we married in six years ago is cordoned off and is swarming with police. "They've found a man's body. He's hung himself, apparently. Give it a rest, you two." I glance at the twins, fighting over a truck. "Gosh, he was only in his thirties. Gives me the creeps." I lower my voice. I'm talking to myself, as usual.

Ed isn't listening. He never is. There was a time when he'd have jumped up and come through when I called him. There was even a time when he'd have preferred to sit in here with me. Most of the time he's in his own bloody world. I rise from the low sofa in the 'playroom,' past my squabbling five-year-olds, and poke my head into the lounge. It's the only room in the house, apart from our bedroom, with any semblance of order – that's because the twins aren't allowed in. "Are you watching the news?"

Ed momentarily raises his quiet brown eyes from his computer. The early evening sunset floods through the bay window, illuminating the thinning hair on the top of his head. He used to get upset about this loss, but he's learning to accept it.

1

"Why? Should I be?"

I really miss my husband. We've grown so far apart since the twins were born and the gulf widens all the time. I sit beside him and point the remote at the TV. "Oh, it's finished. The hotel we got married in. A man's hung himself there." I watch for a flicker of a reaction – that he's at least a bit interested in something I'm telling him. "He was in one of the rooms." That should get his attention. He doesn't realise what I know about his penchant for hotel rooms.

"Oh. Right." His voice is monotone, and his gaze returns to the computer screen.

"Maybe we know him?"

"Maybe we know who?"

"You never listen anymore Ed. What is wrong with you?"

"I'm sorry love. I need to get this finished." He reaches for the remote and clicks the TV off again. "I'll be with you soon. Promise. I'll bath the boys and read them a story if you like. Give you half an hour to yourself."

"I want time with *you*, Ed. Why don't we ask your mum to come and sit with the boys after they've gone to bed?" I brighten at the thought, already mentally planning my outfit. "We've not eaten yet. We could go to that new restaurant we drove past last week. We've not had a night out together for ages."

"Sorry love. I'm whacked."

Whilst he's upstairs bathing the boys, I set about clearing their carnage. We bought our beautiful home whilst I was pregnant with them and I'd never felt happier. But from being somewhere relaxing and wonderful, home has become a place of work. I have progressed from being a newlywed, then a radiant new mother, into a nag and a referee. Something must give. I wish Ed had agreed with my suggestion of going out. I will still try to make our evening special though.

We're becoming like housemates. Apart from once a week - missionary position, usually on a Saturday - and that's if I'm lucky these days. Life still goes on around us, but it feels as though we don't join in anymore. As the earlier news report showed, life is short; we can *never* know what's around the corner.

"They're ready for you." Ed stretches his arms above his head and yawns as he walks into the kitchen towards the fridge. "I think that's earned me a beer. Smells good in here. What are you making?"

"It's the herby veg in the oven that you can smell, and I've got us both a nice steak to go with it." I stand behind him at the fridge, putting my arms around his waist and kissing the back of his neck. It's as far as I can reach.

"Mummy!"

"I think you're wanted." He laughs as he swings around to face me. "I'll check the veg and get some pepper sauce on the go. I'm starving."

"Open a bottle of red too." I walk towards the door. It's good that he's having a little drink. Maybe it will relax him a bit.

The twins are in their own rooms now and they're sleeping better than they were when they shared. However, George is still catapulting around his room when I go in.

"Sleep time, buster."

"But I'm not tired Mummy."

"You will be when you lie down. You need all your energy for swimming tomorrow."

I finally concede by allowing him to lie in his bed with his nightlight on and a book. I kiss his cheek, then go to see Alex. He's nearly asleep with his arms around his sheep. "Night-night sweetie pie." I kiss the top of his head, then head for the bathroom.

I hate the bathroom mirror. The lighting is so unflattering. God, I look a mess today! No wonder Ed hardly looks at me anymore. I drag a comb through my mop, regretting for the zillionth time having it cut shorter, then pull my make-up bag from the shelf for some urgent rectification. Next, I swap my jeans for a skirt from the top of the ironing pile. I hurry downstairs in case Ed's got side-tracked from watching the dinner.

I'm pleased to find he's still on it. He's got the steaks in the pan and two large glasses of red are waiting on the table. I take a large sip from one then set about finding some candles.

"Candles! What do we want candles for?" He laughs as I light them. "Are we planning a power cut?"

"Because we're not just parents." I give him what I hope is a disparaging look. "The boys are in bed and we're having a lovely Saturday evening together."

He turns back to the steaks, saying nothing. He hasn't noticed my skirt, my makeup or anything. He never does. He used to compliment me all the time.

"I wonder who the man is." I stab at my steak, disappointed it's overdone. I won't say anything though.

"What man?"

"The one they found at our hotel."

"Kerry! Do we have to talk about that whilst we're eating?"

"S'pose not." I take another sip of wine. He's right. It's not really the time or the place to discuss someone who's topped themselves. I look at my husband in the candlelight. He's never known how handsome he is with his angular features and long eyelashes framing his eyes. The boys have got his eyes too, which I'm glad about. Mine are piggy and deep set. My self-confidence is diminishing all the time. I guess it comes from having a husband who doesn't notice me anymore.

"Stop staring at me." He laughs, drinking his wine too. "You're making me nervous."

"I love you." I put my fork down and reach for his hand.

"You too. Now let me eat my dinner." He pulls his hand away and picks his knife up.

He always used to say I love you too. Now it's just you too. And he *never* says it first.

We spend the rest of the meal talking about the boys. Then he snaps the big light on. "I'll load the dishwasher. You chill for a bit."

"Can't we chill together?" *God, he's become hard work.* "The dishwasher can wait, can't it?"

"Might as well get it done."

"I'll go and park my arse on the sofa then. Wait for you."

I click the TV on as I pass it. The local news is on again and they're repeating the story about the man at our hotel. I don't normally take much notice of the news, but this time I do as they've added CCTV of him entering the hotel through revolving doors. It's grainy, and the image hasn't been captured face on.

"I don't think I'll be late to bed tonight." Ed flops beside me on the sofa. "Shall we put a film on?"

"Can't we spend some time together?" I snuggle into him.

"We are doing. Choose your film. Anything you like." He clicks the TV onto Netflix, then hands the remote to me.

I settle on *Passenger*. It's got everything. Romance for me and sci-fi for him. We went to see it at the cinema together. It was in its last week, so we had the whole cinema to ourselves. We'd even sat in the back row. Maybe the film will draw us closer. Ed's become so distant. I just want him back.

I'm pleased when he puts his arm around me as we watch the film. I sip at my second glass of wine, feeling a little more content with the warmth and the weight of his arm. Thirty minutes in, his breathing slows, and I realise I'm watching the film alone.

"Ed." I shake him before he becomes too far gone. "Ed. Come on. Let's go to bed."

"Um. Yes. OK love." He stretches and gets to his feet. "You go up.

I'll turn off and lock up."

I'm sick of him calling me 'love' all the time. It makes me feel a hundred years old. Taking the rest of the wine with me, I head up the first flight of stairs to check on the boys. I switch off George's night light and slide the book from under his arm. I lightly kiss his forehead. Alex has kicked his duvet off, so I cover him back up and kiss him too. I climb the next flight of steps to our room, the other room of the house that's usually a child-free zone. Unless we end up with one or both boys in our bed.

It's my favourite room in the house. All cream and silver with a chandelier above the bed and mirrored wardrobes – I wanted a 'boudoir' feel to it. I pull my sexiest nightie from the drawer beside my bed. It's the red, slinky number Ed bought me before I became pregnant. It's snug on me now, so I keep my stomach sucked in. I've started the gym again – I desperately want to drop a dress size. Maybe Ed will fancy me again.

His expression is hard to read when he walks into our bedroom. "What are you wearing that for?"

"You know. I thought…"

"Sorry love. I'm knackered." He sits on the edge of the bed and starts unbuttoning his shirt.

"But it's Saturday." I sink onto the bed, reaching over to touch his shoulder. "What's happening to us Ed?"

"Nothing love. You saw me downstairs. I can hardly keep my eyes open."

"You need to be at home more." I tug my nightie back over my head, hoping that the sight of me naked in the mirrored wardrobes might just do something for him. He doesn't look up but peels his socks off instead. "Through the week, I mean. You're never here. It's no wonder you're always tired."

"There's always tomorrow morning."

I'm stalling before putting my PJ's on, wanting him to look at me.
"What for?"

"You know."

"I'll just lock the boys in their rooms, shall I?"

Ed sighs and pads across the bedroom to the en-suite, closing the door behind him. I sigh too and swing my legs into bed. This has to change. I will make sure it does. No matter what it takes, I will draw him back to me. Make him want me again.

Chapter 2

Ed

I tilt my phone screen towards me in the semi darkness. It's not even seven, and the house is still shrouded in silence, yet Kerry is kissing my shoulders and pawing at my lower naval. She's taken her pyjamas off.

"Kerry, it's a bit early." I want her to get off me. Most blokes are open all hours. I feel guilty, but I don't know how much longer I can do this.

"You said in the morning. The boys aren't awake yet."

She's driving me mad. I'm tired, I've got stuff on my mind and she won't leave me alone. I don't think my 'little man' would be even up to the job at the moment, the way I'm feeling, and I will not put him to the test. I shuffle away from Kerry's advances and slide my legs out of bed until my feet connect with the soft carpet. "I'm off to make some coffee. Do you want one?"

"I don't believe this." She sits up on her pillows, folds her arms across her boobs and scowls at me. "What the hell is wrong with you?"

"I'm not in the mood love. I'm sorry."

"Why? Don't you fancy me anymore?" Her expression is a cross between fury and misery. My guilt-ometer shoots to the top of its range.

I must pause too long because she shrieks at me. "You don't, do you?"

"Course I do. Give over Kerry."

"Mummy!"

"I'll go. You stay there. Read for a bit or something. I'll bring you a coffee up." That was probably the wrong thing to say. Read for a bit. Something hits the door with a bang as I'm halfway down the stairs. Probably her book.

Kerry's bustling around the kitchen, tugging towels from the dryer and stuffing them into the boys' swimming bags.

"He's got more Co-Co Pops than me!"

"He's sitting in my place!"

"I don't want to go swimming. I want to watch *Ben 10!*"

"You've given me the wrong cup."

"Be quiet and eat your breakfast. Both of you."The house is a mess. I sit amongst the chaos, looking forward to the solitude of the gym. How did my life turn into this?

Despite their protestations, Kerry steers the boys into the women's changing rooms whilst I head for the men's. We alternate who takes the boys swimming and who gets gym time every Sunday. We do the same on a Saturday, but it's soft play or the park for the boys, depending on the weather. We're a good team, Kerry and I. As parents anyway.

I'm feeling wired this morning, so I'm glad to get onto the treadmill to warm up before I hit the weights. I take more time, as Carl is in this morning, so we have a catch up as we run side-by-side. He's talking diet, protein shakes and personal bests. He's single and I envy him. Yet I'm in as good a shape as he is, even though he gets tons of time to himself. I'd be here even more if I could be. But, I do weights at home and run a fair bit when I can't get a gym session in.

The weights area is a bit of a man-only zone. There's the odd female body builder but mainly it's blokes, flexing their biceps, competing with who can lift the most, and checking each other out. Carl and I work together today, taking it in turns to lift, whilst the other counts reps. I feel liberated, and an hour passes before I know it.

I fire a text to Kerry from the changing room. *Are you done yet? I'm in the changing room so will be a while yet.*

Boys a nightmare. I'll take them for a drink and something to eat in the bar. x

Good stuff. I've time for a quick swim then. x

She doesn't reply. I think she's still pissed off with me. I don't blame her, really. I'm pissed off with me! Though I feel more like a *man* this morning after the gym. But I'm not feeling it with Kerry anymore. I'm confused with the entire thing to be fair.

I don't bother with a swim. I nestle down into the heat of the jacuzzi instead. There's another three men in there. We all absently stare towards the swimming pool, packed with Sunday morning families. I try to zone out from the noise. I much prefer coming here in the evening when all the little darlings are in bed. Two of the men are discussing football. Which player they have sold to where, and for how much. Yawn. I've never been into football myself. I close my eyes and feel the heat and the bubbles instead. My 'little man' becomes a 'big man' as the bubbles hit the spot. Nothing wrong with my engineering. It's just not working with Kerry. Maybe we should go our separate ways. I slide myself from the pool, hoping no one notices my emergent bulge as I slip into the steam room.

Carl laughs as I sit beside him. "I don't know. I don't see you for weeks and then we bump into each other twice in one session."

"Sorry mate. I didn't realise it was you. Couldn't see through the steam!" Our knees touch and he quickly moves his away.

"Right. That's me." Carl stands up after a minute.

"Something I said?" I'm disappointed. I'd been looking forward to having more of a chat with him.

"No. I'm melting."

"I'd better make a move myself. The missus will be doing her nut with the boys by now."

"I'm off for a pint in the Old Ball with some of the 'cycle-club' if you fancy joining us."

"Sounds good. I'll see if I can get a pass out!"

I shower and dress, then head towards the noisiest corner of the gym bar. There's crumbs and wrappers everywhere. Kerry looks frazzled.

"Right boys. Clear this mess up." I point at their debris.

Kerry's perched on a stool, engrossed with her phone. She doesn't look at me.

"You OK love?"

"Yep. I'm booking some gym classes for this week. I'll leave Mandy in charge of the shop. I need some me time too."

"I know love. I'm sorry I've been longer than normal."

"You've been ages. What kept you?"

I can see from her expression that she's probably worried in case I've been talking to another woman or something. "I was with Carl. Just talking about training and stuff."

"Oh, right." Her face relaxes into a ghost of a smile. "Well done boys. It's looking tidier. Put those wrappers in the bin."

"I'm off to get a cuppa and a sandwich." I fish around for my wallet.

"Ice-cream!" the twins chorus.

As I wait to be served, last night's paper catches my eye. On the front page is the story Kerry's been banging on about. It looks odd, seeing the hotel Kerry and I became so familiar with around the time

11

of our wedding, surrounded by police and crime tape. A bloke, my age, has killed himself by the sounds of it. The rate of male suicide is well documented nowadays – his wife's probably left him or something. That sort of thing hits us men. Often, we can't, or won't talk about stuff.

"What are your plans for the rest of the day?" I'm strapping George into the back of the Range Rover and Kerry's doing the same with Alex.

"Not a lot. Why? What have you got in mind?"

"Carl's invited me to meet the rest of his cycle club, that's all." I slide into the driver side.

"Cycle club?" Her voice is clipped, suspicious.

"Yes. I'm thinking of joining."

She throws her handbag to the floor in front of her feet. "Cos it's not like you're never at home, anyway, is it?"

"Give it a rest Kez. You can do what you want. If there's something you fancy taking up."

"We're supposed to be married. Not leading separate lives."

"That doesn't mean we're joined at the hip. We've got to do our own thing too."

"But we do nothing together. What's wrong Ed?" I can feel her eyes boring into me. "Is there something I should know?"

"Like what?"

"I don't know. You've changed. What's going on?"

"Nothing. But I'm thirty six, not eighty six. I want to *do* things, live a little."

"You've got responsibilities Ed." She gestures with the top of her head towards the back seat. "Them two. Me. We're supposed to be a family."

"A family. Yeah. Not a ball and chain." I regret the words as soon as they've left my lips.

"A ball and chain? Is that how you see us? Cheers Ed."

"I didn't mean it like that. Look, we're not arguing in front of the boys. I'll make it up to you later, I promise."

"Like you did last night. I'm pissed off Ed."

"Mummy swore. Naughty Mummy."

"I'll drop you off at home love. Then I'm off round to the Old Ball. I shouldn't be too long."

"Great. What a fabulous weekend." She pouts, reminding me of Alex. "Are you sure you're not meeting someone else?"

"I'll pretend I never heard that. There's no need for this shite Kerry."

"Naughty Daddy."

I spot Carl as soon as I walk into the pub.

"Ed! Glad you could make it. I was just saying to Darren here that you're interested in joining the club." Carl gets to his feet as I approach the table.

"All right mate." Darren stands up too and offers his hand.

"I'll just get myself a beer, then you can tell me more." I smile at the other lads around the table. "Can I get anyone else one?"

They're all on water or fruit juice, so it's a cheap round. I spend a pleasant couple of hours amongst them, enjoying feeling normal. Well, free might be a better word. I get sick of having to check in, check out and ask permission for time to myself. I twist my wedding ring around on my finger. It feels like a ball and chain. I look around the others at the table. I'm the only one wearing one. Not for the first time today, I feel a stab of envy.

Chapter 3

Kerry

I t's been a crap weekend. I'm so fed up. I walk towards the school
gate, then press my key fob at the car. Peace. Well, until I get
to the shop anyway and Mandy starts wittering away. I've not
got talking to any of the other mothers this morning. I don't want to
hear about the wonderful 'together' weekends they've spent with their
husbands. Like me, although mostly slimmer, they arrive at school
with wiry lycra-clad legs poking beneath long coats, ready for a gym
session, which is where I'm heading once I've opened the shop.

I try to count my blessings. I've got an amazing manager in Mandy.
I can usually grab a bit of me time, especially earlier in the week when
the shop's quieter. My little boutique is doing so well, I'm about to
open a second one. The online sales have really taken off too. I'll be
matching Ed's consultant dentist salary before long if I keep on like
this. I can't grumble about my business, even if it was Ed bankrolling
it that got me going. It's a pity the same can't be said for my marriage.
It's always the same though, when one part of your life is going well,
another falls spectacularly apart, or at least in my experience.

"Good weekend?" Mandy looks up from pricing a new range of dresses.
I reach over to feel the fabric, then hold one up. Size 10. I will make it

my mission to be in that dress within the next two months.

"Not bad. You?"

As Mandy turns her attention from dresses to shoes, she blathers on about the latest man she's met online. I hope my eyes aren't glazing over too much and that I'm making the right 'interested' noises in suitable places. As the mother of five-year-olds, I'm an expert in feigning interest where I have none. Finally, there's a pause long enough for me to get a word in edgeways.

"You don't mind holding the fort this morning, do you?" I grab an armful of dresses and slide their hangers onto one of the rails. "I could do with going to the gym. I've not had a minute to myself this weekend."

"How are those gorgeous boys?" Mandy smiles. "I bet they keep you on your toes."

"And some." I smile back. "They keep me on *my* toes. As for Ed – he still lives the life of Riley."

"What do you mean?"

"Oh nothing. Really. Sorry. Just sounding off." I regret my words immediately. Like I really want anyone to know my marriage might be in trouble. Although sometimes, I feel that if I don't talk to someone, I might explode. Mandy's not the right person though. She's a bit of a gossip.

I've been coming to this gym for a few months now – long enough to make a few friends. With the 'in-crowd' too, it seems. All it took was one of them clocking the Range Rover and, of course, I give them a small discount in the boutique. It's not who you are – more what you've got here. But they're a decent enough bunch and it's lovely to have some female conversation after a weekend with the boys.

"The builders are a nightmare," Claire's moaning as she peels her clothes off. "There's dust everywhere."

"It was the same for us when we had our extension for the boys' playroom and the utility," I smile. "Though well worth it. All that extra space. Have you decided on your blinds yet?"

"The designer's given me some samples." She tugs her trainers on. "I've brought them with me. Thought I'd bring it to the committee!"

"Good thinking." I glance at the clock. "Come on, we're late! We'll have a look afterwards, over coffee."

You know you're one of the 'in-crowd' when you've had a step and your weights put out by one of the others ahead of your arrival. Mine and Claire's steps wait for us, in our usual spots.

"Morning ladies," smiles the instructor. "Don't worry, you've only missed the warm-up."

We spend the next hour copying every move she makes, like lemmings. I push myself harder today. I've got to sort myself out. I want my husband to look at me like he used to.

"I'll go up and order coffee," I announce, having been the first to blow dry my short hair. Now I've got the boys, I've become amazingly fast at getting ready. "Is everyone having their usual?"

We've all learnt each other's requirements. No sugar. Skinny milk. Latte for me. Americano for Claire. Green tea for Alison. Normal tea (weak) for Jo and Expresso for Lindsey. Cath's away in the Seychelles and Lorraine has been on some spa weekend with her mother-in-law, so hasn't got herself organised in time for the gym.

By the time the waiter has brought the drinks, the rest of our little group has gathered on our comfy sofas in the best area of the members' lounge. It's as though other members know to leave this spot for us. We're here nearly every morning. On Mondays it's after step aerobics. Tuesday is legs, bums and tums. I can't get here on a Wednesday as I help at school with the readers. Thursday's class is full of the more mature ladies, so I tend to have a swim, and Friday is body conditioning. I do all this, yet still the weight won't shift. I think again of the beautiful deep-red dress in the shop, and I'm determined to do whatever it takes. I must stop drinking wine and eating chocolate. And the kids' leftovers.

"Sophia's had an offer for Oxford. Unconditional." Jo, the oldest of us all, pours her tea and peers through her fringe for our reaction.

"That's amazing, hon. What course has she gone for again?" Alison's dipping her tea bag in and out of her cup.

"Law. Might be handy having a lawyer in our midst. You never know."

Everyone laughs, but my laugh has a hollow edge. "It'll be quiet in your house come September then. You lucky thing." I sip my latte.

"Don't wish their time away." Jo looks thoughtful. "I wish Sophia was little like yours again. It goes so fast." She points to her upper lip.

I laugh as I brush away my latte moustache. I enjoy being sat here with the girls but will have to get back to the shop soon. I've some stock to order for the new place.

Lindsey gestures towards the newspaper rack by the bar. "Have you heard about that man at the Parkside?"

"I got married there." I blush as no one acknowledges my comment, but carry on talking.

"The one who's hung himself?" Claire looks up from scrolling around on her phone.

"Yeah. Although they're not ruling out someone else being involved." Jo leans in towards us all. "Between us and the four walls, Sophia's boyfriend Dan is a porter there. He keeps hearing bits and pieces about it."

"Does anyone know who he is... was?" Claire twirls a strand of her hair around in her fingers.

"I saw the CCTV on the news," I say. "I didn't recognise him. Poor man."

"And his poor family, if he has one," Claire goes on. "They haven't named him yet."

"There's always a delay in suspicious circumstances," Jo says. "Dan says they're studying all the CCTV and testing stuff they took from the room."

"It'll all be procedure." I unwrap the free wafer biscuit we all get with our drinks. I'm the only one of us who has. "When I saw the news, they were saying suicide. They've just got to rule out anything else."

"There's more to it, according to Dan." Jo taps the side of her nose. "You mark my words."

Lindsey laughs. "This is all getting very heavy ladies. Can we change the subject?"

The rest of us laugh. "You started it!"

"Anyway," says Claire, pulling some fabric swatches from her bag. "I need you to gather round. I have some important decisions to make.

"It's for you Kerry." Mandy passes the phone to me, then returns to serving her customer.

"Is that Kerry Huntington-Barnes?"

"Speaking."

"It's Harlow Boys' School here. We were wondering whether you'd been held up?"

"Held up?" I glance at my watch.

"George and Alex haven't been booked into school club. They're waiting for you."

Anger bubbles. "Their dad was supposed to have collected them. I'm really sorry. I'll come now."

"Thank you, Mrs Huntington-Barnes. Alex has got himself a little upset."

"I'm on my way."

I mutter my apologies to Mandy, grab my handbag and stride from the shop. I have got nothing constructive done today. I shouldn't have spent so long at the gym. I'll have to do some admin once I've got the boys to bed. Bloody Ed! He can take charge of them when he gets home so I can get my work done. Fancy forgetting to pick them up.

The boys sit side-by-side in the plush reception area, leafing through their reading books when I arrive. Mrs Wilkes, the school bursar, looks at me as I buzz to be let in. "I'm sorry."

Alex launches himself at me. George doesn't move.

"I'm sorry," I repeat to Mrs Wilkes. "It was my husband's turn."

"It happens," she replies, her expression cold. "Although if you could take steps to prevent it happening in the future, I would be most grateful. I should have finished half an hour ago."

Snooty cow! I think to myself as I press the door release with the boys on either side of me. I would hope for more respect, given the fees we pay. They've just put them up another hundred and twenty quid a week. Obviously, Ed and I must pay double bubble. We tried for a discount being that we were placing *two* children at the school, but they were having none of it when we were initially interviewed. They kept banging on about their waiting list and how easily they could offer the places to another two families if we didn't want to pay full price.

The boys perk up a bit as we arrive home. They've gone from barely speaking to me because I was late, to fighting over a pencil.

I try Ed's mobile, poised to have a go at him. Voicemail. I ring the surgery and get his secretary. "I'll tell him you've called, Mrs Huntington-Barnes. He's popped out. I don't know if he's gone to a meeting. There's nothing in his diary. I'm sorry."

An hour passes. I try his mobile again. This time I leave a message. "You forgot the boys. Not impressed. Ring me. Or even better, come home."

"Mummy?" Alex pauses his enthusiastic spooning of spaghetti hoops into his mouth.

"What sweetie."

"I got sad at school today. Benjamin Hall-Slater was saying unkind things about you."

"About me?" I don't think I want to hear this.

"He said you look like a boy," George interjects between mouthfuls. "Because you've got short hair now."

I thought I'd be making life easier for myself by having my long hair cut off with two small boys to look after and a business to run. I've never stopped regretting it.

"He said his mummy's much prettier than you. She's got long hair."

Charming. I try not to let it bother me but with the state of things with Ed at the moment, I'd be lying if I said it did not rankle.

"And George got told off today by Mrs Richardson."

"Shush Alex." George frowns at him.

"Why did Mrs Richardson tell you off George?"

He stares into his juice cup. I should take comfort from the fact that he looks shame-faced about whatever he is about to tell me.

"Because I didn't want to work with Ben."

"Why not?"

"I don't like him."

Just like his father. To the point. Cutting. "Why don't you like him George?"

"Because he's brown." George is mumbling and still doesn't make eye contact. "*And* he's got two dads."

"What do you mean? *He's got two dads.*"

"He doesn't have a mum. He's got two dads."

"Right boys. I'm not having this. I don't care if he's got purple skin, six dads, and nine mums, that's no reason not to like him. No wonder you're in trouble."

"I'm not in trouble," Alex protests. "George is. Mrs Richardson said she would tell you next time."

"Well, I don't want to hear any more of it. You can't go around saying nasty things about people."

The rest of their meal continues in silence. George looks close to tears. At least there's some sort of conscience acting in there.

As they splash around in the bath, scrapping over a boat, I rub the steam off the bathroom mirror and drag a brush through my strawberry-blonde hair that makes me look like a boy. I'll grow it again. I *do* look like a boy. I'm not wearing any makeup and I'm wearing a trouser suit. I need a shopping trip. An overhaul is called for. I need to bring Ed back to me. I hope I'm still enough for him. That I can be what he wants me to be. Rooted in the pit of my stomach though, is a knowing that we've gone way beyond that.

It's gone eight by the time the boys are settled. Ed isn't back. I try his mobile again. Still off. I try his office. Answerphone. I wander around for a bit, loading the dishwasher and washing machine and trying to tidy up. Really, I'm just moving piles of crap from one place to another. The house is so cluttered since the boys were born. The twice-a-week cleaner does an impressive job, but there's not a lot she can do with all the paraphernalia that five-year-old twins generate.

He must have gone to the gym. I try to quell the rising fury that he's not had the decency to let me know. I have eaten nothing yet, but don't feel hungry. *Sod it.* I march into the kitchen and pour an enormous glass of wine. I don't normally drink on a Monday, but needs must. I fire up my laptop to do a bit of work. I've the contract for the new lease to go through and some ordering of stock to sort out. After half an hour, I admit defeat. The combination of anxiety and wine means

I can't focus. I go on Facebook instead.

Cath's Seychelles pictures come up first followed by a post with Jo waxing lyrical about Sophia's unconditional university offer. Another of my friends is climbing Kilimanjaro as a fundraiser and my younger brother has won some award or other for his company. It's months since I've seen him, he's too taken up with his work – he buries himself in it these days – he's as bad as Ed. I congratulate him, then share the Kilimanjaro post. Just before I'm about to leave, a post pops up on our village chat page that the Parkside Hotel man has now been named.

Russell Lawson, 36, of Kirby Brompton, was found by a staff member who was servicing the room. His body might have been there for up to two days because of a 'do not disturb' sign on the door.

There's the grainy CCTV video of him emerging from the revolving door at the hotel entrance. About a second before him is a group of men and a couple of seconds after, a couple. There's lots of other people dotted around in the foyer, where the camera pans to. They're all pixilated too.

Police have spoken to most of the guests who either checked in or checked out on the Thursday and Friday and have, so far, not found any information to suggest the involvement of anyone else. However, they are not ruling this out, even though the nature of his death seems to suggest suicide. They are urging anyone, who may have seen Mr Lawson in the hours before his death, to come forward with information.

The clock in the hallway chimes the half hour. 9:30 pm. I shiver. The open plan format of this house means it's always chilly, no matter what time of year. I tug Ed's jumper over my head from the chair beside me. It smells of him. I'd give anything not to lose him. For things to be different. I try to ring him again. Voicemail. I sigh in the silence of the house then walk barefoot from my seat at the dining table across to the fridge for more wine. Where the hell is he?

Chapter 4

For a moment, I forget where I am. I turn over on the leather couch in my consulting room and blink against the early morning sun finding its way beneath the blind. Briefly I wonder what I'm doing here, then I notice the empty whiskey bottle on my desk and it all hits me like a punch. Russell is dead. It was him. The picture I saw on the internet last night. Russell. My Russell.

I stagger to the comfy office chair and fire up my PC. My mouth feels like something's died in it. Whilst I'm waiting for the PC, I rinse out my empty whiskey tumbler, fill it with water from the sink in the corner, neck it, then refill it. Next I rummage around in my desk drawer for some paracetamol, ibuprofen, anything. Though it will take more than painkillers to shift even an ounce of the pain I'm feeling at the moment.

News of Russell has now hit the main news channels and there's a video of Davina, his wife, speaking for the cameras. I click on it and swallow my tablets as the stream buffers.

Russell was my life, she begins. *We've been together since we were teenagers and we've grown up with each other. I'm tired of the speculation that my husband would have taken his own life. Russell would not have taken his own life. Never. Life was too precious to him. Me, his daughter, and his own life too.* Her voice cracks. I wondered if it would. She can be hard-faced at times. *What has happened is simply an awful accident, and I urge the locals and the media to respect the memory of my husband. I would also ask for privacy to be given to my daughter and myself so we can grieve in peace.* She dabs at her eyes with a hanky.

I stare at the computer screen long after the video has ended. Russell didn't love Davina anymore. He had been biding his time. Would there have ever been a good time for him to walk out on her and their five-year-old? Probably not. But, like me, Russell knew he could not live a lie forever. I know that too. As much as I love my sons, I shouldn't have had them. They've just drawn me deeper into a situation I should never have been in. I've allowed myself to become part of this fallacy of being a two-point-four children sort of family man. A husband. The sound of my wife's voice is the most irritating sound in the world, and the sight of her naked body repulses me.

I pluck my phone from the pocket of my jacket. It's still on silent from yesterday's meeting. I plug the USB cable in before it dies and turn the ringer on. Thirty two missed calls. Bloody hell. Most of them are from Kerry's mobile or the landline. A couple are from other people. She will kill me.

Sorry love. I type into a text. *I got wasted and slept at the office. I was tired and got started on the whiskey.*

Within minutes it's ringing. No prizes for guessing who it is. Yes, of course it's Kerry. I'm not speaking to her yet. I can't. I turn the ringer off again and place the phone face down on my desk. The surgery phone rings in reception and I listen as the answering machine picks it up.

I type Russell Lawson into Google. There's a ton of local news reports now. All pretty much saying the same thing. They'll only be allowed to report the official release anyway. *Father of one found hanging in hotel room on Saturday. Police appealing to anyone who might have spoken to him in the immediately preceding days and hours to come forwards. Although his death is being treated as a suspected suicide, they haven't yet ruled out the possibility of a third party.*

I am inclined to agree with Davina. There is no way Russ would have killed himself, but what third party involvement could they be talking about? As far as I know, he didn't have an enemy in the world. I need to know exactly what happened.

I flick through to Facebook, onto Russell's page. His cover banner is one of him and Davina, with Eloise swinging between them when she was a little smaller. The sympathy posts have started.

Russell. A true gent. Gone too soon.

Deepest condolences to Davina and Eloise. Thinking of you. RIP Russell.

I cannot believe it. I only saw him last week. Hugs to Davina & Eloise. x

I can't understand why you didn't talk to me Russ. I will always ask myself this. Gonna miss you mate.

Davina has replied to this one. *If you are speculating that my husband took his own life, then please stop it. He wouldn't and he didn't. Leave us to grieve in peace.* It echoes what she said on the local news.

I jump as there's a knock at my door and my secretary, Annie, pokes her head around. "Morning Ed. Can I get you a coffee before your first patient?" She studies me then lets go of the door. It closes softly behind her as she walks into the room. Her gaze sweeps over my coat-come-blanket strewn on the couch, the still-closed blind and the empty whiskey bottle. I'm embarrassed as I realise that it must stink in here.

"You OK?" she asks. "What time did you get here?"

"Cancel my appointments today Annie, please. Apologise for the short notice." I get up and walk towards the window to let some air in. I can hear the phone ringing in reception again. "If that's my wife, tell her I'm not here."

"But I told her that yesterday." Annie is bearing an expression which

I'm unsure is concern or intrigue. Probably a bit of both. "What if she asks where you are?"

"Tell her you don't know. Sorry, Annie. I've got a few things going on right now."

I ease myself into my Audi. I probably shouldn't be driving yet this morning. I drank enough whiskey to sink a small vessel last night.

I'm pleased the Range Rover's not there when I pull into our driveway. She's probably at work or with her yummy-mummy friends at the gym. I tug my briefcase from the back seat and make the short walk towards the porch, the gravel crunching beneath my feet. It's one of those days that once upon a time, I would have felt glad to be alive. The spring air would once have carried a promise but now just offers misery. Russell is dead. I kick my shoes off. They vaguely land on the shoe rack. I put my key in the lock of the inner door. The usual debris from the boys clutters our large hallway. However, the house is silent and I couldn't be more grateful. I need to be on my own to think.

In the kitchen, I pass over the disregarded breakfast dishes and the spent wine bottles to the Jack Daniels bottle on top of the fridge. Though it's not the most sensible beverage at 9.45 am on a Tuesday morning, it's the only thing that will hit the spot. I pour a generous measure, down it, then pour another. I take it with me as I tread the two sets of stairs up to mine and Kerry's bedroom. Our bed hasn't been slept in by the looks of it. She could have made it, which is most unlikely, so she's probably not come to bed for worrying where I was and passed out downstairs. I try to feel guilty, but I'm struggling to feel anything at the moment. Russell is dead.

The warm water runs over my body as I stand in the en-suite, lathering soap onto myself. Months, no years, of trying to live a life that is not mine have resulted in me taking control of myself in the only way I can. Physically. There's not an ounce of fat on me anymore. Every inch of me is sculpted and toned. I might go to the gym again later, if I can get out of here before Kerry and the boys come back. I can't face her. She'll see how I feel in my eyes. How can she not know who I really am and what I've lost?

Without even drying myself, I crawl beneath the bedclothes. They smell faintly of washing powder and Kerry's shampoo. They used to smell of sex. When I was better at pretending.

Chapter 5

<u>Kerry</u>

"Don't forget to come in and sign off those invoices." Mandy's voice echoes through the speakers of the Range Rover. "And there's a delivery at one o'clock that will need two of us."

"I'll do my best Mandy. I've a few things going on at the minute. It may all just have to wait."

"Is everything OK?" Mandy's voice oozes concern in the silence of the car. "Is it anything to do with you having to shoot off yesterday?"

"I can't talk at the moment." I pull into the gym car park beside Jo's new BMW. I'm slightly late for legs, bums and tums, but obviously I'm not going to tell Mandy that. I had to give George the hard word when I dropped him off at school about saying unkind things. The last thing I need is Mrs Richardson calling me in. I've enough going on. As I swipe my card through the entrance barriers, I check my phone yet again. Ed has not tried calling me back. At least I know he's OK. Worry has given way to fury, and the gym is definitely the best place to work it off. Who the hell does he think he is, staying out all night?

"Late again Kerry!" Alison laughs as I hurtle into the gym studio. The warm-up has finished and the class instructor, who must be covering, looks at me as though she's going to throw me out.

"It's OK," Jo says to her over the music. "She's with us."

I enjoy being one of the in crowd. I had to scrap for it at school and before I was married, but here, it has been effortless. I had to go on a big 'gym shop' to ensure my gym outfits were in-keeping with the others. None of the baggy sweatpants and t-shirts you see some of the chubby newbies wearing. It's a bit of a bind having to put makeup on *before* the gym sometimes though.

At the end of the class, the instructor has a word with me. "In future, if you come into the class late, I won't allow you to join. I do not want injuries from people who haven't warmed up properly."

"You try running around after five-year-old twins from six o'clock in the morning," I reply. "If that's not warming up, I don't know what is." But she's not listening. She's talking to someone else. I make a mental note to complain about her hostility on the way out. After all, we customers are the lifeblood of their business.

"You're quiet Kerry." Jo looks at me as we towel down after our showers. "You OK?"

"Yeah. Early morning with the boys, that's all. I'm fine." I don't want to tell them Ed hasn't been home all night. They've all got perfect houses, perfect children, have perfect holidays and very perfect husbands. I've spent my life trying to fit in and now that I do, I'm not going to blow it.

I'm not at the point yet that the rest of them are, where they can just parade around the changing room naked, like peacocks. I keep myself under wraps beneath my towel. I've another dress size to lose. If Ed carries on like this, I won't have any problem anyway. I've totally lost my appetite.

"I'll just be at the mirrors," announces Lindsey, folding her towel into her bag. "Whose is this shampoo? Is it Jo's?" She glances towards the mirrors where Jo is already blow drying her long curly hair.

Alison lets out something between a snort and a laugh. "Jo wouldn't use that stuff! I don't know who would, to be honest. She only uses

Paul Mitchell from the salon."

I look away as a pudgy woman snatches up the bottles, a gym newbie by the looks of her. She looks like she's tumbled out of bed to be here. I make myself a mental note to check out this *Paul Mitchell* shampoo. For when my hair grows back a bit.

The four of us keep stopping and starting the hairdryers to conduct our conversation. Claire's chosen the fabric for her conservatory blinds, which are now on order. She's going to invite us round for afternoon tea to view them when it's all finished. We speculate about Cath's Facebook photos of the Seychelles. Her bikini bare midriff has taken on a rotund appearance, giving rise to the possibility of baby number three. We wonder where Lorraine might be. Nobody has heard from her.

"Maybe she's just *too* relaxed after her spa weekend," Claire suggests.

"We should all go for one." Alison slips her hair through her straighteners.

"A spa weekend?" Jo replaces the hairdryer into its holder. "All of us?"

"That would be amazing," I say. And it would be. It's just what I need.

"Would Ed look after the boys for the whole weekend?" Alison echoes my thoughts.

"I'm sure I could sort something out."

"My turn for coffee." Jo swings her new Mulberry bag onto her shoulder. "Usual ladies?"

I'm about to order Mulberry in for the shops – I can't wait to choose a new one. We collectively glare at a group of newbies that have taken our spot in the bar. We're forced to sit on the hard chairs near the family area instead of our leather sofas near the fire.

Whilst I'm waiting for my skinny latte, I give the boys' school a quick ring to book them into after-school club, then I fire off a text to Mandy to let her know I'll be at the shop within the next couple of hours. I want to speak to Ed before I go to work.

"That man at the Parkside," Alison begins. "My Anthony works with his wife, Davina."

"I feel so sorry for her." Jo slides the tray of drinks onto the table. "Did you see her on the news?"

"When?" I don't tell them I was too busy drinking wine and searching for my errant husband all evening.

"Last night." Jo passes me my latte. "She's saying he would *never* have taken his own life. Just like I've been saying. Sophia's boyfriend, Dan, reckons something's about to come out."

I change the subject. I don't want to talk about this. I'm feeling better than I was when I arrived and want to hang onto that, not to think about the dead man. It might have happened at my wedding venue but he, and his wife, are nobodies as far as I'm concerned. Especially now. I've got other things on my mind.

My breath catches as I pull onto the gravel beside Ed's Audi. I don't know what is greater – the anger or the relief. I need to know why he didn't come home all night. It's not the first time. I know we're in trouble but it's hard to admit to. I don't want my outwardly perfect life to come tumbling down. I'll do anything to hang onto it. Maybe we need counselling or something.

"Ed?" I call into the silent hallway. The house is just as I left it. That is, apart from the bottle of whiskey that's been moved. He's surely not drinking whiskey on a morning! I ascend the stairs, careful not to trip over a football, a remote control car and a bear. Where is he?

Our bedroom door scrapes across the thick carpet. He's fast asleep. "Ed?" I sit beside him on the bed, feeling the warmth of his body against my hip. I want to snuggle into him. For a moment I wonder if we could take advantage of our twin-free zone. I quell these thoughts immediately. Ed doesn't want me anymore. I could walk in here wearing a basque and a cherry in my cleavage and he still wouldn't notice me.

"Ed." I shake him. "Wake up."

"Huh." He opens one eye. "What time is it?"

"One o'clock," I reply. "Where've you been?"

"What do you mean?" He slides upright and leans against the headboard. He looks rough. His face is lined and I can smell his sour breath even though our faces are several inches apart. "I texted you. You know where I was last night."

"I don't believe you. Why would you sleep in your office when you've got a perfectly good bed here?"

I watch him carefully. There's definitely something up with him. "Talk to me Ed."

"I can't."

"Won't, you mean. What are you up to?"

"Nothing."

"It stinks in here." I get up and push a window open.

"I've had a shower." He pulls the duvet up to his neck.

"Booze," I say. "What are you drinking on a Tuesday morning for? Is there something I should know?"

"Leave me alone Kerry. You're always on my case. I might as well be back at home with my mother."

Relief and bewilderment gives way to anger. "What did you say?"

"You're acting like my mother. Nag, nag, nag, nag, nag. Get off my back. I'm going to sleep for a couple more hours, then I'll collect the boys."

"You're going nowhere near the school in that state." I'm surprised by how much I raise my voice. What have we become? "You don't give a shit about us, do you? I can't live like this."

"I've told you to leave me alone. If you can't manage that, then I'm off again."

"So you're threatening me now?" I notice his clothes, discarded on the floor, in a pile near the en-suite. Normally he folds his clothes before getting into bed. "You can't just check in and out Ed. This isn't a hotel. You've got responsibilities."

"Watch me."

Hot tears stab my eyes. "Why are you treating me like this? What have I done?"

His face softens, but he won't look at me. "It's not you, it's me."

"What's that supposed to mean?"

"I can't do this anymore Kerry."

You don't know the sacrifices I've made for you, I want to say. You don't know how much I want to stay with you. But I'm not going to beg him. He'll come to his senses. Instead I say, "You can't do what?"

"I don't love you Kerry. I don't think I ever did."

I get to my feet. I feel winded. I stagger backwards, looking at him. I'm going to lose him. How will I cope? What will I do? What will everyone think of me? "Please, Ed. Don't say that. Don't do this." Tears are pouring down my cheeks. I can't hold them back anymore.

He swings his legs out of the bed. "Let me get dressed Kerry. Without you watching me."

Rotten bastard. Like I want to watch him dress when he's just admitted he doesn't love me. Really, I knew this. I just thought things could change. I really thought they would after … well, there's no point even thinking about what might have been. I've just got to deal with what's happening. "How about we have a day or two apart and you have some thinking time." I think I'm being generous, under the circumstances. I gaze out of the window as I speak.

"Nothing's going to change Kerry. I'm sorry."

He's dressed and throwing clothes into his gym bag.

"Where are you going?"

"It doesn't matter. I'll be in touch."

"You can't just leave! What about the boys?"

"Just let me get my head straight then I'll come and pick them up. Spend some time with them."

"Ed! Please! Don't do this!" I step backwards, blocking the bedroom door.

"Move out of my way Kerry. I need to be on my own."

"Why?" This isn't happening. Any moment now I will wake up in a cold sweat and find that my whole world isn't falling apart after all. In the end, I've no choice but to let him go. I watch from the window as he throws his bag onto the back seat of his car. Then fall onto the satin-topped bedspread, sobbing hot tears into it as I listen to the engine of the Audi die away.

Chapter 6

Ed

I hadn't really intended to come here and am shocked with myself when I pull up in the car park. What I said to Kerry came as a surprise to me too. But I couldn't bear to sleep another night in close proximity to her. I can't see a way through this and can't keep going through the motions. I need space. To think. And to be able to grieve in peace.

I'm taken aback by the familiarity that envelops me as I exit the revolving doors into the reception area of the Parkside. My face, chilled by the late March afternoon, gets blasted by heat from the wood burner in the corner. My feet sink into the crimson carpet as I stride towards the desk. It has hardly changed since we married here. Kerry had chosen this hotel for its 'rustic' feel. As I check in, I worry that the receptionist may recognise me. My cloak of dread, fear and loneliness weighs more heavily on me than normal.

This is compounded as I dump my holdall onto the double bed in the room. The tea tray is laid for two. I don't normally drink instant but caffeine of any description should bring me round a bit. There's two missed calls from Kerry. I know she'll be gutted, but I feel a tremendous sense of relief from telling her I don't love her anymore. She'll probably be more worried about what her posh friends will think, and any changes to her affluent lifestyle, than losing me.

I'm a decent bloke, in many respects and I love my kids. Nothing will change for them apart from I won't be there. I'll be one of those weekend dads. And if Kerry lets me go without causing a stink, she'll get a decent settlement. I can't imagine that'll happen though.

She'll have probably collected the boys from school by now. I wonder whether she will have said anything to them yet. Daddy's not coming home. I'd be lying if I said I didn't feel guilty about the boys. But how can I think about that at the moment?

The phone's sudden ring makes me jump. It's Annie.

"Ed, I hope you don't mind but I thought I should ring you. Just to check you're OK."

"I'm fine Annie. Just a few issues going on at home."

"You didn't look at all well this morning. I've rearranged all your appointments and Nathan took on the urgent ones."

"I'll definitely be back in the morning." It'll probably do me good to keep busy. Anything to stop me thinking about what's happened. Even for a split second. Thoughts of Russ keep punching me in the stomach.

"Are you sure you're OK? If you need more time off, for your issues."

I take a deep breath. "I might as well tell you Annie. Kerry and I are splitting up. I've moved out."

"What? Oh no! I'm so sorry Ed. I didn't see that coming!"

"We haven't really told anyone yet. It's been on the cards for a while. So if you could keep it to yourself for now. It's all very raw and we've got a lot of stuff to work through."

"Do you want me to say anything to Nathan?"

"No. I'll tell him myself. I'll see you in the morning."

"Right, OK. You take care, won't you?"

I lie back on the bed. It's lumpy compared to our king-size. We spent two grand on it but I don't care. I feel free. The sense of liberation is short-lived when reality clobbers me again within seconds. Russell is dead.

I can't cope with the quiet. I lean forwards for the remote and turn the huge wall-mounted TV on. I would never normally watch TV at this time in the afternoon. *Pointless. The Chase.* Re-run of *Judge Rinder.* Ugh. I keep flicking. The news. That will do. Though it's not long before I'm regretting turning it on.

"Investigations are continuing into the death of Russell Lawson, a thirty six-year-old father-of-one, whose body was discovered in a hotel room early last weekend." I swallow as Russell's face is flashed onto the screen. It's a recent photo. I still can't believe he is dead.

"His death is now being treated as suspicious and anyone who might have any information, particularly if they saw Mr Lawson in the days leading up to his death, is asked to come forward." Suspicious. Oh my God. I feel like I can't breathe.

"The time of death is estimated at between 5 and 6pm last Thursday evening. Mr Lawson checked into the Parkside Hotel on Harrogate Road at 4:25 pm and is believed to have been with a male companion. I swallow. I need a drink. I will go down to the bar shortly. A picture of the front of the Parkside is now flashed up. It's surreal, seeing the building where I am, right in front of me on the big screen.

"Police are keen to pursue this line of inquiry and are conducting forensic investigations. The male companion is said to be white, aged mid to late forties with short, receding dark brown hair. He was wearing jeans, brogue-style shoes, an open-necked shirt and a short padded jacket." I stare as a grainy CCTV picture appears on the screen.

"Police are currently working on an e-fit image of the man they wish to speak to and this will be released shortly. They are urging anyone who thinks they may have information, however insignificant they think it may be, to get in touch by calling one, zero, one and quoting log two, zero, seven, nineteen March."

I grab my wallet and head down to the bar. It's the lull between where people are leaving work and arriving here. This place has conference facilities and a gym, so no doubt it'll be swarming soon. I order a JD then take a spot by the window, well away from the bar and from a group of ladies who are talking animatedly next to it.

There's been two more missed calls from Kerry. I wish she'd leave me alone. I'll ring her tomorrow from work when I've straightened my head out a little. It's done me good to get out of the hotel room – I'm calmer now, though maybe that's the JD. I scroll through the contacts list in my phone and my thumb hovers above Russell's name. I press call, just wanting to hear his voice through his voicemail message. I nearly drop the phone when a female voice answers.

"Hello."

"Erm, I – I was just…"

"Who is this? Ed?"

Shit. My name will have come up on the screen. There's no point hanging up. She'll only ring back or even worse, pass my number onto the police as someone who has tried to call Russell. I only wanted to hear his voice!

"Yes. I'm a friend of Russell's. Is he there?" It's all I can say. Why else would I be ringing a dead man's phone? I can hardly admit to knowing he is dead.

"Don't you watch the news?" Her voice is raspy. We've never met, but I've heard lots about her. I feel such dislike towards her it makes the hair on the back of my neck stand up. "Haven't you heard he's dead?"

"Dead! No! I only saw him a few weeks ago. He can't be! How?"

"I don't know yet. Hopefully, they're on to whoever else was involved by now."

"Are you his wife?" I take a swig of my drink. How on earth did I get into this?

"Who else would I be? Answering his phone, I mean. How did you know Russell anyway?"

"I've been friends with him for a while."

"So how come he's never mentioned you to me?" She asks. "I know all his friends. He's never spoke of an Ed."

"I know him from the gym."

"He'd not been there in ages."

"He was there last week." As soon as I say the words, I regret them.

"You saw him last week? You just said you haven't seen him for a *few* weeks.

"It might have been the week before."

"How well did you know my husband? Well enough to have his phone number, anyway. You won't mind, presumably, if I pass your number to the police officers who are dealing with his death."

"There's no point. I don't know anything."

"We'll let them decide that, shall we?"

Bollocks. Why did I go and do that? Davina's got my phone number and my bloody name.

Chapter 7

<u>Kerry</u>

"Mummy. Wake up."

For a moment I can't open my eyes. I've passed out on the sofa after the two bottles of wine I drank. Two bottles! The TV has timed itself out but the flame-effect fire is still blowing out hot air. No wonder I'm sweating. My head's banging. I can't go on like this.

"Mummy. I'm hungry." Alex is tugging at my arm.

I hoist myself up to seating and feel the room swim around me as I plant my bare feet on the carpet. Ed's gone. He doesn't love me. He never did. I want to cry, but both boys are looking expectantly at me.

I can't cope with them this morning. I'm as stiff as a board after two nights on the sofa and have got the hangover from hell. How on earth am I going to cope with listening to readers at school this morning? Either I will throw up all over one of them or fall asleep. No one tells you about the expectations when your child is at private school. It's somehow frowned upon by the school, and the other mothers if you don't regularly 'get involved.'

"Mummy. Come on." It's like you don't own yourself anymore once you've had kids. Your life is all about meeting their needs and putting yourself last. No matter how bad you're feeling, you've got to carry on. And this morning, I feel terrible.

I stagger into the kitchen, fill two bowls with Co-Co Pops, two beakers with orange juice, then set them on the breakfast bar. "Mummy will be back in a minute." Then I rush to the downstairs loo just in time to throw my guts up. I feel slightly better afterwards. It's like I've purged some of the misery. As I down a cold pint of water, I feel a sense of steely resolve. I'm going to have to fight now. Fight Ed if it comes to it. Fight to keep what I've got.

In the school car park I slide the Range Rover between those cars belonging to the Head and the Bursar, a Jag and a Jeep. I've had a bit of toast and a couple of painkillers, so I'm feeling more human. I won't be drinking a drop tonight. I can hardly be judged for it. It's not every day your husband tells you he doesn't love you. (And never has.) And I know why.

"Good morning children," Mrs Richardson says to the twelve children on the carpet.

"Good morning, Mrs Richardson. Good morning, Mrs Huntington-Barnes."

"My mummy slept on the sofa last night," George announces.

Alex adds, "and the night before."

Cheers boys, I think to myself.

"Is everything alright?" Mrs Richardson asks me, as I'm rifling through the box of reading books a few minutes later. "You look exhausted."

"Erm, you might as well know." My eyes fill with tears. "Ed, my husband, well, he's left me. Please don't say anything, the boys don't even know yet."

"You poor thing," she puts her hand on my arm. "Are you sure you should be here?"

"Don't be nice to me. You'll make me cry." I'm always the same when life is rough – I'm best left alone. The minute anyone is nice to me, I tend to dissolve.

"I'm sorry. Children settle down." She turns and addresses the now-rowdy rabble on the carpet. "Let me speak to Mrs Huntington-Barnes." She turns back to me. "I'm sure you'll sort it out. All couples have their ups and downs."

I nearly smile at the irony of what she says. Then I recall Ed's words. *I don't know if I've ever loved you.* "I don't think so," I say.

"Get yourself home," she says kindly. "Have some time to yourself."

"I think I need to keep busy."

"I'm sure you can keep yourself busy in an environment more conducive to holding it all together than here."

"OK, I will do, and thanks. I'll be OK for next week. You won't say anything to anyone, will you?"

"Of course not. You take care."

I'm still fighting the tears as I walk down the school corridor towards the revolving door.

Mrs Wilkes looks quizzically at me. "Is everything OK, Mrs Huntington-Barnes."

"Yes, thank you. I just need to leave."

"Very well." She releases the door and I make towards my car with tears sliding down my cheeks. It's what I need, a good cry, and as soon as I'm around the corner from the school, I pull up and bawl my eyes out. He doesn't love me, I say over and over again. What am I going to do?

I jump as a passer-by with a dog taps on the window. "You alright?" she asks. I nod in reply, then drive off. The concern they have afforded me this morning, whilst it's reaffirmed the goodness in human nature, has made me feel worse.

I arrive at the park. It's quiet, apart from a few dog walkers. I do a double take at one of them as he approaches me head on. For a moment, I think it's Adam, my brother. I should ring him. We used to be close as kids. He followed me everywhere, and we told each other everything. Problems with our parents, schoolwork, love-lives, the lot. He was great. I say *was* as though he's dead or something. I guess the brother he was, *is*. He's become someone else now – work obsessed and in denial of where he came from. I've heard from our mother that he doesn't visit her very often, but I'm just as bad. Having said that, I've got more of an excuse – I live much further away from her and I've got the boys to organise.

Adam left home as soon as he possibly could. Fed up of living with damp and furniture that was falling apart. Tired of having to hide from debt collectors and watch our mum work her fingers to the bone. We never used to bring friends home – it was too embarrassing. Our dad was at death's door for years. When he finally went, it was almost a relief. It's hard for both of us to go back though. Our childhood was filled with such hopelessness and misery. Mum's picked herself up a bit now. She's retired with a bit of a pension and she has her own life at last. But every time I see her, it depresses me. She represents who I never want to be. So that's another reason I don't visit as often as I could.

The March wind dries my face and I'm pleased Mrs Richardson advised me to take some time out. This is what I needed. With each footstep, my thinking becomes clearer and I feel stronger. I will fight for Ed. I'm not giving up. This is just a blip. It's all been a blip. Once everything has settled down. We can get back what we used to have. What I hope we had anyway.

"Kerry." The voice in front of me sounds familiar, but I can't place it. "What are you doing here? I thought you helped at school on a Wednesday."

I squint in the low sun at the hazy figure coming towards the bench I've sat on to have a rest. "Jo. Hi. I nearly didn't recognise you without your gym kit on!" She looks really nice in skinny jeans and designer trainers. With her perfect make-up and hair wrapped in a bun, she looks better suited to a night out than a dog walk.

She laughs. Then she looks more closely at what is probably a tear-stained face. "Are you alright? Have you been crying?"

"Don't be nice to me." Fresh floods erupt and I'm aware of my make-up-free face, unkempt hair and less-than-perfect clothes. No wonder Mrs Richardson gave me my marching orders from school. I got dressed in such a hurry this morning, especially by the time the boys had finished pratting about.

"What on earth is the matter?" She sits beside me on the bench and puts her arm around my shoulder. "Is it Ed?"

I nod. "How did you know."

"Well, it's usually a man at the root of all upset, isn't it?"

I laugh, despite my misery. "Have you time for a coffee?"

"A quick one," she says. "I'm taking Sophia clothes shopping in a little while. I just wanted to get this one out for a walk first." She gestures to her spaniel, sitting beautifully, probably awaiting further movement.

"Latte? You stay with Maisie. I'll go and order."

I take the dog lead and sink miserably onto the seat outside the café. It's a touch too blustery to sit outside but we've got the dog. I feel like I could do with more wine. Take the edge off this hangover. God, it's 10:30 am on a Wednesday morning and I'm thinking about wine! I watch Jo at the counter. What I'd give to swap places with her. To have a straightforward, happy life, with older kids and a husband who loves me. I'm sinking fast. I wanted things to come to a head. But not like this.

"Right then. Spill." She sets the tall, glass cup in front of me.

"Not the latte, I hope." At least I can still crack, albeit bad, jokes.

"Ed's left," I then say, staring at the steam curling from my drink.

"Left? Why?"

"I don't know."

"When?"

I've got her full attention. This is every woman's worst nightmare. Especially when you live the lifestyles we do. With the appearances we must maintain.

"Yesterday." I look up at a jogger as he passes.

"Oh, he'll be back." She puts her hand on my arm. "What happened? Did you have a row?" Then she reaches down and strokes Maisie. "Good girl."

"Not really. It's been all wrong for a while."

"Why didn't you say something?"

"I couldn't. I haven't told anyone." My voice wobbles. "I thought it would sort itself out."

"That's what friends are for." She touches my arm again. "To listen."

"There's not much to tell really." I gaze into my lap. I can't look at her. "I'm not sure what's going on myself, to be honest."

"Have you tried talking to him?"

"I have. Yes. He won't. He just clams up."

"What about counselling?"

"I can't imagine he'd try that in a million years."

"Men."

"I know. Look. I'm alright, honest. I just need to keep going. I'll try talking to him again."

"You're not on your own, you know. We're all here for you if you need us. Do you mind me telling the others?"

"I suppose they will find out eventually." I'm gutted. They'll all be judging me. I'll be different.

"We'll all look after you, you know."

"Thanks."

The conversation then turns to more normal matters; Sophia's prospective halls of residence, Jo's impending holiday, her dad's arthritis, the twins. Then Jo drains her cup.

"Right, I'd better be off. I'll drop you a text later to check on you."

"Thanks. I'm glad I bumped into you." I am. Although it's hard to admit, I'm often in danger of drowning in my own company.

She hugs me, which makes me want to cry again. Then she's gone. I don't know how long I sit there for. I feel at peace but utterly displaced. My life has changed beyond all recognition. In a few hours it will be twenty-four hours since I've spoken to my husband. I've tried to ring him several times, but he won't pick up. He can't do this! We've got two sons to think of! I'm going to try him again.

"Kerry," he says, surprising me by answering.

"So you're picking up now, are you?"

"What do you want? I said all that needed to be said yesterday."

So he definitely meant it. Part of me had been praying it was heat of the moment stuff. "Ed. I love you. I want you to come home."

"I'm sorry Kerry. I'm not coming home. I've had a long think. I can't do this anymore. I want a divorce."

I feel sick again. "You can't! Why!" The anguish in my voice attracts the attention of a passing dog walker, who pauses, looks at me, then continues. "You can't possibly have made a decision like that since yesterday. At least give yourself a few days to think about it."

"It's been coming for a while. I'm sorry."

"And that's it? Just like that? What about the boys?"

"I'll still be their dad."

"You really mean this, don't you?" I feel like I've been punched. This is horrendous. "What about the house?"

"Look Kerry. Give me a couple of days to straighten my head out a bit. Stop ringing me for God's sake. We'll talk at the weekend."

"At the weekend? But that's days away!" The days I'll continue to be in limbo stretch before me like an abyss.

"Please. I need some space."

"And what about me, you selfish pillock. I'm just expected to hold it all together and look after the boys, a house and a business, am I?"

"Kerry, I'm staying in a bloody hotel room. I can hardly take the boys overnight at the moment."

"Your choice. Why don't you come home? You could stay in the guest room. Surely we can sort this out." I think back to what Jo said. "We can go for counselling. Relate are supposed to be very good." I know I sound desperate and I hate myself for it.

"You don't understand. You never have. I'm not who you think I am."

"I know exactly who you are." I snap back at him before ending the call. Fuck him. That's the last time I grovel for him to come back. I just can't believe how much I've invested in this relationship. How much I've sacrificed. For it all to turn out like this.

Chapter 8

I pull into the car park, a few cars away from the police van. You'd have thought five days was long enough to find whatever it is they're looking for in the hotel room. It's been good to keep busy today. Annie and Nathan have been great. They both know about the 'Kerry situation.' They've asked no questions and have just let me get on with it.

Nathan's taken all the emergency cases on, leaving me with only routine appointments to deal with. Obviously, I've got to maintain my professionalism when dealing with patients. They can't know that my life has fallen apart. I had a brief time earlier when I was so immersed in work stuff that I realised half an hour had gone by without me thinking of Kerry, or the boys, or even Russell. The police haven't called me since my phone call yesterday with Davina. I'm sure they would have done by now if they were interested in me.

The receptionist smiles as I retrieve my key card from her. She asks no questions, and if she recognises me from our wedding, she never says so. She'll know from her computer that my home address is less than two miles away, but I guess it's part of her job description to be discreet.

Rather than taking the lift to my room, I go for a wander. I look at the gym and the pool area. They gave us three months use in the run up to our wedding so I know it's worth using. I might give it a go later today, or maybe tomorrow. My energy levels are low at the moment, so probably tomorrow. I walk through the bar, which I'm definitely going to return to today, then past the French doors that open onto the garden. It's getting lighter every evening now. I remember that the clocks go forward this weekend, which normally lifts me, but right now, it would take a crane to lift me from where I'm at.

I find myself on the first floor landing, outside the room. There's a do not disturb sign on the door handle and police tape at either side of the door, right across the corridor. I pause. All is silent, apart from the sound of my own breathing. He died in there. Russell. *My Russell.* I close my eyes, trying to bring to mind what his last moments might have been like, feeling close to him, being outside the very room, yet feeling miles away. He has gone.

A porter emerges from nowhere and eyes me curiously. "Can I help you sir?"

"Erm no, I was just…"

"Are you lost?"

More lost than you could ever know. "I think I've got out of the lift at the wrong floor. I should be up again."

"As long as you're OK sir."

I swallow hard and walk away from him, soon within the now-familiar surroundings of my hotel room. My makeshift home, for now, at least. This is going to cost me a fortune. Thank God for my private consultancy work.

I make a coffee and stretch out on the bed, smoothing the Yorkshire Evening Post out over my legs. The same photos that were on the local news yesterday look out from the bottom of page two, accompanying the same story. I stare at them. They could be anyone, really. Mr Average. Short dark hair, no real distinguishing features and the out of focus CCTV shot is hardly worth the paper it is printed on. They're clutching at straws. I'm interested to learn what they might be examining in the hotel room. No doubt that will come out shortly.

My phone beeps beside me. Bloody Kerry. She just can't leave me alone.

The boys are upset. I've told them you're not living here anymore. They've been asking where you are and want to see you.

For a moment, I consider not replying. But I've got to, really. *I'll take them out on Saturday and spend some time with them. I'll explain. Give them an enormous hug from me.*

You should be giving them one yourself, she fires back. *I can't believe what you've done to us all.*

I'll talk to you on Saturday.

I owe her that much, I guess. I'll get my mum to have the boys and take Kerry for a coffee or something. Perhaps it's time I told her everything.

Hi Mum, sorry I've not been in touch for a couple of weeks. Just wondering if you're free on Saturday – late morning, I think. X

Mum always replies quickly. I'd worry if she didn't. *Yes, I think so. Why? X*

I need to talk to you. And then I need you to look after the boys for an hour or so. X

Sounds ominous. Is everything OK?

I'll talk to you on Saturday. I'll be round at 11. X

Are you sure you're alright? You've got me worried now! X

I'm fine. Honest.

Whilst I'm in a texting mood, I send one to Carl. *Alright mate. I'm staying at the Parkside for a few days. Wondering if you fancied joining me in the gym sometime. We could have a beer afterwards?* I hope he replies. I could use some company on an evening. I want to tell him that I will join the Farrier's Cycle Club too, but I guess I should get my shit sorted first.

I remember when I first met Kerry. I'd got to thirty and mum was always on at me. *When are you going to meet someone? You're more married to your work!* I met Kerry online. It was five weeks after we 'matched' before we met. We took it slowly and only met once a month for the first four months. I liked her, and we got on well with each other, but she didn't make my pulse race. For a while I managed to suppress the 'real me.' She was a good-looking woman. She still is. More so then, when she had longer hair and was slimmer. Not that any of that really matters to me. I was more interested in her astute mind and her ambition. She works hard, and she's a wonderful mother to our boys. Even my mother approves of her, and she always takes some winning over.

But I'm not attracted to her. I never was. She was a decoy. A smokescreen. Someone to hide behind. A person, I hoped, who might be able to change who I really am. Allow me to live a normal life with the detached house, regular holidays and two point four children. I tried, I really tried and suppose that what I've done to her is unfair. A person can't change who they are inside. What they are. It's all been a sham. A lie. For I'm gay. There I've said it. I've admitted it. And the only person I've ever truly loved, is Russell.

Chapter 9

<u>Kerry</u>

I pull up outside the shop. I've no gym class this morning, so am showing my face here. I've not been in much this week with everything that's been going on. Then I'm going for a swim and a steam. I need to calm my racing mind and chill out for a bit. I can't eat. I can't sleep. I feel awful.

I've resisted the urge to text Ed since last night. I'll do as he's asked. Give him space. Hopefully before long, he will miss us and see sense. I really don't have any other strategy to try. His departure has left a gaping void. My life feels as though it's hanging by a thread and I can't bear it. I want it to be Saturday to see what he's got to say, but at the same time, I don't want it to be Saturday as I know I won't want to hear what he's going to tell me. Everything will become final.

"Morning Mandy." I let myself in and dump my bag on the shop counter. Mandy's as impeccably turned out as always. She always wears our clothes, I give her a new outfit every month from stock and she can buy whatever she wants at a fifty percent discount. She works hard for her perks. I know how lucky I am to have someone I can trust. It's a shame the same can't be said for my husband.

"Whoa, Kerry. Are you alright hon?" The concerned way she is looking at me invites the all-too-familiar tears to my eyes. "You look exhausted."

It's probably a combination of the fact that I have drunk at least a full bottle of wine, every night, for the last five nights, and have now got the boys sleeping with me, as they're so upset about their dad. At least I'm back in our bed instead of on the sofa. The boys are keeping me going. When you've got five-year-old twins, what else can you do?

"Kerry?"

"Ed's left us." A tear rolls down my cheek and I angrily swipe it away. I will not lose it in front of my shop manager.

"Oh, my God. Why?"

I see a million questions in her eyes, not least probably ones about this shop and the forthcoming new shop opening, and her job. Ed's a silent partner in it all and has put up a considerable amount of capital. Depending what he says on Saturday, I should probably see a solicitor.

"I'm not sure at the moment. I just need to crack on. I'm speaking to him at the weekend, so I'll know more then."

"You poor thing? Are the twins OK?"

"A little upset. They'll be fine."

"Are you OK?"

I turn away from her and reach for the cheques and papers that need a second signature. "I'm going to get through these and then I will have an hour or two at the gym." I hope my voice conveys the message that the subject of my marriage is well and truly closed.

"Sure." She picks up her duster and resumes her polishing of the mirrors, which she was doing when I first arrived. "But you do know, don't you, that if there's anything I can help you with, even if it's just a listening ear..."

"Thanks. I appreciate that."

"Are you able to manage everything? On your own, I mean?"

"I'm doing lots of the paperwork and new stock ordering in the evening when the boys are in bed. I've just got to do what I can, when I can, at the moment. Work it around the boys."

"Of course. And you don't ever have to explain to me. You're the boss."

Alison's at the counter when I arrive at the gym, arguing with the receptionist about her daughter's lack of a swimming place. I try to walk inconspicuously through the turnstile, but the receptionist acknowledges me, averting Alison's attention enough to turn around. Really, I want to be on my own this morning – going up and down the pool normally clears my head.

"Kerry," she exclaims. "Have your two had their swimming places restored?"

"Ed sorted them out," I say, feeling bereft as I speak about him as though nothing is wrong. "Where are the others?"

"I've not seen anyone yet." She turns back to the receptionist. "I'll pop back to see you on my way out. Can I leave this with you?" Then, without waiting for a reply from the receptionist, she links arms with me. "Have you time for a coffee?"

"I might as well tell you," I say as I stir my latte. "Ed's moved out. I'm OK. At least, I will be."

Alison's heavily made-up eyes widen. She always attends the gym looking like she's ready for an evening out. "I had no idea anything was wrong. Why?"

"He hasn't really said yet. I just wanted to let you all know. In case I'm a bit quiet. I bumped into Jo yesterday. So she knows." There's no way I'm going tell them any more than this.

Alison takes a sip from her drink. "How awful for you. I'm glad you've said. At least if we all know what's going on, we can look after you."

54

"Thanks." I bend forwards for my latte, wishing I still had long hair to shield my face. The tears are threatening to return. They're never far away. I really didn't see *this* coming. Not like this. I can't believe how bad I feel.

"Bloody men," Alison continues, obviously meaning well.

"I'm just going for a quiet swim this morning." I'm not getting into slagging Ed off. I'm feeling too numb at the moment. "I need to clear my head."

"Do you want me to tell the others what's going on if I see them?" She crosses one perfectly formed lycra-clad leg over the other.

I stare enviously but am also smugly aware of the *divorce diet.* My appetite is non-existent so if Ed doesn't come back, the weight will be tumbling off me. *If Ed doesn't come back.* The thought crushes me. "You might as well. Though I'm barely sure myself what is going on right now. I'll keep you posted."

"You must." She looks at me with such concern that I want to cry. I stand up, swallow hard and say. "Right. I'll go and get that swim. I need to keep busy."

"I'm off for a run round the track whilst they get this swimming lesson thing sorted. I'll see you tomorrow. Keep your chin up."

I hurry away. I just want to be on my own.

I'm pleased that the swimming pool is quiet. My eyes sting, not only from the chlorine but from the tears that have frequently plagued me. Last time I was here, we were still a family. It's less than a week ago. I knew we were in trouble, but I could still pretend then. I've heard somewhere that divorce is like a grief and you go through all the stages, as if someone has died. I'm probably in the shock phase at the moment. I hope things don't go any further, or else everything we've worked for and been through will have been for nothing.

I've no energy to swim. I plod up and down the pool a few times, trying to still my thoughts. Swimming usually helps me. If Ed doesn't come home, I wonder if he will keep his gym membership here. The thought of us bumping into each other as a separated couple fills me with misery. I don't swim for as long as normal. Suddenly, I feel cold and head for the steam room. That will make me feel better. I sit, my brain still whirling with the steam, thinking about whether I should have left things as they were. Maybe everything would have blown itself out.

I feel marginally more human as I return to the changing room. I've had a soak in the jacuzzi and a rest on one of the poolside loungers. I think I even drifted off for five or ten minutes. I had felt lulled by the intermittent splashes of the few swimmers in today and still a bit hungover. The changing room's quiet but I still transfer my belongings from the locker into one of the three corner changing cubicles. I don't want to make conversation. With *anyone.* I drag the curtain across, glad of the solitude.

I hang my coat on the peg and sink to the seat whilst I have a quick look at my phone. *Nothing.* I towel down and smooth body lotion over myself. Then I hear two familiar voices nearing. Just as I'm about to pull the curtain to one side and say hello, I'm stopped in my tracks.

"Do you think she'll be able to afford to keep the house on?"

"Who knows? She's got the smallest house of all of us, but it must easily be worth half a mil."

"She's only got that shop, and it's probably him who funded it."

It's Jo and Alison. No prizes for guessing who they're talking about. I transfer my shoes from the floor to the seat so they don't notice them under the curtain. I might as well hear what else they have got to say.

"You've got to feel sorry for her. It's one of the worst things that can happen to *any* woman. And she's got those two little ones." At least Jo's saying something half-supportive.

"Didn't you see it coming? I did. I've always thought there's something shifty about him. And it always seemed to be a marriage of convenience."

"What do you mean?"

"That dinner party Claire had. They arrived separately and he seemed distracted all evening. Like he didn't want to be there. They hardly spoke to each other. Carl's all over me when we go out. He never lets go of my hand."

"How does it make it a marriage of convenience? Maybe they'd had a row or something."

"He kept her. She kept up appearances. You watch this space. It'll all come out."

"But who will keep her in Botox now? That is the question."

I can't believe Jo has said that. As they both laugh, I feel winded. Yes, I've started to have a few injections. So what? They then move their conversation to the hairdryers and I can't catch much of what they're saying. I think they've grown bored with discussing me and have moved onto something or someone else. I'm gutted. I thought I was part of their group.

I stay in the cubicle until I know they've gone. It doesn't take me long to blow dry my hair, and wish once again for it to grow back and that I hadn't had it cut. I haven't been wearing make-up this week but stick a bit of eyeliner and mascara on. Words my mother said when I'd been dumped in my teens return to me, *fake it till you make it. Shoulders back, chest out, stand tall.* I miss her all of a sudden.

"Kerry!" It's Alison's voice, echoing from the coffee bar.

I'm heading towards the exit turnstiles. They wouldn't have seen me, had they been sat in their usual sofa spot. Someone must have taken it again. The two of them are sat in full view of the exit. For a moment, I contemplate pretending not to hear, but I don't think I'd get away with that. I swing round and walk towards them.

"Hi," I say, probably a little too brightly.

"I didn't realise you were still here," Alison says, placing her lipstick stained cup onto its saucer. I think it's more of a question than an observation.

"I think I dropped off on the rest beds!" I laugh, hollowly. "I'm exhausted at the moment."

"You must be." Jo's face oozes with concern. Though I'll never trust her again after what I just overheard. Another thing my mother used to say was *eavesdroppers never hear any good about themselves.* Definitely true.

"Are you having a latte?" Alison reaches for her new Gucci bag. We all fawned over it a few weeks ago when Carl bought it for her birthday.

"No, not for me thanks. I've got a million things to take care of at the boutique. I've been here long enough." *Long enough to overhear you two bitches,* I want to add.

"OK, but you take care, do you hear."

"Don't be overdoing things," Alison adds.

Half of me wants to laugh at their mock concern. The other half of me wants to go to sleep and never wake up.

You have memories with Ed Huntington, Facebook informs me. I'm sat in the cocoon of my Range Rover. I would have fancied a coffee but I couldn't bring myself to sit with Alison and Jo. Against my better judgement, I click on the notification.

Two years ago. Fab Easter Monday out with my gorgeous family, I've smugly written. There's a photograph of Ed with three-year-old Alex and George on either side, all poised to roll eggs down the hill.

Four years ago. *With Ed Huntington at Leeds Bradford Airport, feeling excited. Florida bound with my handsome husband and boys.* The picture is of Ed leaning over the double buggy, smiling in a way I've not seen him smile for a long time.

Seven years ago. *With Ed Huntington at Windermere Lake, Cumbria, feeling loved. Romantic meal. Love it here.* There's a picture of the sun going down over the lake. That was such a good weekend away. We'd only been together for a year or so.

I scroll through the top posts on my Facebook feed. There's a post from West Yorkshire Police on the 'Our Town' page with a new CCTV picture from the hotel.

There are a ton of comments on the post.

Tina Westerman *I knew him. I think I went to school with him.*

Darran Franks *Me too. Always thought he was OK.*

Lee Sellars *Who? The dead man or the one in the photo?*

Tina Westerman *Russell. Don't know who the other one is.*

Lee Sellars *I've heard he was gay. Leading a double life.*

Tracey Fellows *What a waste, he was quite a hunk xx.*

Tina Westerman *He looks gay.*

Lee Sellars *Who, the dead man?*

Tina Westerman *Both.*

Tracey Fellows *The other one looks tasty too xx*

Sara Billes *I think you people should have some respect and take your comments down. How would you feel if it was your loved ones?*

Cat Butler *Hear, hear.*

Kev Lyle *I've heard it was some kind of sex game gone wrong. That's how he died.*

Debi Hughes *That's hardly suspicious circumstances.*

Kev Lyle *Depends.*

Debi Hughes *What's it called? Auto Asphyxiation.*

Kev Lyle *What's that?*

Debi Hughes *Google it. I'm not explaining it here.*

Tracey Fellows *A kinky sex game. You should all try it xx*

Diane Williams *OMG. What's wrong with you people. Admin – can't you do something?*

These comments have just been posted. I reckon they'll be taken down before too long. His wife is bound to have something to say about them. I wish I'd never opened Facebook. The whole thing has sent a chill through me.

Chapter 10

Ed

Mum is sat by the window as I pull up outside her house. I'm relieved to see that only *her* car is on the drive. She's been seeing Alistair for nearly a year, but she must have got rid of him ahead of my visit. He's alright, good to Mum, I suppose, but he doesn't really bother with her family. Though, to be honest, anyone's an improvement on BF (biological father.) I can't bring myself to refer to him as *dad*. Not after what he did to me.

Mum waves as I lock the car and head towards her porch. She's in the hallway by the time I walk in. "Hello love. So, to what do I owe this pleasure?"

I laugh. "Let me get through the door Mum." I go towards her and give her a hug, feeling slightly better just to be around her, and in the familiarity of the house I grew up in. It still smells like home, despite the bad memories. Mum did her best. There was always plenty of everything, especially love, which is more than can be said for BF. I hook my coat at the foot of the banister and kick my shoes off.

"I remember when I'd have to go on and on at you to take your shoes and coat off in the house." Mum laughs. "Though I do miss those days sometimes. I'll put the kettle on."

I follow her along the sunlit hallway towards the kitchen. It briefly crosses my mind that I could stay here; she'd probably be fine with me staying in my old room for a bit. It would certainly save on hotel fees. Then I think of Alistair and decide against it. To be honest, the prospect of staying in my old room leaves me cold. Once you've left home, you can't go back. Then there would be the memories. It's alright visiting, but sleeping here is something else altogether.

"Are you OK?" Mum's voice cuts into my thoughts. "I've been worrying about you since you messaged me the other day. How are the boys? Where are they?"

"With Kerry." I sit at the breakfast bar. "Where else would they be?"

"You should have brought them." Mum fills the kettle and places it on the stove. "I haven't seen them for ages."

"Well," I take a deep breath. "That kind of ties in with a favour I need to ask you. I was hoping you'd look after them for an hour or two whilst I go for a walk with Kerry. I need to talk to her."

Mum slides some cookies onto a plate, then places them on a tray beside the teapot. She always makes an occasion out of having a cup of tea. She's in good shape for her age, my Mum. She doesn't look as though she's approaching sixty. She still dyes her hair and teaches aerobics classes. Kerry's always been envious of her figure. She looks at me over the top of her glasses.

"Why do you need to go for a walk to talk to each other? You live in the same house."

"We've separated."

"You've what?" She looks at me with such worry that I feel guilty.

"I left on Tuesday."

"Why? What's going on?" She comes around the breakfast bar and pulls a stool up beside me. "Why didn't you tell me before? Tuesday! That's four days ago!"

"I don't love her Mum. It's a mess." For a moment I want to tell her everything, but I resist. She doesn't need to know. What right have I got to put the burden on her.

"Since when?" Mum says. "I thought things were fine between you. You all seem to have a good life together."

"It's OK. On the surface. But not really." I feel like a prat. We did have a good life, to an outsider, looking in. Two amazing, healthy twin boys, a beautiful home, exciting holidays, and with my job, money's never been an issue. But that was before Russell. However, I can't tell Mum that.

"What about George and Alex?" Mum's looks at me as I turn the Audi around in her cul-de-sac. "How are they with all this?"

"I don't know." I sigh. "I haven't seen them for a few days. Kerry says they're upset."

"They're bound to be. Have you thought about going to Relate? I'd look after the boys whilst you go."

"Things have gone too far for that." I nearly overshoot a junction. I slam on. My concentration is non-existent.

"You can't walk out on your wife and two five-year-olds, Edward. Haven't I brought you up better than that? After everything that happened with your father."

"Let's not get started on the past Mum. We've managed to get beyond that, haven't we?" The last thing I want to think about right now is BF.

"Perhaps the past is more relevant than you think here, Edward."

"I don't want to go there Mum."

"Well, at least come and stay with me then, whilst you get yourselves sorted. I don't like the thought of you staying in a hotel."

"I'm sure Alistair won't want me hanging around." I don't add that I'd prefer being at the hotel. I feel closer, somehow. To Russ.

"Never mind Alistair. He'll understand. It's not forever. You're my son still, no matter how old you are."

"Thanks for the offer, Mum, but I'm fine where I am. I'm close to the boys and to the practice, and the gym."

"Is work OK?"

"It's the only thing keeping me sane. With all that's going on, I mean."

"I don't know what you mean, Edward. You haven't really told me anything."

"You don't need to know anymore. Really, Mum. Trust me – I know what I'm doing."

"I almost feel sorry for Kerry and I never thought I'd say that. You've always been so closed, Edward, so autonomous. That's why I think you should go for counselling. Sort out what's going on in that head of yours."

"It'll take more than counselling to sort my head out Mum. Thanks for coming though. The twins will be glad to see you." What I mean is *subject closed.*

"Well, with a bit of luck, it will distract them from things."

I walk behind Mum to the porch, feeling anxiety swirl in my stomach. If I'd been on my own, I'd have rung the doorbell. Mum walks straight in, as always. Kerry has always been irked by Mum's failure to use the doorbell first. She once said, w*hat if I want to walk around with no clothes on?*

I've only been gone a few days, but it doesn't feel right just walking in. It's *never* felt like home to me though. Home is the who, not the what. I remember the celebration when our offer was accepted on this house and we counted the weeks down until we could move in. That, was quickly followed by the birth of the twins. It was an exciting time, however, it didn't take long afterwards for the whole situation to become a noose around my neck.

"Yoo-hoo," Mum calls into the hallway, unable to mask the look of disapproval on her face. I've never noticed it before, but I do today. The house is in its usual state. Coats, shoes, toys, papers and other paraphernalia everywhere. It's familiar, yet alien, all at the same time, making me feel even more displaced. I catch sight of myself in the mirror at the end of the hallway. I've lost weight and need a haircut. My thin on top patch always looks more visible when my hair needs cutting. It all seems pointless though now. Part of me is not here anymore.

"Granny!" George and Alex launch themselves at Mum, once her presence has been allowed to cut into whatever crap they're watching on the telly. Kerry and I had so many rows about it. *The electronic babysitter,* I called it. But I'm hardly in a position to challenge her. Effectively, I've made her a single parent over the last week. She would argue that she was one even before then. Which is crap.

"Where's your Mummy?" I watch as Mum fishes two packets of chocolate buttons from her handbag.

"In the shower." Alex thrusts the packet towards me, presumably to open. "Why have you not been sleeping here Daddy?"

It's a fair question. "Mummy and I have just got a few things to sort out love."

"And then will you come back Daddy?" George says as he crams a handful of chocolate buttons into his mouth.

"Don't talk with your mouth full. After I've had a chat with Mummy, I'll sort something out so I can spend some time with you boys."

"You can always bring them to my house," Mum says as she lowers herself to the sofa, patting the space either side of her. The boys dash to sit with her and, as always, start fighting over who will sit on her knee. "I can sort the spare room out."

"You've got it all worked out, haven't you?" The frosty voice of Kerry startles me. "Shouldn't you check with me before you arrange to take George and Alex to your mother's?"

"We haven't arranged anything yet." I swing round to face her. "Mum was just…"

"I just want to help, love." Mum stands up. "I don't know what's going on but you two clearly need to talk."

Kerry drags a brush through her damp hair. She looks knackered. If I know her correctly, she's probably been hitting the wine all week.

"Shall we go for a walk?" I say. "I'll buy you a coffee."

"Can we come?" Suddenly I've got the twins at my feet. "Granny too?"

I laugh, despite the conversation I know I'm about to have. No matter what's going on and the distance I feel towards Kerry, I love my sons and I miss them madly. They're what has kept me here. "I'll have a chat with Mummy first." I raise my eyes from Alex to Kerry. "Can I take them to the park for an hour after that?"

"What about your mother?" She says. I hate her for her rudeness, but she obviously can't separate Mum from me at the moment.

"Don't worry about me," Mum says gently. "I can always get Alistair to pick me up. Or I can come to the park with you, Edward. You two just go for now."

"Well?" We've barely got to the end of our drive and she swings round to face me. "What is it you couldn't say to me in front of your mother and the boys?"

"It's not about what I need to say to you Kerry." I continue walking. I'm not rowing with her in full view of the neighbours. They must have noticed I've not been here, anyway. "It's more that we've got things to discuss."

"Too right we have." She quickens her pace after me. "You've been an absolute arsehole, Ed. Who do you think you are, just leaving us?"

"I can't do it anymore."

"Do what."

"Be married. I want a divorce."

"You've already said. But I don't understand why. You can't just want a divorce all of a sudden." Her voice rises, but she's less angry than I would have predicted. Perhaps she's seen it coming. "And you reckon I'm just going to roll over and let you do everything you want."

The postman walks past us. I'm sure he raises his eyebrows at me.

Kerry continues, "if you think I will just let you just throw away the life we've built up and the home and everything." She pauses. "I've put everything on the line for you."

"What are you talking about? I'm not exactly going to make you all homeless."

"Too right you're not. And if you think you're having anything to do with either of the shops."

"Just remember who financed them, Kerry, before you start with your ultimatums."

"You've left me to do all the work on them. Run the current one. And look after the house, and the boys."

"Don't worry, you'll get what you deserve." My tone is more sarcastic than I meant for it to be.

"What's that supposed to mean?" She rounds on me again.

A lady looks up at us from where she's knelt doing something or other in her garden.

"You leave us, and I'll take you to the cleaners. I mean it Ed."

"Keep walking Kerry. I don't want the entire street to hear us." My temper's rising a bit. I might have known she'd start making threats. "I'll remind you of what you brought into the marriage, shall I? When you were Kerry Barnes. Not a lot, as a remember."

"I work bloody hard. And all for a husband who doesn't love or want me anymore."

"You got that bit right." I feel like a right bastard, but she's got to hear this. I can't live this lie anymore. I can't live with who I am, with what's already done and I'm not sure I can live with all that's going on now or yet to come either. I'm an utter mess.

"So when did you decide you didn't love me anymore?"

"I never did." I might as well keep being honest. It's turning into a no holds barred conversation. I want to go the whole hog and tell her exactly what I've been up to over the last few months. But part of me suspects that she already knows.

"What? So why did you marry me in the first place?"

"I don't know."

"You can't treat people like this. I won't let you. If you're hellbent on seeing this through Ed, you'll regret it. I mean it."

"If you think giving me ultimatums is going to make things better - I thought we could talk like two civilised adults."

"About working things out, not getting divorced." Her whining voice reminds me of George when he's not getting his own way.

We're approaching the park gates. The thought of sitting with her in a café in the mood she's in doesn't appeal. She'll end up making a show of us.

As it happens, I'm saved by the bell. But not in the way I would have chosen. Kerry's watching me intently as I pluck my ringing phone from my top pocket.

"Is that Edward Huntington?"

"Speaking."

"This is West Yorkshire Police. My name is Detective Inspector Terence Milner of the Serious Incident Team at Weetwood. We'd like to speak to you as soon as possible."

"What about?"

"It's not something I can go into on the telephone. We've tried calling at your house and were told you were not in."

"When?"

"A short time ago. Are you free today? I can send a car for you if you like?"

I glance at Kerry. I am not having this conversation in front of her.

"Can I ring you back, please? I'm just in the middle of something."

"We need you to come into the station Mr Huntington. As soon as possible, please."

"I'm just about to pick my sons up. Can we say tomorrow at 2:00?"

"We would like to see you today if you don't mind."

I might as well get this over with. Plus, I want to get away from Kerry, to be honest. "I can be there in half an hour." I ring off and face her.

"Who was that?"

"Just somewhere I need to be."

"What? Now?"

"Yes, I'm afraid so."

"Where? What could be more important than taking your sons to the park, like you've promised them?"

"Nothing normally. Maybe I can come back later?"

"Don't bloody bother."

Chapter 11

<u>Kerry</u>

"Where's Edward?" Marie looks up from where she is sat on the conservatory sofa, reading to the twins, surrounded by toys. The house is a pigsty but I don't care anymore. "The police were here before, looking for him."

"He even had a police car," adds George.

"What's going on?" Marie puts the book to one side and stands.

"Where's Daddy?" Alex jumps up as well. "Can we go to the park now?"

"I don't know what's happening," I mutter as I head towards the fridge and wrench the last bottle of wine from it, making a mental note to nip out and get some more. I can't believe Ed has walked off again.

"Do you not think it's a little early for that, Kerry?"

"No, I don't, actually." I spin around to face Marie, who's come up behind me. "And what's it to you anyway?"

"You've got two little ones to look after." She leans against the breakfast bar. I know she's right, but I feel so shitty that I can't help myself. And I want to know what Ed's phone call was all about. He just walked off and left me at the park. He's taken off in his car without even saying anything to his mother.

"It's none of your business Marie."

"They're my grandsons Kerry. Look, I don't know what's going on between you and Edward, but drinking wine early on a Saturday afternoon isn't the answer. And I want to know why the police were here before."

"I've no idea – you'll have to speak to your son. If you can find him, that is."

"When can we go to the park?" George is tugging his wellies out of the shoe box.

"Daddy's gone," I say flatly.

"Gone where?" asks Marie. "Whether you like it, or not, I'm part of this family and I have a right to know what is going on."

"Hasn't he said anything to you? He must have."

"No. But I'm guessing something pretty big must be going on for him to have moved into the Parkside."

"He's staying at the Parkside!" I absolutely can't believe it. Of all the places he could choose to stay. Talk about being close to the bone.

"Yes. Didn't you know? I've tried to get him to come and stay with me but he's having none of it."

"He doesn't tell me anything." I fill a glass of water, secretly wanting wine but not Marie's judgment. "He won't even answer the phone to me. I don't know how I'd get hold of him if there was an emergency with one of the boys."

"Well, at least he's not far away. And he's staying somewhere that means something to you both."

"I knew he was in a hotel, but not the Parkside. You'll be happy now, won't you, Marie? You never did think I was good enough for your precious son."

She looks genuinely hurt. We've always had a bit of a fractious relationship. It's healed a little since the twins came along though, from its worst point.

"There's no need for that Kerry. I just want you all to be happy."

"Well, talk some sense into your son then!" Maybe she can? Perhaps he'll listen to her.

"I'll try. I will. The last thing I want is for you two to split up. Look, why don't I take the boys with me tonight. Give you a break?"

The void of the rest of the day stretches out in front of me. Part of me can't bear to lose the company of my boys, part of me wants to just get slaughtered into oblivion, and the rest of me is already wondering what I could do with a day to myself.

Marie must sense I'm willing to accept. She says to the boys, "Instead of the park, would you like to come to Granny's house. We could do some baking."

They are still leaping around in excitement as I go upstairs to fill an overnight bag for them.

By the time I return, there is a taxi waiting. Marie, Alex and George have got their coats on. I kiss their little faces before turning to Marie. "I'm sorry. For what I said before, I mean. About you being happy."

"It's OK. You're under a lot of strain. I'm sure everything will be OK – you'll see."

"I hope so."

"I'll bring them back tomorrow afternoon. You make the most of the break. And I don't want to lecture you, but put the wine away. At least until later!" She takes hold of the boys' hands.

"Bye Mummy," they chorus as the door bangs. I listen to the car reverse and then its engine fade away. The house is suddenly silent, and I burst into tears. I never thought it was possible to feel this lonely.

Eventually, I haul myself to my feet. I resist the urge to refill my water glass with wine and grab a packet of crisps instead. Then I reach for my mobile and dial Ed. Voicemail.

I don't know what you're playing at, but I want you to know how pissed off I am with you. We were supposed to be talking and yet you take a phone call, then just do one. I can't take much more of this Ed. I want you to come home. Your mum's taken the boys for the night. Why don't you come around? We can talk.

By the time I press the end call button, fresh tears are sliding down my face. I wait a few moments. He doesn't ring back. Then clicking open my e-mails, I notice there's a flash sale at the gym's beauty salon. Without a moment's hesitation, I ring and book myself in for nails and a facial.

I'm incredibly relieved that I didn't start on the wine and feel slightly better as I lock the house and walk towards the Range Rover.

I slip through the gym reception. The classes are all finished for today, so it's unlikely I will bump into any of the crowd. Normally I would seek them out but I'm still wounded from being talked about. The scent of Ylang Ylang oil and the soft piped music calms me the instant I walk into the spa area.

"So what colour are you having?" the beauty therapist asks in her high-pitched voice.

I stare at the array of Shellac options like a child in a cake shop, unable to decide. My mind is so fuddled, I can hardly choose which shoes to put on right now. Ask me what my name is and I would have to think twice.

"The champagne orange is really popular at the moment," she advises. "Perfect for spring. And look, it's got a shimmer in it."

I stare at it.

"Or you could go for the sorbet. Or the rose." She pulls two more bottles from the display. "Would you like to try them?"

I'm tempted to go for black at the moment. "I'll have the rose," I say instead.

"Perfect." She rolls the bottle between her palms.

I spread my hands before her and gratefully accept the coffee I am

73

offered from another lady.

"So are you enjoying your weekend so far?" she asks as she files my nails.

"It's not been too bad." What a load of crap. What do I say to this slip of a girl? *My whole life is falling apart. My husband has left me. All of my friends are gossiping about me.* "It's *certainly* got better now I'm here," I try to say cheerily.

"There's nothing like a little pampering."

I enjoy the silence for a few moments until she cuts into it. "So have you any holidays booked this year?"

The ultimate salon question. "No, not yet, have you?"

"I'm just waiting to see what time off my boyfriend is going to get. I guess it's the same for you. You're married, aren't you?"

"Erm yes." *For God's sake, leave me alone.* I look at her rosebud mouth and perfect figure. She's at least ten years younger than me with her entire life in front of her. Mine feels like it's over.

"What does your husband do?"

That's what we're all measured by here, within this gym community. What we do. Who we're married to.

"He's a consultant dentist."

"Wow. How about you?" She starts applying the base coat.

"How about me, what?" I hope she's not going to keep talking throughout the whole manicure.

"What do you do?"

"I own a clothes shop and I'm just about to open another one."

That piques her interest. We spend the remainder of the manicure talking about fashion, interspersed with quiet moments I make the most of. I'm grateful to lie down on the couch in the treatment room. At least I'll hardly be spoken to whilst I have my facial.

It's the fastest two hours ever. It's good to have someone's hands on my face. Other than the boys, no one ever touches me, *ever.* Whenever

Ed's given me a hug over the last few months, he's felt like a piece of wood. And as for anything more than that, no chance. I nod off as I'm left to enjoy my face mask.

I make another appointment to return next week for a massage. I've got to look after *me*. No one else is going to. Bloody Ed can take the boys next Saturday.

I order a coffee in the bar. I can't get Ed out of my mind. Every time my brain wanders, he pops into it. The brief relaxation I've felt, is replaced by fury again. I speculate what might have been so important. His earlier phone call led him to abandon what was supposed to be an important talk between us. And he didn't just let me down, he let the boys down as well.

I pull my phone from my bag to try him again. This time it rings. He doesn't answer. "Ed, will you bloody ring me back," I hiss into the phone, aware of my quiet surroundings. I click onto Facebook, the ultimate distraction.

Marie's posted a photograph of the boys covered in flour. *Saturday kitchen with my two favourite little people*, she's written. I try to swallow the pangs of jealousy that they're having fun without me. I'm not exactly much fun anymore, am I? I can't remember the last time I smiled. Sometimes when I look around at people smiling, I wonder what on earth there could be to smile about. I should be grateful to her, but it heightens my current sense of aloneness. I would ring and check on them, but there's no need. They're obviously OK.

I scroll on. My brother Adam has a new girlfriend. She's tagged him in a photo. I wonder how long this one will last. He tends to scarper from women once the seriousness crosses a certain line – he's always been a bit of a 'lone wolf,' especially since he left home.

And then there's the usual banging of the Facebook drum in relation to the Parkside death, now dubbed the Parkside hanging.

Terry Speight *They've taken someone in.*

Francis Kaye *Really. Who?*

Terry Speight *My brother-in-law's brother knows someone in the police and has said they're questioning someone.*

Francis Kaye *They've said all along they thought it was suspicious.*

Wendy Cullingworth *I've heard it was a sex game gone wrong. That's not suspicious. It's an accident.*

Eva Harrison *How can you die from a sex game?*

Claire Steeton *If you must troll a private bereavement, do you not think you should take your nosy conversation to a private message rather than air your comments in the public domain?*

Susan Johnson *Admin, can't you do something about this?*

Matt Taylor *I used to know Russell. I want to know who they've lifted.*

Francis Kaye *It'll all come out.*

I click onto the West Yorkshire Police page. Nothing.

Chapter 12

Ed

"Have you any idea why we've asked you to come in Mr Huntington?"

"Not really." There's two of them, Burnley and Milner - one speaking, one taking notes. It's not a proper interview, apparently. I've come in voluntarily and I'm free to leave anytime.

"We had your number passed to us by Mrs Davina Lawson," says the fair-haired CID. "Does her name ring any bells?"

I suspected as much. I couldn't have imagined why else they'd want to speak to me. "Yes, though I don't know her personally."

"But you know her husband?"

"Her husband?"

"Russell Lawson. You telephoned him two days ago. At 15:42."

"Yes, she told me he was dead. I didn't know what had happened to him. I still don't." I glance around the interview room. Shit, it's warm. There isn't even a window in here.

"How well did you know Russell Lawson?" The CID loosens his tie slightly.

"Just from our gym. We were friends."

"For how long?"

"Only for a few months."

"And you met at the gym?"

"Yes."

"What is the name of the gym?"

"Fountains Hall." I watch as his colleague writes this down.

"And did you see one another anywhere else?"

"Not really." The fluorescent light is making my head ache.

"Not really. What does that mean?"

"We sometimes sat together for a coffee after a gym session."

"And that's it?"

"Yes." The questions and answers bounce between us like a ping-pong ball.

"What surprises me, Mr Huntington, is that you rang his mobile after his death."

"I wasn't aware of his death."

"Even though it's been all over the news?"

"I've been having some problems at home. I've not really been taking much notice of things."

"What sort of problems?"

"Look, I'd rather not go into it. It's a private matter."

"As you wish, Mr Huntington. Where were you last Thursday, the seventeenth of March, between the hours of four pm and eight pm?"

"I'd have been working. You can check with my surgery if you like." The note taker writes down the work details I give him.

"If we need to talk to you further, can we find you at your home address, eight Hawthorn Close, Farndale?"

"Erm no. I separated from my wife a week ago. I'm at a hotel. Until I sort something more permanent." I'm aware of my voice wobbling a little. I hope they're not going to read something into where I'm staying. Maybe I should have got a solicitor involved here. They gave me the impression though that this was just an informal 'chat'.

"Really? Which one?"

"The Parkside."

The two officers look at each other. "Interesting."

Burnley speaks. "Any particular reason you've chosen the Parkside to stay at?"

"It's close to my boys and to my office. And I got married there actually."

"I'd have thought that would be the last place you'd want to stay then, given your marital separation."

"That doesn't bother me. It's just convenient."

"And yet you still claim not to have known anything about Russell Lawson's death. Despite the police activity there?"

"To be honest, I've been so wrapped up in my own problems. You know what it's like…" My voice trails off.

"We may need to speak to you again, Edward. May I call you Edward?"

"Yes, if you like."

"Fine. Thank you Edward. We'll be in touch after we've made a few more enquiries."

Back in the sanctuary of my car, I let a lengthy breath out as I reach for my phone and switch it back on. I'd be lying if I didn't admit to being a little worried about them wanting to speak to me again. I just want to feel some sense of normal again, that's if such a thing exists. The only time I feel anything like me anymore is when I'm working.

My mobile immediately buzzes with an angry voicemail rant from Kerry. I can't blame her, really; I did leave in a bit of a hurry. There's a text from Mum to say she has the boys. I point my car toward her house, eager for a bit of company.

The boys pounce on me as soon as I walk in, wanting hugs and attention. They're desperate to show me something they've baked and lead me into the kitchen, one dangling from each arm. The smell of food makes me feel a little sick. I've hardly eaten today.

"Cup of tea?" Mum asks, opening the fridge as I follow her into the kitchen. "Or a beer? You look as though you could do with one."

"Just the one. I'm driving, aren't I?"

"You might as well stop here, Edward. I'm keeping George and Alex overnight."

"Sounds like a plan." I've paid for tonight at the Parkside, but the prospect of an evening here with a bit of company is more inviting than a silent hotel room and my racing mind. The boys are obviously bored already at our conversation, and run back to the lounge.

"You can tell me what's been going on, can't you? And what was so important that you rushed off this afternoon. Have you eaten?"

Typical mum. It always comes back to food. "How come you've got the boys?" I take the top off my beer. "Stop it you two." I call out. They're arguing over biscuits. "They'll argue over anything." I laugh, despite my anxiety.

"Stop changing the subject Edward. What has happened at home?"

I take a long drink of my beer. "Where do I start?"

"I've got all night." Mum sits beside me at the breakfast bar. Her concern adds to my misery. No matter what, I'm sure she will always be here for me. "Start from the beginning. You haven't answered my question either."

"What question?"

"Have you had anything to eat?"

"Not really." No matter what age I am, or how advanced in my career I am, it's something she always asks me.

She jumps up and begins preparing a sandwich. It's the last thing I feel like, but I know that I've got to try and keep on going.

"George has nipped me!" Alex shrieks, running into the kitchen.

"No, I didn't. He's got *my* biscuit!" George runs after him.

"Give him his biscuit back Alex. Now!" I can feel myself losing my temper.

"Go and watch the end of your programme," Mum says. "Your dad needs a little peace, then we'll run a bath. You've still got cake mix in your hair George."

Thankfully my anger at the boys subsides quickly. I'm glad Mum's taking charge of them, as I realise I haven't got the volition, or the energy, to do so properly. With all that's going on, I don't know what to think, how to feel, or what's coming next. I feel better being around her though. She has a cool air about her that always calms me down. And it's great to be near the boys, despite my lack of get up and go.

"You never said why you ended up bringing George and Alex here? Was Kerry going out?"

"She needed a break," Mum slides a plate with a packed sandwich in front of me. "She looked exhausted."

"Are you not having a glass with me?" I raise my beer and ignore my sandwich. I can do without my mother taking sides with Kerry or feeling sorry for her.

"Perhaps after the boys have gone up." She wraps her hands around her mug as she sits back down next to me. "I'll put them in the double in the guest room, and you can have your old room."

I'm not sure about that but it sounds as though she's got it all planned out. I can't imagine lying in there, staring at the same ceiling as I did at sixteen years old. Perhaps it won't hurt as much, now I'm in my thirties, and a father myself. But it's more likely that I'll be somehow taken back there, listening to BF moving around outside my room. I'll stiffen, unable to breathe, waiting for him to come and drag me out of my bed like he did back then.

After their endless nagging, I end up bathing the boys. As I'm sat on the bathroom floor, absently watching them, I hear the front door slam, then Alistair's voice downstairs. He's the last person I want to see this evening. We're civil, in a superficial way, but I get a sense he resents anyone who takes Mum's attention away from him. I shush the boys so I can catch what he's saying. They seem to think it's a game.

"Why are you shushing us Daddy? Alex shouts.

"Why didn't you ring first?" Mum's speaking.

"I shouldn't have to. Is this how it will be when I live here?"

"We haven't decided on that yet Alistair."

"Is this going to be a regular thing now? Them lot – here?"

I don't catch Mum's reply, as George squirts Alex with cold water, making him shriek.

"Boys!" I hiss. "Shush. Just for a minute."

"Their problems are nothing to do with you." He's on one already, is Alistair. "We've got our own lives to lead, haven't we?"

"My son and grandsons – nothing to do with me? Sorry Alistair. What do you expect me to do?"

"He's big enough and ugly enough to sort his own mess out. And to not come running to Mummy." Hatred drips from his voice. Why does my mother have such rotten taste in men?

"I can hear you, Alistair!" I shout from the bathroom door. Who the hell does he think he is?

Within moments, the door's banged and I hear his car engine die away down the street. I'm glad he's gone.

"What on earth was up with him?" I say to Mum as we help George and Alex into their pyjamas. "Does he really resent us all that much?"

"His evening has been scuppered, that's all. We were going to have dinner together."

"I'm sorry Mum, that we've interfered in your evening. You should have said."

"It's fine. Family comes first." She rubs at George's hair with a towel.

"It always will. Alistair will get over it."

"I don't understand what his problem is. With us, I mean."

"You know what he can be like. He likes one to one. Not lots of people. He's not the most sociable person in the world."

"I don't care. He's rude."

"I know. I'll speak to him. You get another beer. I'll take the boys up with some milk."

"Can we have a story Granny?"

I'm glad I've had a few beers as I lie in my old bed. I've told Mum enough to appease her curiosity. She'd suspected I don't love Kerry. I guess she knows me more than I give her credit for. Hopefully she doesn't suspect anything else. I can't believe I *chose* this room when I was a teenager. There's barely enough space for a single bed, bedside table and wardrobe. It's at the other end of the landing from Mum's room though, which she used to share with BF. I think that's the reason I wanted it.

I couldn't bear hearing his voice through the wall. If I close my eyes, I can hear him now. I open them again. This is why I don't enjoy staying here. It all comes flooding back. I'll never forget that final night. When he was arseholed, and dragged me out of this bed in my boxers. His jeering outside the door had woken me. All about *what I was* and *what he thought of me.* I had buried my head beneath my pillow, but then the bedroom door had slammed into the wall and I had become aware of his fists pummelling at me through the duvet. I curl into a ball, like I did then. I was a gangly sixteen-year-old, all limbs. I'd had a ridiculous floppy fringe at the time which had given him something to get hold of. I remember hearing Mum scream as he'd pulled me down the stairs. I was no match for him. He was built like a brick outhouse. He'd kicked ten bells out of me in the garden. I woke up in hospital with a cracked cheekbone, three broken ribs and two teeth missing. I had a concussion from where he'd kicked me in the head and I needed surgery on my knee. It came out in court that he'd had his steel toecaps on. I've not seen him since, but I think I'd take a knife to him if I did. Particularly if he ever tried to come near George and Alex.

I shouldn't have stayed here! This house is full of ghosts. A tear rolls down the side of my head and pools in my ear. I wish I could talk to Mum. I can't talk to anyone. And Russell is dead.

Chapter 13

Kerry

"You don't have to ring the bell!" Marie holds the door open for me. "You're family."

Her words cheer me slightly, but I'm too depressed to raise a smile. "For now," I reply. "If Ed has his way, we'll be divorced soon." I follow her through the hallway into the kitchen.

"I'm sure it won't come to that." She flicks the switch on the kettle. "And no matter what, you're the boys' mum. You'll always be my daughter-in-law, too. No matter what happens."

"Thanks." I'm suddenly aware of tears rolling down my cheeks. Shit. I'm sick of crying. And I feel an idiot in front of Marie.

She comes rushing over and wraps her arms around me. "Oh, you poor thing! It'll be fine, I'm sure it will."

"It won't. It really won't. I'm sorry for getting upset." I try to wipe the tears away with the back of my hand, but they keep on coming. I sob into her shoulder, grateful that someone is hugging me, even if it is Ed's Mum.

Eventually, I pull back, so Marie reaches for the kitchen roll.

"Have you spoken to him?" I dab at my eyes with the piece of kitchen roll she has given me. "Ed, I mean. He still won't answer the phone to me."

"I've tried. You know what he's like. He's a bit of a closed book at the best of times. And it's been difficult to talk much with the boys being around."

"Where are they anyway?" I glance around. "They're very quiet." I suddenly feel ashamed. I'm that wrapped up in my misery that I've not registered their non-appearance when I came to the door.

"Oh, Edward's taken them to soft play for a couple of hours." Marie walks back to the kettle and places two mugs next to it.

"He has, has he?" I feel irked about this.

She must read this in my expression. "At least they'll have worked off a bit of energy before you take them home."

"I guess so. Thanks." The smell of the coffee she places in front of me makes me feel slightly queasy – a combination of last night's wine, lack of sleep and not enough food.

"Let's take these through to the lounge, shall we?"

I obediently follow her through. The sight of the photographs on her windowsill depresses me some more. Ed and I on our wedding day. Ed and I with our newborn twins. Ed as a boy. I look away.

"Blooming *Peppa Pig.* The music from it will be with me for the rest of the day!" She points the remote at the TV, bringing up the local news. "I'll just leave this on. I want to catch the weather forecast. I'm supposed to be walking with Dorothy later." She puts her cup down and flops into a chair. "Gosh, they're still talking about this man."

"What?" I follow her gesture to the TV. It's the first item in the news bulletin.

"This Parkside death. I can't believe it's happened in the place you got married. It's a bit too close to home if you ask me."

"I know." I look at her, then quickly back to the screen, wanting to shush her and listen to what's being said. In between her comments, I catch bits of the report.

Police have several people helping them with their enquiries.

Investigations have now been concluded in the hotel room where Mr Lawson's body was discovered on Thursday, seventeenth of March.

Police are suspecting foul play.

Ligature.

Strangulation.

That gets Marie's attention. "Isn't that sort of practice what gay - I thought he was married?"

"Probably a smokescreen," I say miserably, resisting the urge to draw parallels.

"I feel so sorry for his wife," she goes on. "Apparently, he's got a daughter too. They only live in the next village. Just goes to show, doesn't it?"

As she witters on, I notice Ed's Audi pull up behind our Range Rover. My anxiety levels immediately rocket. "Ed's here."

I walk to the front door, ready to greet the boys. As they run towards me, I notice that Ed's getting back into the Audi.

"Hey. You're not going, are you?"

"I've got things to do." He doesn't look at me. "Sorry."

"Marie, would you mind taking the boys inside. I'll be back in a few minutes." I march towards Ed and he climbs back out of the car.

"Not now Kerry. I've got to go."

"Go where? This is important Ed. Does our marriage not count for anything?"

"I can't do this now." He looks at the ground.

"Then when. Why won't you talk to me?"

"I'm a bit of a mess at the moment. I need some time to myself."

"You've got two kids to think of! And I'm your bloody wife! You're treating me like shit! Who the hell do you think you are?" I'm aware of my voice ringing out around the cul-de-sac, but I don't care.

"Go back inside Kerry. Your kids need you."

"But I need you!" I'm crying. Again. I can't remember the last time an entire day went by without me crying.

"It's over. You need to start accepting that. I'm not coming back to you."

"But-. I don't understand. He's gone now. We can go back to how things were."

"Who's gone? What are you on about?" Ed's raising *his* voice now.

"You know exactly who I'm talking about." I know I've gone too far, but here we are.

"Come on you two, I've got to live around here." Marie's behind me, taking hold of my shoulder. "Come inside love."

"Get off me!" I swing around to face her. "You said you'd talk to him! You know the truth, don't you? Who he really is? You must do."

"What do you mean?"

I don't answer her as I storm inside. "Come on kids. Get your stuff together. Now! We're going home."

"Why are you crying Mummy?" The concern on Alex's face sets fresh tears off.

I hear the roar of Ed's engine. His answer to everything. Run away.

Marie's back behind me again. "Kerry. Look at you. You're not driving in this state."

"Watch me."

"You're not taking the boys in that car until you've calmed down." She reaches for my car keys on the table, but I get to them first and slam my palm on them.

"They're my kids, not yours. Sort your own son out."

"What's that supposed to mean? And what's *'who he really is'* all about? You're talking in riddles. George, Alex, go and put *Peppa Pig* back on for a few minutes."

"Don't pretend you don't know Marie."

"Don't know what? I really don't have a clue what you're talking about."

"That he's on the other bus. Bats for the other side." I can't believe it's my bitter voice leaving me. "Whatever you want to call it. By all accounts, it's a miracle you ended up with any grandchildren."

She's quiet. And I can tell by her face that what I've just said hasn't come as a complete shock. We hold each other's gaze for a few seconds. Then she looks away.

"Are you ready boys?" She unhooks their coats from her coat rack.

"So we're allowed to leave now, are we?" I look at her. "This subject is not closed," I hiss. "It's shelved, for now."

I'm calm, maybe numb would be a better word, as Marie and I strap George and Alex in, without speaking to each other.

"Give Granny a kiss," Marie says to George, then walks around the car to do the same with Alex. She says *drive safely* without looking at me. Not that it's *me* she cares about, just the boys.

I arrive at home, unable to recall my journey. The boys are asleep. Marie probably let them have a late night. I tug my phone from my bag. Nothing from Ed. I click through to WhatsApp to read the conversation my 'friends' have been having.

Jo Is anyone going to the gym today? I fancy a swim and a coffee.

Claire I might join you. I'll check with Simon to see whether he can have the kids. X

Lindsey Sorry ladies. I'll just have to see you tomorrow. We're having a family day. x

Claire Ooooh. Are you doing anything nice? X

Lindsey We've got to visit my mum in the care home, but then we're having a drive out. Thought we'd have a walk and a pub lunch somewhere. X

Lorraine I can't come either. We've got the in-laws today. I'm knee deep in peeling spuds as we speak! x

Jo What about you Kerry? What are you up to today? x

I feel like typing, *I'll be spending the time trying to survive until I can put my twins to bed and then I'll open a bottle of wine because I make my husband's skin crawl.* Instead I reply,

Kerry *Just spending time with the boys and catching up on jobs.*

Alison I'll definitely be there tomorrow. I've got a bit of gossip for you all ladies! x

Lorraine Exciting! What????

Alison You'll have to wait until tomorrow. It's not in the public domain yet.

Lindsey You can't keep us in suspense for a whole day! x

Jo No you can't. Spill! x

Claire Yes!!!

Alison OK, OK. You know how my husband works with Davina?

Claire Davina????

Alison The wife of the Parkside man. She's apparently off work at the moment, but on Friday, she went in to speak to their head. She came out really upset so my Anthony had a chat with her.

Jo And????

Alison He took her to the café over the road in the end. He was on his PPA time but none of the other teachers were around. She was in a right state.

Claire Do they work at Harlow?

Alison No the other one. The one with the horses.

Lindsey Anyway. What's the gossip? x

Claire Yes come on – out with it!

Alison You've got to keep it quiet as Davina told him in confidence. X

Jo Of course we will. X

Alison Davina's husband. They've found out what he died of.

Jo Wasn't it suicide?

Alison Nope. Apparently not.

Lorraine I heard on Facebook that it was a sex game gone wrong.

Lindsey Yeah, I've heard that too.

Jo I never believe much of what I see on Facebook

Alison Not just any sex game though.

I can imagine her face, full of glee at imparting her salacious gossip. At least it's moved them on from talking about me and my current marital predicament.

Alison It was gay sex, apparently. He's been leading a double life.

Lorraine Gosh. Did she know anything? Before he died, I mean?

Alison I'm not sure. Anyway, the police have let her know what's about to come out in the papers.

Claire Pardon the pun.

Alison It's awful though, isn't it? Poor woman. She won't be going back to work anytime soon.

I decide I should probably join in the conversation. Everyone will be able to see that I have read the comments.

Kerry Enough of that now. Have you all had a good weekend?

Jo Fabulous, thanks. You? x

Kerry Suppose. Is everyone OK for the gym tomorrow? X

Lorraine I'm not. Someone's coming to measure up for the loft conversion. x

Jo That's a shame. x

"Mummy, are we home now? Can we put the TV on for a bit please?"

I walk my two sleepy boys inside and brace myself for another evening of loneliness.

Chapter 14

I park up for a bit, my head buzzing. I can't cope with this anymore. I've got Kerry in one ear and I can still hear Russell in the other. My kids provided a welcome distraction but now, the remainder of the day yawns before me. I feel like I should be doing something. Solving something. Making things better somehow.

I realise that I am outside Russell's house and am not sure how I got here. I'm parked at the other side of the road, staring at the front door he probably painted, the garage he will have driven in and out of many times and windows he will have stared from. I feel closer to him here.

No! I recognise Davina from the local news – she's parted a downstairs blind and she's staring back at me. I pick up my phone, try to look nonchalant but before I know it, she's at the side of the car. I wind the window down. "Can I help you?"

"I could ask you the same thing. You've been staring at my house for the last ten minutes."

She's prettier in the flesh than on TV. I'm able to think that about women, even though I'm not attracted to them. She looks exhausted and for a moment I feel the drag of responsibility.

"Have I? I'm sorry. I was just thinking. I didn't mean…"

"OK. Well, so long as you know you were making me nervous. I've just lost my husband." She walks around the front of the car.

The momentary exhale of relief is quickly replaced by a sharp inhalation again as I realise she has clocked my number plate. ED H321.

"It's you, isn't it?" She returns to my open window.

"What?"

"Ed. The man who's been ringing my husband. Pardon the euphemism."

"Yes. I spoke to you last week." I decide to sidestep her sarcasm. "When I didn't know he had passed away."

"Passed away! You make it sound like a gentle death!" She starts to cry.

Oh God! Why the hell did I drive up here? What an idiot! I get out of the car and step towards her. I never can stand to see a woman crying.

"Get away from me! I shouldn't even be talking to you! I've given your phone number to the police."

"I know." I step back.

"Have they spoken to you yet?"

"I'm not saying." In the pit of my stomach, I know this conversation is very, very wrong.

"I'll be telling them you've been up here. There's laws against this sort of thing." I notice a couple of her neighbours watching our altercation.

Talk about making things worse for myself. "I'm sorry. I didn't mean..."

"What are you hiding Ed? Apart from your relationship with my husband."

"We were friends."

"Yeah. And the rest." Her misery is replaced by venom as she stares at me with a slight curl to her lip. "You'll get what's coming to you. Does your wife know?"

"Know what?" I shouldn't have got out of the car. I shouldn't be here. I wonder now if she will go running to Kerry with this. I'm certain that Kerry, at least, suspects my relationship with Russ.

"Mummy!" A little girl, with hair the exact colour of Russell's comes hurtling down their drive. It hurts to see her. The little girl with half his blood running through her veins. He talked about her frequently.

"Stay there!" Davina shouts at her, running back across the road towards her.

I jump back into my car and take the opportunity to drive off, cursing myself.

I enter the now-familiar revolving doors and stride towards Parkside reception to retrieve my key. There's the usual throng of people in the bar next to the desk and the low hum of conversation. I smile across the counter, but the usually friendly receptionist doesn't meet my eye.

"I won't be a moment Mr Huntington. The manager wants to speak with you."

Seconds later, she's back with an impeccably suited, unsmiling man. "Mr Huntington," he says. "If you could just step this way."

He leads me to a side room. He holds the door open, inviting my entrance. He's so tall that he has to duck under the doorframe. I'm baffled to see my suitcase on the table.

"What's going on?"

"I'm afraid we will have to ask you to vacate your room at Parkside, sir."

"What? Why? I don't understand." My already high anxiety levels rocket. I don't want to drive again. I just wanted to settle down for the rest of the day. I want to get a JD and coke down me, fast.

"It's to do with your involvement with the Russell Lawson case. We think it's better if you leave."

"I fail to see why."

"Perhaps I should explain?" He glances at the door, then back at me. "I had hoped, though, that an explanation wouldn't be necessary."

"I think you should. I haven't done anything." Jumped up idiot. He's barely out of his twenties. I can't believe I'm being treated like this. After the money I've spent here over the years.

"We know you're helping the police with their enquiries to do with Mr Lawson's death. And that is enough reason for us to ask you to leave." He walks towards the table. "They've been in here, studying CCTV and asking lots of questions about you. I am sure you don't need me to spell out the possible disruption your being here could have on our business." He picks up my suitcase and stands it upright, in front of me. "We would therefore like you to settle your bill and check out, with immediate effect."

"But I'm paid up until next weekend. You can't make me leave. You've no grounds for it. Yes, I've spoken to the police. Russell was an acquaintance. But that's it."

"All guests stay here at the manager's discretion. There are other hotels nearby. We feel it's appropriate that you no longer are staying at this one. You, of course, will be reimbursed any monies you have overpaid."

"But this is where I got married. You were OK taking my money then, weren't you?"

He doesn't answer that one, but gestures to my suitcase. "Would you like me to get a porter to help you, Mr Huntington?"

"You had no right, going into my room and touching my belongings. I will be complaining about this."

"Fair enough. I will give you the address to put it in writing." His voice is infuriatingly even.

I grab my suitcase and follow him back out into the reception area.

"Ellie, give Mr Huntington a head office compliment slip, would you please. "Then he nods to a man stood by the door. "Daniel, would you take Mr Huntington's case to his car please?"

"I can manage." There's no point creating a scene. Several people are staring. "You haven't heard the last of this."

The porter presses the button on the disabled access door, which springs open. I hoist my case into the boot then sit in my car for a few moments, trying to work out what the hell I'm going to do next. My phone beeps. If it wasn't for the boys, I would block Kerry.

Your mother knows, doesn't she? About you. You're nothing but a liar and a cheat. You've ruined my life Ed - I'm going to take you to the cleaners.

No, you're not. Time to get one step ahead. She came into the marriage with bugger all and she's getting nothing beyond the house, the car and her business as it stands *now*. Russell is gone, and it's time to fight. Tomorrow I'll get some advice. There are some shit hot solicitors in Harrogate. I point the Audi in that direction.

Thirty minutes later, I drive into the palatial grounds of the Old Swan Hotel, complete with its spa and near £200 a night price tag. I might as well enjoy a bit of what I've got.

"Can I help you sir?" I stand before the oak and brick desk. A huge grandfather clock chimes next to me. I can't believe it's 4 pm already. It's been a hell of a weekend.

"I'm in town on business," I reply. "I'm not sure how long it will take to wrap things up. I need a room indefinitely."

"Certainly, sir. Is it just for yourself?"

"Yes."

"And will you be requiring a table in the restaurant this evening?

I realise I have not eaten since the breakfast Mum plonked in front of me this morning. "Seven pm. A table in a quiet spot, please."

"Will anyone be joining you, Mr...?"

"Huntington. No. Just a table for one, please."

I notice the well-spoken receptionist looking at my left hand.

Probably wondering if I'm an eligible bachelor. I'm still wearing my wedding ring. I think the time has come to remove it. I've lived a lie for long enough.

Chapter 15

<u>Kerry</u>

I turn over in bed, instinctively reaching for Ed. I have fleeting moments when I forget that he's left me. Either when I first wake or when I'm really immersed in something. If I'm to be honest, there's a part of me that always suspected this could happen, but I learned to ignore it. We once had a heart-to-heart about a year after we'd met, and Ed told me about what he called a bi-curious incident when he was sixteen.

Though he didn't offer details about the incident itself, he went into much more depth about his dad, who he calls BF, and his reaction. At the time, I dismissed it as teen stuff. After all, lots of teenagers get confused about sexuality and all that. But within a couple of years, it reared up again. I remember us driving somewhere and right out of the blue, he said, "Have you ever been attracted to a woman?"

It was just after we had got engaged, so the question took me aback. "Can't say I have. Why do you ask?"

"So, you're telling me you've never even wondered?"

"Wondered what?" This wasn't the Ed I knew. He was a bit of a missionary position, Saturday night kind of man. I wondered if he was suddenly having fantasies of me with another woman or something.

"What it would be like to be with a woman, instead of a man?"

"No, I haven't." I looked sideways at him. His gaze remained steady on the road. He didn't look back at me.

"I read somewhere that eight out of ten people experiment in some way at some point in their lives." He changed gear with a hand I hoped would only ever touch me, but the way he was pushing this conversation was making me worry.

"Experiment with what?" I wanted to change the subject, but another part of me needed to know what was going through his head. However, I also knew that I could cope with anything. I loved him beyond measure, and he was the man who would be my ticket out of normality. He had already promised me 'the house.' He had also promised that he was going to finance my boutique business. With him, I would have the holidays, the car, the lifestyle. No way was I letting him go.

"With people of the same sex." He glanced at me then. "So, even if you haven't thought about experimenting already, chances are that you will do, at some point."

"Ed, I'm one hundred percent heterosexual. I'm marrying you. I'd never be unfaithful with anyone, woman or man."

"I don't think it counts as unfaithful. If you went with a woman, I mean."

I laughed, but it sounded hollow, even to me. "Well, I won't be doing. What about you? Is that what you're trying to tell me? That you're going to be unfaithful?"

"Hopefully not." He looked at me now. "Sorry love. We've just got engaged, I know. It's just forever is a long time."

Hopefully not? Something twisted in my stomach. I couldn't lose him. "Are you getting cold feet Ed?"

"No, of course not. Don't worry. I was just thinking out loud."

But it rattled me. I couldn't get the conversation out of my head. And ever since then, I've looked for signs. I have always been more threatened by his friendships with males than with females. People I know remark on his sensitivity and campness. At the start, this was part of why I had fallen for him.

When, on our wedding night, he was unable to rise to the occasion – I put it down to all the champagne he had drunk. He was constantly tired when we were on honeymoon, blaming the stress of wedding preparations, apart from twice – in two weeks. I was miserable about it. He must be made of stern stuff though because one of those times resulted in me becoming pregnant.

He wouldn't come near me when I was expecting the twins. I accepted it at the time; I was huge, and knackered anyway. For several months afterwards, I was a definite *no sex zone*. However, we stayed like that. He had never had a high sex drive, but we had begun to dwindle from Saturday nights to whenever I chased and nagged him enough. I noticed that he had to be drunk to come near me. It was soul destroying. In the back of my mind, the 'gay' conversation lingered.

I get out of bed and cross the carpet to the en-suite for water. As always, the nightly wine that is now my medicine, has left me dehydrated. I can see the moon through the skylight which casts a silvery glow across our beautiful bedroom. I love this house and will fight for it, but it feels so empty without him.

I can't believe what I've done with my life. Marrying someone when, deep down, I always knew he'd stray. And with someone I could never compete with. How desperate I must have been. I've no idea how many times he might have strayed with different men. And the thing is, I loathe gay men. Well, not the men themselves, but the act. I normally keep my opinions to myself – it's not particularly politically correct to feel this way. My dad was the least politically correct person I ever met – referring to gay men as 'queers.' Some of his opinions had been inherited by Adam.

When I first introduced him to Ed, Adam was frosty. I'd gone into the kitchen at Mum's to sort the dishes. Adam followed me in whilst

Mum stayed in the lounge, talking to Ed. She seemed quite taken by him.

"So what do you think to him?" I'd asked Adam.

"Seems alright if you like that sort of thing."

"What sort of thing?" I'd hissed back.

"He's on the other bus." He made no attempt to lower his voice as he rammed dishes into the dishwasher. "And you know what I think about his sort."

"Who? *Ed?* Don't be so ridiculous. We've just got engaged."

"You mark my words." He looked at me with the half smirk he'd always reserved for when he told on me for something. "I recognise them a mile off."

"He's not. He's just in touch with his feminine side, instead of being a Neanderthal like you."

"You're gonna get hurt sis. I'm telling you."

His words pierced me with fear, but it felt warm to be called sis by him. It was years since he'd shown me any affection. Since anyone had, really. Looking back, I guess I thought Ed was all I deserved and that the material gains might make up for everything else that was lacking.

He was reserved around women. This surprised me for a man who seemed reasonably close to his mother. His friendships were always with other men. Old school friends, work acquaintances, blokes from the gym. Their conversations had a depth I'd never seen with my previous boyfriends. I'd sit with him in bars and coffee shops, listening as he struck up conversations, or I would overhear him on the phone, talking animatedly. I recalled from my two serious relationships prior to Ed, men who discussed the footy, the price of beer, their latest car.

At first Ed's level of conversation gave him an edge. I loved how interested he was in other people and how intently he listened to them. His subjects were religion, philosophy and human rights. I noticed how tactile he was with his friends. Hugging, touching them as they were talking. When someone had Ed's attention, it was like they were the only person in the world that existed. Apart from me. I could never get that. I'm not sure why he ever married me. Now when I think about it, perhaps it was the awful beating and endless taunting he received from his father that forced him to suppress something in himself.

I kept wishing that perhaps his orientation was bisexual and I could somehow swing him in my favour. After I'd had the boys, I felt as though I would have the appropriate leverage. He would settle for the family life.

I turn over in bed and slam my head against the pillow. I need to sleep. It helps me to escape from my whirring thoughts. I'm sick of lying here, without him, going over and over things in my mind. The hate I feel consumes me. It won't allow me any peace.

Chapter 16

This hotel suite is the business. The porter leads me in and the first thing I notice is the huge jacuzzi bath. The sitting room leads into a bedroom which looks over the golf course.

I tip him then unpack the meagre contents of my suitcase to help me feel as though I'm living somewhere. I make a mental note to pick up some more stuff from home. Home – I don't really feel as though I have one anymore. Yes, it's a hundred and eighty quid a night but I can afford that. Plus, I might as well spend the fruits of some of my investments before Kerry tries to get her hands on it all. She doesn't know about everything I've got, and I plan to keep it that way.

I sink onto the comfy bed with a sigh, folding my arms across my chest. I'm lucky I've got money. I think of the countless men who must leave their wives for whatever reason and spend every night, like I did last night, holed up in their childhood bedrooms or in some awful bedsit somewhere. Memories of BF come bubbling back and I rub at the scar on my forehead. I don't want to think about him. I really don't. I force myself to turn my thoughts elsewhere, and inevitably, they swerve towards Russell.

I first met him at triathlon training. The twins were babies, and Russell's wife was expecting their first child. I'd been impressed watching him perform handstand press ups. He was ripped and had a body most men would die for. We showered side my side afterwards, and I had to force my gaze upwards as we chatted. He invited me to have a beer in the gym bar with him.

"I'm making the most of the freedom, whilst it lasts," he had laughed, holding my gaze as he sipped his pint. "How are you finding the parenting lark? Is it as hard as it looks?"

"Life's never the same again," I replied, watching a group of younger men burst into the bar. "Look at them. I used to be like that. Full of energy and liberation. I vowed the whole children rigmarole would never capture me."

His eyes crinkled with amusement. "You've got twins, haven't you?" Really deep blue eyes.

"Yep. One minute, I was Ed, career minded and getting my kicks out of new cars and holidays, the next I've got two kids, a goldfish, a mortgage and a family-sized car. I often think *how did that happen?*"

"What about your wife?" Russell asked.

"What about her?"

"You never mentioned your wife. You are married? Aren't you?"

I realised that I didn't want to talk about Kerry. I was more interested in this blue-eyed, fair-haired man in front of me. I liked the way he ran his fingers up and down his pint and I loved the way he was looking at me. "Yes, I'm married. In name, anyway." What was I saying?

"Have things gone a bit awry since the kids came along?" The way he looked at me. It was like he could see right inside me. Right through to my core.

"I don't think things have ever been right. I think I just got swept along with what I thought I should be doing. What was expected of me. God, I can't believe I'm saying all this to a virtual stranger. It's just…" My voice cracked. "You're so damn easy to talk to."

"I'll take that as a compliment," he replied. "I've a feeling we might be doing a lot more talking.

The triathlon training lasted over six weeks. It became a thing. Russell and I, having a pint together. I looked forward to Wednesday evenings immensely. It was on the sixth week when I made time before the gym to have my hair cut. I also found that I was putting out-of-character thought into what I would wear for our drink after training. I realised I was in trouble, but then, I couldn't help who I was attracted to.

"I'll miss our drinks together," Russell said. "There'll be no more training sessions after Saturday's triathlon.

"We can still meet, can't we?" I became alive when I was around him. I hadn't felt this way since being sixteen. When what happened, happened, before BF ruined it all and made me feel *dirty* for who I was - am. Even though I was betraying Kerry, it felt so right.

"Davina could have the baby anytime now." He stared into his glass. "But I'll see what I can do. She and I have an understanding, if you know what I mean?"

Something lurched within me. "No, I don't know what you mean."

"She knows who I am. What I am. But she loves me. And she wants to stay with me. At all costs. Especially now we have the baby on its way."

"What you are?"

"Come on Ed. You and me. We're cut out of the same piece of cloth. Just bear with me for now, and somehow we'll make this work." He cupped his hand over mine, sending waves of electricity shooting through me. Kerry had never, ever had an effect on me, that came anywhere near it.

I sit up on the bed. I need to get amongst people. I need to get out of this room. I can't be arsed getting a shower. There's little point making much effort. Russell is dead. And it's his face on the front of the local newspaper again. I pluck one from the stand at the bottom of the staircase as I make my way into the dining room.

See page five, instructs the caption under his photograph. I order wine and tell the waitress that I will order food in half an hour or so.

Police Release More Information in Relation to Hotel Death

Further information surrounding the last moments of Russell Lawson was revealed yesterday by the two detectives investigating his death. At first, his death was thought to have been either suicide or an accident. The cause of death has been cited as asphyxiation due to hanging.

Evidence found in the hotel room, and on the thirty-six year old man's body has now suggested the involvement of a third party. And CCTV footage at the Leeds Parkside Hotel, has showed him moving through the hotel with another man. Originally it appeared that they may have entered the hotel separately, but this is contradicted by the recent emergence of CCTV footage on a second camera, close to the room where his body was discovered.

Reporters have today spoken to his wife, Davina Lawson. She is said to be outraged at rumours that her husband of six years was living a double life. Stories have escalated on social media that Mr Lawson may have died through gay sexual experimentation after being found naked and hanging from a ligature. Toxicology tests are still being carried out on his body.

Further examination of CCTV has not shown the same man leaving the hotel who entered with him. Inadequate coverage within the building might have meant he could have left the hotel by another exit.

Police are still appealing for anyone who saw Mr Lawson in the hours preceding his death to come forward. A number of people are now helping police with their enquiries.

Chapter 17

<u>Kerry</u>

"**M**ummy!"

I used to love the feel of two warm little bodies clambering into bed with me but nothing makes me smile anymore. I'm exhausted, having been awake for nearly three hours in the night.

That Ed's not here once again hits me. My misery is compounded by the fact that, if I'm honest, I always knew this was coming. I haven't only messed my own life up, but also that of my boys. I should have sat him down before we got married. Demanded the truth. Admitted to myself that I could never be enough for him.

"When can we have breakfast?"

I stroke Alex's hair as he lays his head on my chest. One day my little boys will become strapping men, hopefully turning out a different way to their father. I've heard these things can be genetic. Not that there's anything wrong with being gay, just I'd prefer they weren't, in today's society. The truth about Ed keeps whacking me around the head with a slap.

"How are things, Mrs Huntington-Barnes?" Mrs Richardson asks as I bustle around in the cloakroom. "For a class of nine children, they're making a right racket this morning."

"Much the same. You've got your pumps on the wrong feet." I look down and try to smile at George.

"Has your husband not come home yet?"

I frown at her over the top of George's head as I try to push his foot inside the pump. "No, not yet." I notice one of the other mothers stiffen, probably listening for the latest. Gossip spreads like the common cold in this neighbourhood.

"Will you be alright to come and hear readers on Wednesday morning? Or should I get a stand in? Children – be quiet." She turns and calls through to the rest of the class. "I will be there in a moment. Run along boys," she says to George and Alex.

"I'll be here," I say. "Best to keep busy."

"You look tired," Mandy observes as I stride into the shop. "Are things any better?"

Why is this the first thing everyone is asking me? Do they care or are they just being nosy? "Ed's not come back, if that's what you mean. He's not going to either."

"Are you sure?" Mandy's threading prices onto a pile of dresses on the counter. I always feel calmer when I come in here. I love the soft lighting, the relaxed décor and the smell of new clothes. "Have you thought of getting some counselling or something?"

"There's no counselling that will fix this one!" I laugh a hollow laugh. "I'm sorry I've been hit and miss lately – I've just got so much to deal with. How's everything been?"

"Pretty good to be honest. Now the weather is warming up a little, people are coming in droves for spring wardrobe pieces. It's a brilliant time to be opening the second shop. Have you got a manager sorted yet? For the other shop?"

"Can you organise an advert for it today? I can always manage it myself to start with, if needs be."

"Will it still be a May first opening?" She racks the dresses and starts dusting the glass shelving where the shoes are displayed.

"Yes. The sooner the better. In case Ed tries to stall anything. Do you want a coffee?" I walk past her towards the back room.

"Yes please. Are you not going to the gym this morning?" She glances at the clock.

"No. I'm going to get on with making sure our new shop will open." I continue through to the back of the shop and flick the kettle on. I'll stay in here, as I could do with making some phone calls. I might nip out for a swim or something later. There's no way I feel up to joining in the gym small talk about holidays, extensions, conservatories and the like. I long to be back in that safe, insular world I used to inhabit. But I seem to have left it behind.

"One of your gym friends was in on Saturday, right before I closed." Mandy calls from the shop. "Lorraine, I think, she said her name was. She was asking if I knew anything."

"About what?" I poke my head around the corner back into the shop.

"Don't worry. I didn't get involved. I don't know anything, anyway. She was with another woman. She introduced her but I can't remember her name."

"What did she look like?"

"Tall. Glam. Perfect figure. Blonde hair. Looked like it had been highlighted."

Mandy pauses for a moment, as though she's considering something. "She was talking about that Parkside death that happened the other weekend. Reckons, the wife of the man, works with her husband. Apparently someone had been taken in for questioning."

"Alison," I reply. "Watch what you say to her. She's a right gossip." Like you. I want to say. But I need Mandy right now. She's holding it all together whilst I'm barely able to.

"Have *you* heard any more?" She's still on about it. I want to change the subject.

"About what?" She's looking at me in a way I don't like.

"About the man who's been taken in?"

"How should I know?" I can tell from her expression that she knows it's Ed. He and I haven't discussed it directly, but Davina will no doubt have spread the word. Part of me wishes Mandy would just say what she wants to say, but I know she won't.

"I just thought you might have heard something. Especially with it having happened at The Parkside."

"No. I haven't."

I think of my cold childhood and fraught teenage years, compared to the life I've carved out and carefully constructed since, and I can't shake the feeling that it is all about to fall apart.

It's lunchtime when I get to the gym. I'm familiar with the routine of the others and know they'll be gone by now. I'm glad to be here. I descend the steps to the changing room and pull a cubicle curtain closed behind me. I'm no longer ashamed of my body. In just a fortnight, the weight has tumbled from me.

The cubicle though, offers the solitude I need. I don't want anyone trying to make small talk with me. I need to think, and I'm struggling to feign pleasantries about the weather or holiday destinations. Then I hear an unwelcome voice.

"She obviously never saw it coming." It's Alison. Is she talking about me? Again?

"I know, but it can happen to anyone. None of us can ever know what's around the corner."

"Always the big *I am*. And she's still strutting around like she's something she's not. I hope she gets a good solicitor. I knew her when she was plain old Kerry Barnes. Believe me, it's him who's put her where she is."

"They must have been unhappy for a while. It's their kids I feel sorry for. Hopefully, he'll do the decent thing and let them stay in the house." The gentleness in Jo's voice balances the abrasion in Alison's. I can't believe they're still here, at this time. What are they playing at?

"Something will come out, something big and juicy." Alison's voice is loaded with glee. "I was talking to her shop manager the other day."

"What did she tell you?"

"Enough. It ties in with what Anthony has told me about Davina."

"Davina?" Jo sounds puzzled.

"The wife of the dead man at the Parkside."

"But what's he got to do with Kerry and Ed? I don't under..."

"You should check who's listening before spouting your gossip!" I rip back the curtain and step toward them.

"Kerry. I thought you weren't here today." Jo looks horrified.

"Evidently. This isn't the first time I've heard you all bitching about me." I snatch up my bag, no longer in the mood for a swim.

"We weren't!" Jo steps towards me. "We just feel sorry about your situation. Come on Kerry. Let's go for a coffee. We can sort this out."

"Leave me alone." I stride from the changing room, angry tears stabbing the back of my eyes. Great. When I most need my friends, I've managed to fall out with them. I feel like I'm back at school.

"Are you OK?" The girl on reception looks startled as I head towards the revolving door. "You've only just got here."

I ignore her and storm towards my car, ignoring Jo's voice behind me. "Kerry. Wait!" She's running towards my Range Rover as I screech from the car park.

I pull up in a layby a mile from the gym, turn off my engine and allow the tears to fall. I'm so sick of crying.

My phone beeps. *Kerry. I'm so sorry. We do care about you. It's just... we've been so shocked about what you're going through. Please ring me.*

A notification comes through to say Alison has commented on a post on the 'Our Town' group on Facebook. With a feeling of dread, I tap on it. It slides straight to her post. *We should stop speculating about this. These are actual people's lives.*

That's rich, coming from... I type but then delete it. Instead, I scroll up to look at the rest of the conversation. There's a pixelated still of Russell Lawson in a corridor with a man. I tap on it to read the article, then scroll down the comments.

Claire Aylesbury *Am sick of hearing about this now.*

Jo-Ann Bowyer *Don't be so awful. This is someone's husband and father.*

Claire Aylesbury *So what. People die all the time.*

Jo-Ann Bowyer *But he was strangled.*

Kev Lyle *He did it to himself, didn't he? Whilst he was getting off?*

Claire Aylesbury *??????*

Kev Lyle *Same way as that rock singer died. What's it called? Sexual Asphyxiation.*

Lee Sellars *But he wasn't on his own. That's what all this is about.*

Dawn Henley *That man looks familiar.*

Sally-Ann Turner *He looks like my dentist!*

Jo-Ann Bowyer *Lol.*

Ruth Kettle *I only stayed there last month. This can't be doing the hotel any good.*

Lee Sellars *No such thing as bad publicity.*

Alison Hughes-Watts *We should stop speculating about this. These are actual people's lives.*

Life feels shit. Life is shit. Nothing is as I thought it would be. But I've got a feeling that it's all about to get even worse.

Chapter 18

Ed

"Good morning sir. Did you sleep well? Is everything alright for you?"

"Yes, thank you." I can hardly respond by saying that I tossed and turned half the night and my world has fallen apart. It's damage limitation now. I've got to protect what I've got left and allow things to run their course.

"If you'd like to help yourself to the buffet sir. A full English is available from the hot counter or you may prefer the continental option. Can I get you some coffee?"

"Yes, please." I rise from my chair. I'm not hungry, but I need to keep going. Plus, it's costing me enough to stay here. I might as well eat. I'll make use of the rest of the facilities when I get back later.

As I pick at a croissant with one hand, I use the other to type into Google, Mark Smeaton-Barrie. Then click through to his website. I've heard associates talk about him. He comes at a price but he's shit hot. And I've got a lot to lose. I take a slurp of coffee. Although nothing could compare with what I have already lost. I don't need to read the reviews – he's the man. I click on the book an initial consultation button and am pleased to see that he has a half hour slot later this morning. I'll have to rearrange a bit but sod it. This is important.

The waiter returns to me, his footsteps silent across the thick carpet. "Is everything alright for you sir?"

"Yes, thank you." I ignore BBC Breakfast bumbling away on the big screen above me. I've enough shit of my own going on. A nearby couple are holding hands across their table. I think once more of Russell. He would have liked it here.

"Morning Annie." I notice her blonde head bent over her computer screen as I stride into the surgery and head straight towards the coffee jug.

"Morning Ed. How's your weekend been?" She glances up and starts rifling through bits of paper in a tray on her desk. "I've got a few messages for you."

"Don't ask. How about you?"

"Good thanks. We went to the coast." She gestures towards the photo of her kids as she speaks. I feel a pang. She's taking her kids to the coast whilst I've walked out on mine.

"Annie, I need a favour. Can you shuffle my appointments around? I need my two late mornings moved to the end of the day or rearranged completely."

"Sure - I'll do my best."

"Thanks. I've got an urgent appointment to get to at eleven in Harrogate."

"Are you alright, Ed?"

"It's just family stuff. Anyway, I'd best go, and get on. My first appointment will be here soon."

Laura, my assistant, is assembling tools in my surgery as I walk in. "Morning Ed." Her voice is high pitched and reminds me of Kerry. "Good weekend? It's just gone so fast. I can't believe how nice it's been."

She witters away and I say yes in the right places. She's a likeable girl. Only young. She talks too much, but she's good with the patients and always manages to put them at ease. I'm probably a touch aloof, preferring just to give instructions and get on with my job.

I still check my phone as often as I was doing when I was expecting texts from Russell. I was surprised at myself - feeling a thrill when he sent so much as a heart-shaped emoji. I went daft for a time. I'd give anything to feel like that again. There's a text from Mum. *I need to see you. Lunch?*

I wonder what it's about. I only saw her yesterday. Perhaps she's been speaking to Kerry. I type back. *I've got a 30 min mtg in Harrogate at 11. Can you meet me there after that?*

Only if you treat me to morning coffee at Betty's.

Done. See you soon.

"Good Morning. Mr Smeaton-Barrie's office." I sit, listening to his secretary on the phone as I wait, feeling somewhat nervous. The waiting room is well furnished. I suppose it would be, given the fees he charges.

"Mr Huntington." He's exactly the same as his website picture. Salt and pepper hair and a smile that says *don't mess with me.* He's a good looking man. But I shouldn't be thinking that. I'm in enough hot water.

"Have a seat Mr Huntington." He gestures to a couch in the corner. His office is not unlike mine. Around the same size, but he doesn't have models and pictures of teeth in every corner. I bet he never has to sleep in here either.

"Call me Ed."

"Call me Mark!" He laughs. He's got a reputation. He's thrashed out some amazing settlements for many divorcing men. He's got a reputation for making sure grasping ex-wives do not take his clients to the cleaners.

"Thanks. I've separated from my wife," I begin. "Divorce is probably on the cards but for now, I need to put some things in place. The house, assets, that sort of thing."

"OK. This is just a thirty minute consultation to get the ball rolling. After that, my fee is four hundred and sixty pounds per hour."

I nod. "OK. I'm happy with that."

"So for today. I'll get a few details from you. Make sure I can take you on, and then we'll make a proper appointment."

"Sounds fine."

"Right. What's your full name?

"Edward Anthony Huntington."

"Date of Birth?"

"Fourth of the second, eighty seven. I'm thirty-one."

"Address?"

"I'm currently staying at the Old Swan."

Michael lets out low whistle. "In Harrogate?"

"Yes."

"What's your home address?"

"Eight Hawthorn Close, Farndale, Yorkshire." I watch as his silver pen flicks across the page.

"What's the value of the house?"

"Around nine hundred and fifty thousand. Well, that's what it was five years ago, when we moved in."

"I'll take more information about your assets in my next appointment. It's just the initial paperwork today."

"Wife's name?"

"Kerry Ann Huntington-Barnes,"

"And what's her date of birth."

I have to think. I never could remember her birthday. "Sixth of

July. Nineteen eighty six," I reply after a few moments. "She's a year younger than me – thirty."

"I take it she's still at the marital home?" His phone beeps. He picks up and says, "take a number for me," then turns back to me.

"Yes, with our two boys, George and Alex."

"Is their surname the same as their mothers? Huntington-Barnes?"

"Yes. And they're twins. Five years old."

"Thank you. So what's the reason for the split?" The question hangs for a moment whilst I wonder how truthful to be.

"We've been growing apart for a while. I don't love her."

"Was anyone else involved," he asks the question, all-matter-of-fact.

"Yes." I speak in a low voice. He needs to know the truth.

"Does your wife know?"

"I'm not sure."

"Is the other woman still in the picture?"

"No." I could tell him it's not a woman and that the person I loved is now dead but I feel that's best left for another meeting.

"So what do you want doing at this stage?"

"I need to protect what I've got. What I've worked for. I've known associates whose wives have gone to town on them." I think of a former colleague, Nigel. His wife had been the one having an affair, yet he ended up homeless, having to thrash out access arrangements for his kids and with the CSA laying claim to a third of his salary.

"Do you and your wife have a substantial joint account?"

"It depends what you mean by substantial. I have a monthly standing order going to it. It covers all the household expenditure, a personal allowance for my wife and anything my boys might need."

"What about a mortgage?"

"We own our house outright. I did very well out of Bitcoin."

"Yes, a few of us did! Does your wife have an independent income?"

"She does, but it was me who set up her business. Really, she came into our relationship with nothing. She runs a successful clothing boutique and I'm in the process of financing a second one. I'm willing to see that through if she's willing to play fair. At the moment, she's threatening to take the house and everything."

"Did you have a pre-nup?"

"No." Out of habit, I reach for the finger on which I used to twist at my wedding ring. I haven't got used to not wearing it yet. I regret that now. At the time, a pre-nup felt cold and clinical. Hindsight is a wonderful thing." I pause, thinking of Russell. "As I said, Kerry entered our marriage with very little and whilst she's worked hard on her business and takes care of our boys, she has an affluent and easy lifestyle. And that's down to *my* savings, *my* investments, and *my* business."

"What do you do, Ed?"

" I'm a consultant in cosmetic dentistry. I have a private practice in Ilkley with three partners who've bought in."

"What are you drawing from that? Per year?"

"It varies. Around £300,000. I have an income from my property portfolio too. Then I have savings and a fair bit tied up in investments. I'm concerned that my wife will get half of everything. I don't mind doing my bit; I certainly don't mind her being in the house with my sons for now, but to give her half of everything I've worked for, well, it doesn't seem fair." I feel like such an idiot now for not insisting on a pre-nup.

"I agree. Do you know if she's appointed a solicitor yet?"

"If she has, she hasn't told me. Probably not."

"OK. Well, I suggest, in the first instance, we write to her, advising that you've set the wheels in motion. That should give her the impetus to appoint her own solicitor. This is assuming, that you've definitely decided to instruct me?"

"Yes. Of course. Can she spend all my money in the meantime

though, or move it somewhere else?"

"Well yes, any accounts she has access to could be emptied or moved."

"But most of what I have, she can't get at. There's our joint savings account. I might move some funds out."

"As you wish."

"OK... so... where do we go with this now?"

"We'll probably set up mediation to start with. With your income, it's a given, that she will be entitled to stay in your martial home for as long as your children are in full-time education. What school do they attend?"

"Harlow Boys. Poole-in-Wharfedale."

He writes that down. He's got two pages of notes. "Right, Ed. I'll write to your wife, copying you in. I'll also draw up your contract and terms of instruction. We'll get another appointment booked for next week, for which payment on account will be required. Is that acceptable to you?"

"Yes. I'm just relieved to have the ball rolling."

"Where can I write to you?"

"The Old Swan, for now. I'll let you know if I move from there."

"Good. I'll need to see your marriage certificate, and if you could make a list of your exact assets, joint and separate, that would be helpful. Now, and at the time of your marriage." He rises and shakes my hand. "We'll get the assets sorted first, like you said, then we can push forward with the divorce."

"Thank you for your time."

"You're welcome. My secretary will book you another meeting."

We've been dead on half an hour. I swap the air-conditioned office for the early April heat. It feels like July in terms of the sunshine, yet I could liken my bleakness to January. I do feel lifted by taking some control and seeing Mark, but I'll always feel wretched at walking out on my boys. I'll have to find somewhere to live soon so I can start having them to stay. I can't exactly take them to the Old Swan Hotel.

Mum echoes this as we queue in Betty's. "Why you don't come and stay at home with me," she says. "The boys would be welcome anytime. It must be costing you an arm and a leg to stay at the Old Swan."

"You're only jealous," I laugh as we follow the pristinely dressed waitress to a table in the corner. "So what's urgent enough for you to *have* to see me."

She looks at me in the way she always used to when I'd done something wrong as a boy. "I don't know how you can laugh Edward. You should be trying to put right the mess you've created."

Great – I'm here for a lecture. "Cheers Mum. I thought you were meant to be on my side."

"It's not about sides. But if it was, I'd be on the side of those two boys of yours. Do you think it's right, leaving them like this?" She glares at a woman on a neighbouring table, dressed from head to toe in beige, who's clearly listening to the conversation we've struck up.

"It's not about the boys Mum. It's about Kerry. You know I can't love her." If the woman doesn't stop staring soon, I will be asking for a table move.

But Mum's undeterred by her. "I don't think you realise the consequences of your actions. How you've affected so many lives. Including mine."

"*Yours?* How do you work that one out?"

"They're my grandsons, Edward. I don't understand why you went through with it all in the first place."

"With what?"

"Can I take your order please?" Before Mum gets chance to answer, the black and white clad waitress is before us, pen poised.

"You should eat something." Mum shoves a menu at me. "You look like a coat-hanger. I'll have soup with a roll and a pot of tea please."

"Thanks for the compliment Mum. You're on form today. Same for me please." I place the menu back in its holder.

"Don't you want to know what soup it is, sir?"

"No. It's fine thanks." She lingers for a moment but responds to my glare, turns on her heel, then walks away.

"I don't know why you went through with marrying Kerry."

"I know what you're saying Mum."

"Let's not go there right now. The walls have ears." She looks again at the beige woman who immediately busies herself with her stack of sandwiches and cakes. "It's something else as well." She looks down and lowers her voice. "Your father has been in touch."

Something twists in my gut. "I haven't got a father. Not after what he did."

"I wanted to warn you. He knows where you live and where you work. And he's still blaming you for getting him sent down."

"Warn me! Why? Hasn't he done enough damage?"

"I couldn't believe it when I opened the door to him."

"He's a complete narcissist. Whatever he does in life, it's always someone else's fault."

"I know. He's a nasty piece of work. I'll never forgive him for what he did to you."

"It's been years. Why now?"

Our conversation is thwarted again by the stony-faced waitress, who proceeds to smooth out a napkin in front of each of us before laying down soup spoons and butter knives. "Your order won't be long."

"Thank you." I return to Mum. "What does he want?"

"He said he knows something and was quite menacing with it. Said he wanted to speak to you, to set the record straight. I wish Alistair had been there."

"What do you mean, he knows something? About what?" Having lunch in Betty's is supposed to be a pleasant experience. With its

121

pianist in the corner and the coffee and cake aroma, I can't believe we're having this conversation. My immediate thoughts are for my boys. BF knows my address, and obviously I'm not there. But they are...

"We should warn Kerry." Mum takes her phone out of her bag, checks it and puts it back again. That's not like her. She normally bollocks me for phone checking when we're together. "It's shaken me so much that I feel like moving house."

"Was he threatening you? Maybe we could get an injunction on him or something."

"It was his manner more than anything - not enough for an injunction, I wouldn't have thought. We don't know where he lives anyway, to have anything served on him."

"We could find out." Crockery and conversation echoes around us. "How's he found out where I work and live anyway?"

"You're not exactly hard to find Edward. Your business is all over the internet. Thanks." She smiles weakly at the waitress who places a bowl of soup before each of us.

"No sir." As I try to select a roll from the proffered basket, the waitress produces a set of tongs from within her apron. "We don't handle the food."

"Good grief." I watch her retreating form. "With the reputation this place has got, you'd think they'd employ friendlier waitresses."

"Never mind all that." Mum dangles her spoon above the soup. "Your dad..."

"I said don't call him that." Several of the other diners look at me. I lower my voice. "He ceased to be my dad the day he beat me to a pulp and put me in hospital."

"You don't know how guilty I feel about that." Mum still hasn't touched her soup. "After all, it was me who told him. About your being confused, I mean."

"I wish you'd stop describing it as *confused*." I feel bad snapping at my mother. However, I feel like she's always been ashamed of me. And she still is. I can see it in her eyes. "Did he say anything else?"

"He was just ranting, you know, like he used to. The usual *white noise.* I couldn't take it in."

"I remember it well." He'd keep talking, talking, talking. Repeating himself so no one could reply or offer their own view.

"Well." Mum puts her spoon down. "He kept saying *I know what he is, and I know what he's done.*"

"What's that supposed to mean? What does he think I've *done*?"

"I don't know Edward, but he was adamant that a time has come where you're going to experience some of what he has, whatever he means by that."

I watch as the waitress plonks a tray laden with silver jugs and teapots at the edge of our table. "Can I get you anything else? Sir? Madam?"

"No thank you. You sound like you're on *his* side Mum."

"Don't be so ridiculous. I just want to know what he was on about. Is there anything you need to tell me, apart from the obvious?"

"No. Eat your soup Mum."

"Are you going to tell Kerry, or am I?"

"I'll let you do it. I'll only get my head bitten off. Especially after she receives a letter from my solicitor in a day or two." As if I haven't got enough going on right now.

Usually I enjoy the company of my mother. Her calm air always grounds me. But I don't like the way she's looking at me today. Either she's completely sided with my soon-to-be-ex-wife or she thinks she knows something about something else. But whatever it is, she's not saying. If BF comes anywhere near me or my boys, I'll run him over. I'd probably be judged to have acted out of diminished responsibility for it, after the way he behaved.

123

Chapter 19

<u>Kerry</u>

"What do you want?" I hesitate before answering the phone to my mother-in-law. She knows more than she has ever let on.

"Oh Kerry. There's no need to be like this. I want to help if you'll let me."

"I'm sorry. I've just had enough of everything, to be honest. And I haven't slept well."

"I'm not surprised. Look, I'll take the boys again for you at the weekend. Let you have a bit of time to yourself."

"Is that why you're ringing? Wait a minute George." I turn away from him and walk to the lounge window, watching the next-door neighbours kiss one another before getting into their respective cars. I feel a huge stab of envy. "Ed should be having them, Marie. These boys are his responsibility too. He's just left us to it."

"I know. It's just with him staying at a hotel, it's difficult. As soon as he gets sorted, he'll take them for you, I'm sure."

"For me! They're his kids too!"

"I'm sorry love – I didn't mean it like that."

"You always stick up for him though, don't you?"

"Mummy!" Alex tugs at my skirt.

"Just give me five minutes. I'm talking to Grandma."

"I'm sorry to ring you so early Kerry, when I know you'll be getting the boys ready for school, but I really need to talk to you."

"What about?" My heckles are immediately up. *What now?*

"Can we meet up for coffee?"

"When?"

"This morning – if you've time. Caffé Nero, on the High Street?"

I sigh. "I'm supposed to be doing a gym class." Yet, I'm glad of an excuse not to go. Not to have to face my, so-called friends. With their lives that are oh-so-bloody-perfect, that it gives them the right to speculate about mine.

"It's important love."

"Is it about Ed?"

"Kind of. But I don't want to go into it over the phone."

"I'll drop the boys off, call into the shop, and then I'll see you. About half past ten?"

It's just after ten when I arrive. I don't seem to be rushing around quite as much as I did before Ed left. As for being early anywhere, it was unheard of. Apart from with the boys, I seem to have lost my sense of purpose. Mandy's taking good care of the shop. Perhaps when the new one opens, I should think about upping her salary a bit.

I sit for a while, suddenly realising that my head is in my hands as I stare into my Americano. I am surrounded by soft strains of jazz and pleasant conversation, and have never felt so lonely. My life is unrecognisable from what it was a month before. Losing Ed is like a physical pain.

I shouldn't be drinking coffee. The syrupy sweet smell around me is sickening my already queasy stomach further. My Fitbit shows my heart rate as being ninety-six beats a minute. Maybe that's down to caffeine on an empty stomach, but more likely, nerves at what Marie wants to talk to me so urgently about. Either way, I should have ordered chamomile tea.

I watch a couple across from me as the man reaches over the table to take hold of his companion's hand. I recall when Ed was like that, in the beginning, and without warning, tears fill my eyes. Yet perhaps he had always been destined to leave, and maybe I'd always known the truth about him.

Two men take their places on the table beside me. One squeezes the other one's thigh and I feel like throwing my coffee at them.

I watch as Marie approaches my table. She looks amazing for her age, despite the marriage I know she endured when she was younger.

"Do you want another one Kerry?"

"Yes please. Can I have chamomile tea please? Any more coffee and you'll be peeling me off the ceiling!"

We were friends when Ed and I first got together, and now I feel like I'm losing her, along with Ed. I can't help but push her away now, it makes me feel more in control in a situation where suddenly, I've no control whatsoever. I guess that no matter what, she'll be there for Alex and George. I look at her as she stands in the queue. Her loyalty will always be with Ed.

My mother doesn't even know we've split up. Neither does my brother, Adam. Soon I'll have to tell them and brace myself for the I told you so's. But for now, I kind of like them not knowing. It makes it less real somehow. When I first arrived here, the jazz music felt mildly calming. But now it's starting to grate.

Marie slides a tray onto the table and smiles at me, though it's a weak smile. "So how are you?" She puts a cup, saucer and teapot in front of me and a glass full of iced water in front of herself.

"I've been better. You?"

"Same." She does look tired. I never noticed before. Though other than her married, father-of-two son being secretly gay, I can't imagine what she's got to be stressed about. She seems to have a settled enough life.

"So what's so important that I had to miss my gym class?" I've surprised myself really. A month ago, I wouldn't have missed my class and my friends for all the tea in China. The weight's falling off me now though, whether I go to the gym or not. I've no appetite. I don't enjoy food anymore. I don't enjoy anything anymore.

"Ed's real father has been to the house."

"Really? When?" I've never met the man. I know he terrorised Ed and put him in hospital once. Ed wouldn't really discuss it, or him.

"On Sunday evening. It's a shame Alistair wasn't there. He was a bit intimidating to say the least."

"How?"

"I can't really tell you anything concrete, just that I want you, and obviously George and Alex, to be careful." She's avoiding my gaze and keeps looking at the door.

"What do you mean *careful*? We've never even met him!" I'm baffled now. Like I don't have enough hassles of my own at the moment.

"He's gunning for Ed." Marie takes a sip of her water. "He served eighteen months for what he did to him. There seems to be something else that's bugging him now."

"Why did he do what he did? Beat him up, I mean?" I steel myself. Will she be honest, or not?

"Ed wanted to come out. He'd been seeing someone when he was younger."

"A man, you mean?" I feel sick. Marie had known, even back then. Why couldn't she have warned me? Though really, would I have listened?

"Well, a boy. I had just thought it was a teenager thing. A phase. At

127

least I hoped so. My ex-husband was the most homophobic person I had ever known. It stemmed from when *he* had been younger – something had happened."

"Go on." I stir my chamomile around in the tea pot, hoping it will calm me down.

"He was followed home from a youth club when he was thirteen. Two men. They'd taken it in turns with him. And it was never dealt with. He'd been too ashamed to report it. And his own father had turned on him. Another homophobe. And a bit of a brute, by all accounts. His mother had a rotten time with him."

"I didn't know any of this. Ed wouldn't talk about him." I pour my tea. "Is she still alive? She'd be George and Alex's great grandmother, wouldn't she?"

"No. She's long gone."

"So how come you married Ed's father? Knowing how screwed up he was?"

"I didn't know back then. I was young and naïve. He had turned on the charm and promised to look after me." She sighs. "It was as Edward was growing up that I saw his true colours. I was always having to protect Edward from him."

"Is that why you didn't have any more children?"

"I guess so. I'd have loved a daughter, but there was no way I'd have risked having any more children."

"Why did you stay so long? I mean, Ed was sixteen. That's a lot of years to waste." We're not so dissimilar, I nearly add, thinking of the years I've wasted so far.

"I know." Her eyes are downcast. "It took Edward being beaten up by him before I found some fight in myself. I thought I could fix him. My ex, I mean. I made excuses for him. The bottom line is that you become so ground down with living in an awful marriage, and you start to believe that's all you deserve."

"I can't imagine you living like that. You seem so strong."

"Thanks. I guess I've done a lot of work on myself since." She rubs at her head. "And I've had to forgive myself for staying so long - putting Edward through it all too."

"So what's he come back for?"

"I'm not sure. He's claiming he knows something and was also shouting about Edward owing him. I didn't listen to him for long. But I heard enough to discover that he knows about you, and the boys, and where you live."

"Where I live? But he doesn't know me!" My voice rises to a pitch where people at other tables look round at me.

"I know. I just wanted to warn you. He's a nasty piece of work. There's probably nothing to worry about, but you've got a right to know what's going on – just in case."

"But Ed's not even living with us." Hope suddenly shoots through me. This latest development might bring Ed back. "Did you tell him? His father, I mean. About us splitting up?"

"Of course not. I just want you to be careful. You and the boys. If he wants revenge on Edward, he might target those he cares about most."

"You mean the boys," I say, bitterness trickling through my voice. "He doesn't care about me, anymore."

"I'm sorry about what's going on." Marie reaches across the table and squeezes my arm. "It's a mess. But I'm here to help you. I'm not going anywhere, I promise."

"Thanks." I know she means it. "What do you mean – target?"

"Unfortunately, I can't answer that. Just be vigilant for a week or two. Keep the doors locked and don't let the boys play in the garden."

"You're kidding." I glance out of the window at the beautiful spring day. "They're hyper enough without being cooped up inside! Surely they're not in any danger from a man who is technically their grandfather."

"That's precisely why they are." Marie drains her glass.

"Maybe Ed will move back in. If not for me, for them." I feel faintly hopeful. If we can all be back under one roof, perhaps he will want his old life back. Maybe we can work things out when things settle down. He's been mixed up about himself before and returned from it.

"I was thinking the same thing." Marie tucks her purse into her handbag.

"Do you think he's definitely gay, Marie? Is there any chance he's still confused?"

"I'm sorry love. As his mother, I think he's worked through the confusion. I think he is gay but has buried it for a long time. It's an awful situation and I really feel for you."

"Perhaps he's bisexual?" But even as I say it, I know I'm talking rubbish.

She shakes her head, a sad expression on her face. "I don't think he would have moved out like he has if that had been the case."

The little bit of hope I'd just felt, instantly fades. "I just can't cope with it all." I rub at my temples, feeling the urge to break down and weep, right here in Caffé Nero. I've had enough.

"You'll get through this. I promise." Marie moves around the table to my side and sits next to me. "Why don't you and the boys come and stay with me for a few days?"

"Thanks, but there's no way some weirdo man is driving me out of my own home. I'll be careful though, like you said."

"Well, if you change your mind, you can just turn up anytime."

I arrive early to pick the boys up and can't help checking around me for nasty looking, middle-aged men. I feel detached from the hum of conversation which echoes around me as I stand in the playground, waiting. I've buried myself in work all day, swatting away Mandy's attempts to find out the latest. She's efficient and trustworthy, as a manager, but as a fellow female, she's nosy, gossipy and I don't trust her.

I've always felt displaced from other mothers at this school. It's as though they suspect where I came from, and today, I'm plain old Kerry Barnes. To one side of me, the conversation centres around how many degrees centigrade a certain holiday destination is likely to be and how fabulous the hotel is. On the other side, A-Level stress is being discussed in relation to a university offer, and behind me, two ladies are discussing an invitation to a wedding and what they might wear. I swallow memories of my own wedding and watch the classroom window. There's a flurry of activity inside as the children all get organised with coats, shoes, book bags and paintings. Alex waves at me through the window. The teacher pulls the blind down. I feel my heckles rise at that.

"Sorry to hear about what you're going through."

My breath catches in my throat as I turn around. "Erm thanks."

It's the mother of a little boy who is friends with George and Alex. "It must be really hard. I can't imagine…"

"Don't even try. But thanks anyway." The little display of kindness makes me want to cry, there and then. I've been reasonably strong since Ed walked out, but today I'm feeling seriously wobbly.

The double doors of the cloakroom swing open and we surge forwards. There are two reception classes with nine children in each. I watch for my two. I notice a couple of sideways glances at me. Loaded with pity, I think. No one else speaks to me. In fact, over the last couple of weeks the other mothers have spoken to me even less. Like your husband walking out on you is something you can catch.

Holding the hand of each twin, we walk towards the Range Rover. I'm still scanning the vicinity for anyone lurking around. I can't believe I'm having to do this!

I can't face going home. "How do you boys fancy going to Ikea?" I try to load cheer into my voice as I strap them both into their car seats.

"What's Ikea, Mummy?"

"We can have some tea there and buy some new toy boxes for your bedroom."

"Can we buy some new toys as well?"

I laugh at that. "George, you've got lots of toys. You don't need any more. Mummy wants to look at some things for the new shop. I will put a new office in the back of it, and I need some furniture." I feel brighter. Maybe I can look to the future.

I'm hoping they don't spot the play area and ball pool as we walk in. But of course they do. "Can we go in?" they shriek in unison.

"If you're really good boys, you can have some time on the way out. Come on."

"Aww!"

"I'm not sure what time the café will close. And we want some tea, don't we? But the ball pool is open really late!"

At first the twins are interested in all the mocked-up rooms as we follow the arrows around. Some of them are impressive. Before we set up home, Ed and I once wandered around, taking photos of layout ideas and planning what we would be buying. We laid on a bed together, with our feet dangling off the end, and I remember feeling happy and excited about what our future would hold. I see a young couple now, a similar age to us then. He's stood behind her with his arms around her middle and she's taking a photograph of a kitchen. He kisses the top of her head and I want to cry again. Ed never loved me like that.

But he gave me my sons. I watch them now, dashing around a set-up studio apartment, laughing together, and my heart swells. They're lovely boys and I can take them anywhere, knowing they'll always behave. They can be boisterous but they're polite and to a point, they do as they're asked by adults. It's amazing what advantages a good start can offer. They've had the best of everything so far, unlike the poverty I knew as a child. At the moment, they seem relatively unscathed by their father's departure. It's as though he's working away or something and they're used to that.

Perhaps, before long, I can persuade him to return. Particularly now there's the threat of his father turning up. I'm unsettled by this possibility, but not scared. So he might say a few nasty things but seriously, what harm can he do? I'm through the worst of it, I'm certain of that.

I have to believe for my own sanity that Marie has got it wrong about Ed. He may be mixed up about his sexuality but I can win him back. Just a few days in the house will show him he can have a happy, normal life with us again. Lots of people are bisexual. Maybe I can live with that.

It's like a school canteen in the Ikea dining hall. I queue with the boys behind a family. Watching their easy interaction brings the all-too-familiar lump to my throat. The man squeezes the woman's bum, which part of me is amused by, yet another part feels so lonely that I want to scream at the injustice of it all.

"No, you two are not carrying a tray." I swipe it from Alex. "Mummy will hold it, otherwise tea will end up all over the floor."

"I'm hungry." We stand in the queue for five minutes, waiting to pay. I pat George's head. I'm starting to feel impatient. Their food will be cold by the time they get it, although they can be such slow eaters, they're used to cold food anyway. I'm glad I got a sandwich, although my appetite isn't what it was at all. I feel sick with nervous energy all the time. Since Ed has gone, I feel a sense of displacement. I struggle to focus on anything and don't feel like me anymore.

"OK, boys. Once we've eaten this, we're going to look at toy boxes. That means you'll both have to tidy your rooms."

"Then can we go to the play area?"

"If you're very good whilst Mummy looks at the office furniture. I need to look at some pictures too."

I've got a fair order by the time I get to the warehouse and payment area. I will get it all delivered to the new shop. I'm signing the lease next week, so it's safe to get it all ordered now. There's space for a proper office there, rather than the little desk beside the sink we have at the current shop. I've ordered a small filing cabinet, an electronic sit/stand desk, an executive leather chair, a shelving unit, pictures and a rug. And the toy boxes for the boys and a bookcase to tidy their books onto – they have tons of them. I feel a flicker of excitement at the thought of assembling my office at the new shop. If only my personal life could be going as well as my business.

The boys are fractious as we wait in the lengthy queue to pay.

"Remember what I said about the play area!" They immediately stand to attention. I smile at them. It was an excellent idea, coming here. I feel better than I have in weeks, despite the conversation I had with Marie this morning. I hand my debit card to the cashier.

"Sorry, it's been declined." She rips off a receipt. I stare at it, as though that might change something.

An echo of when I was younger envelops me. It used to be the norm that I always had insufficient funds, usually because of a bank charge or something. "I can't understand that." I say, "can you try it again, please?"

"Certainly Madam. If you'd like to pop the card back into the reader."

I do as she asks and type in the PIN for the joint account really carefully. Almost immediately, it flashes up transaction declined. "Maybe my husband's changed the PIN number." I feel my face flame.

Shit.

"No, the PIN is fine, it would have said *incorrect PIN* if it wasn't. Do you have another payment card, madam?"

I wish she'd stop calling me madam. I slide another one from my purse and put it into the machine.

"Mummy!"

"Just a minute sweetie-pie."

I type in my number. "This one will be fine." I try to smile at the assistant, but it's probably more of a grimace.

"I'm sorry. I'm afraid that one's been declined as well."

She looks bemused and I hear tutting from the queue that's snaking down the aisle behind me.

"Would you like to try another payment method?"

"Mummy. Come on!"

I want to disappear. This scenario is far too close to the bone. I can't think straight. Both our joint accounts. He must have emptied them or something. The card for the business account is at the shop and I'm waiting for a replacement debit card for my own current account. "Do you offer credit facilities?" I'd pass a credit check. I don't know what else to do. I don't know why I don't just walk away from here. Everyone is looking at me.

"I'm sorry madam. We don't. Perhaps you could pay by credit card?"

"I don't have one." We've never needed one. We've always had enough money, thanks to Ed. Fucking Ed. As if he hasn't hurt me enough.

"Would you like me to call a manager?"

"I'll leave it thanks. Come on boys." I catch the hands of George and Alex and walk away from the pictures and toy boxes piled up on the conveyor belt.

"What about our things, Mummy?"

"We'll come back for them another day."

"Can we go to the play area now please?"

"No." I just want to get home, pour a large glass of wine and find out what the hell is going on.

"But, Mummy, you said…"

I literally have to drag them both to the car park, wailing in unison. Everyone is staring at us. By the time we reach the car, I'm nearly wailing with them. "Shut up, both of you!" I snap as I struggle to strap them in. They both cry harder. I would not normally tell them to shut up, but I'm at the end of my tether. By the time we reach home, they're both fast asleep and I've spent the entire journey with tears coursing down my face. Serves me right for feeling momentarily normal in Ikea.

"Straight to bed tonight boys," I say as I lead them towards the door, swiping up the pile of letters from the doormat as we go in. "Go and get your pyjamas on."

"But what about our bath?"

"And our milk?"

"I'll bring some up shortly and you can just have a flannel wash tonight."

"And a story?" Alex looks at me.

I feel so guilty. I've no energy for them tonight. "Just go upstairs. I'll be there soon."

As they walk away, I flick through the letters in my hand. Most of them are for Ed. One is stamped MSB Solicitors and addressed to me. With a thudding chest, I rip it open. It's straight to the point.

We have been instructed by Mr Edward Huntington of his intention to commence divorce proceedings. We are writing to you in order to recommend that you obtain independent legal advice for yourself if you haven't already. You should provide your appointee with our details, in order that both parties can be represented. We await a response at your earliest convenience.

Chapter 20

Tony

I never dreamed I would end up in this line of work. It all came about when I was strapped for cash in my late twenties. *Very strapped for cash and in a fair bit of trouble over a debt.*

My mate, Laura, I say mate, but I fancied her really, was getting a massive amount of grief from her husband. By all accounts, she'd started to *walk into a few too many doors.*

It was her Mick, her brother, who paid me to deal with him. I wasn't supposed to take him out completely, just give him a pasting he'd never forget. But a white rage, fuelled from what I'd been through myself in my teens, took over me.

Not long after that, Mick had a run in with someone who owed him a lot of money. It had been a bit of a shady deal and his associate was threatening to go down official channels to resolve it. This time I was briefed and paid for the 'full monty.'

Next, one of Mick's mates wanted to see the permanent back of his girlfriend's ex, then another mate, of mine this time, had someone who had defrauded him. Word was spreading. People knew I did a thorough job. And was discreet.

Really, I see myself as a provider of a service. Weeding out the dregs of society. As the years have passed, I've been able to increase my fee substantially - after all, I'm a lone wolf and it takes a lot of thought and preparation to do what I do. Not to mention personal risk. Anyway, I'm digressing here.

It was the first time I'd be paid to take someone out in this way. *Sexual Asphyxiation.* With a man. Made my stomach churn. I really had my doubts about this one, even though I was to be paid double what I would normally make. Ten grand up front and another ten grand on completion. It had to look like a sexual act gone wrong. And something he might have decided to do on his own.

Russell Lawson wasn't the usual sort of bloke who would have a contract out on him. When I started fact-gathering, I couldn't believe it. He lived in the sticks of Yorkshire and was an average family bloke with a steady, well paid job.

I'd been told there was more to him than met the eye, but I still wasn't convinced, at least to start with, that I was doing the right thing. He had a young kid, for God's sake. However, an increase in the fee did the trick. An extra ten grand. Ta very much. Thirty Grand.

In the week I surveyed him, he was putting it about a bit, probably spreading God-knows-what around. I watched him meet six different men and take four of them to hotel rooms. He must have had some kind of sex addiction. It would make my job easier than I thought it would be. Far easier. And I would be doing society a huge service.

I set up a fake profile on Grinder and arranged to meet him in a pub opposite Leeds Parkway. If only it was as easy to persuade women to meet me.

"You look a bit different from your profile picture," he'd said, looking at me. We were sat in the corner, me, with my back to the room. There was nowhere else to look other than at him. He was nothing special but he had a swagger about him. I could see why he had no trouble pulling people in.

Like I've said, I hate queers, and with this one, there was something piercing about the way he looked at me. It awoke something that made me furious, in fact, it made me despise him, if I'm truthful. Which wasn't a bad thing really, given the task ahead of me.

"Amazing what a haircut and a good night's sleep can do," I'd replied, holding his gaze, hoping he couldn't see the loathing in my expression. I'd found the picture of 'me' on Google images - it wasn't that dissimilar. I'd used a variety of cafés and libraries to research Russell Lawson and message with him once we'd matched. I never doubted we'd 'match' – he obviously shagged anything that moved - man or woman.

"So do you bat for both sides or are you an all man kind of man?" He crossed one leg over the over as he brought his pint to his lips.

"Just starting out, to be honest. I've always been a bit mixed up about myself." I can be a bloody good liar when I want to be and this was an Oscar-winning performance. To the rest of the pub, we probably looked like two mates out for a drink after work.

"So how far have you gone? With a man, I mean?"

"Not got to first base yet." Fuck! Am I really having this conversation? I felt sick to my stomach. "I'm kind of looking for a no strings, showing of the ropes."

"Well, you've come to the right place." He ran his thumb and forefinger up and down either side of his throat as he spoke.

"I'm nervous, to be honest." *Not as nervous as you'll be when you're gasping*, I thought.

"Don't be." He licked beer froth off his top lip. "Fresh meat. I like that."

Fucking Nancy. I hated him. "So what have you got in mind?" I glanced around. I'd suggested this place because I knew the new side entrance was free of CCTV. Russell had gone to the bar to order when we'd first arrived, and I'd been glad of a beer to settle me down a bit.

"There's a pleasant hotel over the road." He tipped his head and his eyes seemed to wander to my crotch as he spoke.

"Nice?" Get your fucking eyes off me.

"You know. Convenient. It's a room. One where we can lock the door. Enjoy the rest of our afternoon." Because he was so blonde, I could see he had flushed to the roots of his hair.

"I've got a lot to lose," I said.

"Wife? Kids?"

"Both." I had neither. I did once but I fucked it up. I've stayed single since as it would take a certain type of woman to understand what I do.

"We can be discreet."

"That's what I was hoping you'd say. I'll go with you. As long as we go into the hotel and make our way to the room, one at a time."

"I've made the reservation." Russell smiled.

"How very presumptuous." But I smiled back. I had a role to play, after all. And I was doing it very well.

"I could tell you were ripe. From your messages, I mean." He drained the last of his pint.

"Ripe! You make me sound like a peach! I take it we're not getting another?" Part of me wanted to stall what was about to happen but the other part of me knew I had to get it over with. I wanted more beer really. However, it would have to be a soft drink, clear head required, and all that. I'd also have to get Russell to go again. I couldn't risk the bar staff getting a look at me.

"Nah. I think our time together could be better spent, don't you? I'll go first. Room twenty-four. Ground floor. Through the revolving door, to the left, follow to the end of the corridor then go right."

"You've obviously done this before."

Russell tapped the side of his nose. "I've already checked in. I've left a few bits and pieces in the room. Make things more interesting."

I pointed towards my holdall on the floor. "Me too." *Wouldn't you just love to know what's in here?*

"So what are we waiting for?" He stood, his arms bulging out of his shirt sleeves. "If you want to follow on in a few minutes, I'll be waiting."

"Can I come straight in? Do I need to say anything to reception?" I already knew the answer to this. I'd seen that this was Russell's favourite location once he'd pulled, and I'd checked out the hotel's layout on their website.

"Yeah, I've got the keycard." He patted his top pocket. "Just follow me in."

I watched him stride to the main entrance, exuding confidence. He pulled the door open, turned, and grinned at me before leaving. I necked the rest of my pint. My chest ached with tension. I swallowed. This was the most nervous I'd felt during a contract. Though I'm getting to be an old hand at this game, this situation was a first, with a lot of money riding on it and a lot of shit within myself to overcome. *Get a grip Tony – fuck's sake,* I said to myself. I took a couple of long breaths before slipping out of the side door.

Either Russell had lingered, or I'd been too quick off the mark. Either way, as soon as I got through the revolving doors of The Parkside, I spotted him, only just disappearing around the corner. I slowed my pace and avoiding anyone's eye, headed nonchalantly in the same direction.

I'd caught up with him before we made it to the room.

"Fancy seeing you here," he grinned.

"Fancy." I kept my head bowed as we progressed along the corridor to the door of room twenty-four.

"So here we are." He slid his card into the door handle. "I can think of worse ways to spend a Thursday afternoon."

"Me too." Like jumping into a bath full of acid.

I dumped my holdall on the bed, taking in the items he'd brought. Lube, some kind of vibrator, massage oil, what looked like clamps, condoms. I now knew what the expression *made my flesh crawl* meant.

He noticed me looking. "I always practice safe sex. I've got a wife too."

"Does she know... about all this?"

"Kind of. She knows I've got needs she can't fulfil. I've tried to be straight. Can't resist though." He sank to the bed, watching me the entire time. "What's in your bag of tricks then?"

I unzipped the holdall and pulled out the ligature. "I've always wanted to try this. I've heard you shouldn't do it on your own." I thrust it towards him. "Thought you might be the man who could show me how it's done."

"It's been a while since I had a go at that." He took it from me and inspected it. "It's mind blowing. Come here."

I sat beside him on the bed, stomach churning. I've taken people out over and over again, barely breaking a sweat. But this was something else.

"No, right here."

"I'd like to watch *you* first," I said. "I want to see you naked." I could hardly believe these disgusting words were leaving my mouth. Thirty grand. Thirty grand.

"Fair enough, as long as you promise to join in with me."

"Remember. This is my first time. I need to ease myself in."

He began unbuttoning his shirt, then his jeans, his eyes not leaving mine the whole time. I hardly knew where to look as he removed his boxers, revealing his excitement.

"Carry on." You've already had ten grand. You can do this. Service to society. Service to society.

He took himself in one hand and reached out with his other for me.

"Not yet. Let me watch for a while." I took the lid from the oil and held it towards him.

Moaning, he rubbed it over himself.

"Stop." I said, after a few moments. "Let me watch you really go to the brink." I pointed to the leather strap on the bed.

"Really?"

"I want to try it too. But I want to watch you first."

"Fuck me. Straight in for the jugular. You'll have my back, right?"

"Of course." I stood. "Thump your chest if it becomes too much. That can be the signal."

"Why don't you make yourself comfortable? He reached towards my flies. I want to see what you've got for me."

"All in good time. Don't forget, I'm new to this."

He was so turned on that he was far easier to talk into it than I ever thought he would be. Taking the strap from me, he moved towards the en-suite door. He studied the strap for a moment, before opening the door a little and hooking it over the door and through the automatic door closing mechanism.

"Once I've watched you. You can help me get to the same place."

I watched as he fastened the collar to the belt, then poked his head through the collar, tightening the buckle around his neck. This was playing out like clockwork.

"It's been a while since I've done this, but as you'll soon find out, it's the business."

"Like I said, I've always wanted to try it. It's supposed to be better than heroin."

I stood before him as he took himself in hand again. Within a few minutes, he was dangling from the collar with slightly bent knees, his feet skimming the carpet, panting, groaning, rubbing at himself frantically. His eyes were closed, clearly he was in his own world. I didn't want to be watching but with another twenty grand riding on it, this had to be seen through.

I slipped around the other side of him and moved the door with my shoulder, so it was slightly more ajar. As I'd tested already, the strap shortened and he was now really dangling. Even if he straightened his legs he'd be on tip-toes. He started to gasp. I moved further behind the en-suite door as he shot his load. I pushed the door further open so his feet could no longer connect to the floor. He began to really struggle then, trying to get his feet back down, thumping his chest. I kept my shoulder pressed against the door, holding it open as he writhed around, making a gurgling sound like I've never heard. It was the first time I'd taken someone out by strangulation – it's normally a good beating with a baseball bat or a quick and easy shot.

It felt like forever before he lost consciousness. Handsome Russell was not a pretty sight. Cock still in hand, his face was purple, his tongue lolling from his mouth. He was still gurgling, though the sound had faded. I decided to leave it a few minutes before making my exit.

I heard some women pass outside the door of the hotel room and noticed the closed curtains billowing in the breeze. Thirty grand. It was the most I'd ever been paid for a hit. Easy money, even if I had to compromise myself a little more than usual. I could *say* that now it was over. I just had to get out of here.

I wanted to check his pulse but didn't want to risk touching him. I hadn't touched anything in the room. Retrieving my holdall, I fought the urge to wretch as I stepped over the spunk trail and left. I've normally got a stomach of steel but this one had got to me. I knew I'd probably hurl somewhere but needed to get well away first.

I'd already recced my departure. I was close to where the corridors joined the spa changing rooms and knew I could leave via the veranda doors, near the outdoor hot tub. I'd checked, and the CCTV camera was directed towards the hot tub and not the exit.

I disappeared into nearby woodland, which emerged at the edge of the park. I swallowed bile, trying to get further away. I couldn't be sick there! I started running, then realised that I'd draw attention to myself. Breathe. Breathe. It was no good. Within moments, I was bent double, spewing the pint I had drunk, and the sandwich I had forced down earlier. I chucked a load of foliage and bark over it, cursing myself. Hopefully, there'd be no searches done down here.

I'd planned this carefully enough. It looked like a solo sex game gone wrong. End of story.

Chapter 21

<u>Ed</u>

I t's almost seven thirty when I arrive back at the Old Swan. I've worked late to make up for the appointments that had to be rescheduled from yesterday. Working keeps my mind off things a bit. Russell is never far from my thoughts but I get less 'sledgehammer' moments whilst I'm seeing patients, when I suddenly remember that he has gone.

"Good evening sir." The man behind the reception desk recognises me now. "Will you be dining with us this evening?" He glances at the grandfather clock. "We're serving until eight thirty."

"Thanks but I think I'll take advantage of the swimming pool." I glance through the glass panel to where it waits, still and inviting. There's just one person in the jacuzzi. "I'll nip out to one of the local restaurants later."

"That sounds like a fine plan for the evening sir. Oh, before I forget, I must give you these." He reaches beneath the counter, then places an envelope and a message slip before me.

The envelope has been franked with MSB Solicitors and the message slip has my name at the top, the personal caller box has been ticked and the time of call has been given as 17:30. No message left. I look up at the man. "There's not a lot to go on here."

"I know. I'm sorry sir. Your visitor didn't leave his name."

"So it was a man? What did he look like?"

"I don't know. About your height, I guess. Dark hair, receding at the top a bit."

"How old?"

"I'm not very good with ages sir. Middle aged? He sounded local. Gosh – I should work for the police!"

"What was he wearing?" I don't like the sound of this. No one knows where I am staying.

"Ah now that I can remember! Because we get so many businessmen here, I was struck by the fact that he was wearing jeans and trainers."

A woman standing behind me sighs. She can sigh all she wants. "How did he ask for me? Did he sound like he knew me?"

The man laughs. "So many questions! I think he just used your full name."

"Not Ed?"

"I don't think so."

"Thank you."

"I'm sure that if he really wants to speak to you, he'll be back."

The woman gives me a dirty look as I stride away from reception. I think back to yesterday's conversation with Mum. Surely BF wouldn't have the audacity to just turn up here? I'm totally unnerved by the prospect and wish whoever it was had left their name. I won't rest until I find out.

I take the lift to my room, then sink into the armchair to open my letter. It's confirmation that Mark Smeaton-Barrie will be acting for me, with a page full of terms and a copy of the letter he's sent to Kerry. I wonder if she's had it yet. I feel an unexpected twinge of guilt. Perhaps I should have warned her it was coming. I wrestle with the urge to help myself to a whiskey from the mini bar and instead tug my trunks and a change of clothes from the wardrobe. I stride towards the door and let it softly close behind me.

By the time I've done a few lengths, I'm feeling calmer. I'm the only person in here and I feel lulled by the sound of my arms powering through the water as I pelt up and down the pool. I can finally allow my mind to wander a bit. I think of the boys and the last time I took them swimming. I miss them hugely and know I need to get the situation sorted out. But Kerry, for all her faults, is an exceptional mother and I know she will be taking good care of them.

I notice a figure standing at the window near the hotel reception. It looks like Russell. I still imagine I see him everywhere. I've heard that's common when someone you love has died. I remember our triathlon training each Wednesday night and how fantastic he looked. By the time I've turned at the end of my length, the figure has gone. I feel like I'm going through the motions at the moment, lacking purpose and joy. It's as though everything I had to live for has died with Russell. Splitting with Kerry has displaced me as well. Even though I could not stay with her, she grounded me – I had a sense of normality and routine. Right now, there's only work that is any sort of constant.

As I turn again at the near end of the pool, I see the figure clearly now. He's aged somewhat and seems smaller somehow. It's been fifteen years but there's no mistaking BF, stood watching me with the same hate in his eyes he harboured for me before. I'm a grown man with two boys of my own, but an unplanned fear rises in me. He's an evil piece of work and is capable of anything. I don't know how he has found me, but here he is. According to Mum, it won't be a social call. I have to get out of here. There's no one around and if BF comes into the pool area, he's likely to try to drown me or something. Especially if his past actions towards me are anything to go by.

I need to get to where there are people around. He'd have to swipe his room card to get into the pool area but if he tells the man on reception that I'm his son, perhaps he'd let him in. Son! The thought makes me angry. I've only got about ten lengths in. I grab my towel and pull on my jeans. They're hard to get on over wet flesh but I must get out of here. I poke my head through my t-shirt, slide my feet into flip flops and make for the pool exit. There's no sign of him as I emerge in reception.

I gasp at the woman behind the counter. "The man, who was here before, have you seen him?"

"What man?" The young girl flicks her blonde hair as she sweeps her gaze from one side of the foyer to the other. "I'm sorry – we've just changed shift. I haven't seen anyone. I've just come out of handover."

"It's just-there's a man-he might be here to cause-he's my-." I'm not making any sense. I need to calm down. "I'm sorry." They'll be asking me to leave here as well if I'm not careful. I take the stairs to my floor, where I will be able to see the door to my room from the top of them, and get back down if he's waiting there. The lift faces the other way. By the time I've run up all six flights, I'm panting for breath. I glance up and down the corridor. No sign, so I run towards my room and let myself in.

I scan the car park from my window then pull the heavy curtains across. I turn a tumbler over on the drinks tray, fill it with a whiskey from the mini bar, then down it in one. Another one would be good but I'm probably best getting out of here. He knows where I am. Think, Ed, think. What if he's gone to Kerry's next? I hope Mum's warned her by now! He could have been checking on my whereabouts, before going to her. I chuck all my belongings into my case. I'll have to return home. They need me there.

The receptionist looks startled when I tell her I'm checking out. "Is everything alright sir? I thought you were staying indefinitely."

"Something's come up. If I could just settle my account please."

"Certainly." She presses some keys on her computer.

I glance towards the doors. "If anyone comes looking for me, please don't give them any information as to whether I've checked out."

"We wouldn't, sir." She slides a piece of paper from the printer and places it before me. "Everything is confidential."

"Good." I hand her my payment card.

I pull up outside the familiarity of home, feeling nervous. The Range Rover is on the drive so I know they're in. There's no sign of life within the house but it's after nine, so George and Alex will probably be in bed by now. It dawns on me that I probably should have let Kerry know I was coming. I glance around. There's no sign of anyone hanging around, or any cars I don't recognise. I lock the Audi and head for the front door. Locked. I decide to ring the doorbell, rather than use my key. After all, we're separated now. No reply. I ring again. The house is silent. I take my mobile out and try Kerry's number.

"What do you want?" she snaps after one ring.

"I'm outside," I say. "Can I come in? I need to talk to you."

"Is it about the letter?"

"No. It's about my father. He's hanging about. I need to talk to you."

"Well I've got nothing to say to you, you heartless bastard."

"Kerry. Just let me in. We can talk about all this."

"No chance. Do one Ed." She hangs up.

I put my key in the door and push. She's bolted it on the inside. *Cow.* "I own this house," I shout. "You can't lock me out."

"You should have thought about that before you emptied all the bank accounts." her voice sounds from the hallway. "You just wait!"

"Mummy!" I hear Alex, his voice sounding small from the floor above.

"Go back to bed Alex. Mummy will be up in a moment."

"Kerry, please." I plead.

"No, Ed."

I feel empty. What the hell do I do? I could go to another hotel. I want to be here, protecting them, but if she won't let me in... I return to my car and head towards my mother's house.

Chapter 22

Kerry

It took ages for the boys to go back to sleep last night. I had the doors and windows locked up like Fort Knox. The front door kept going all night. It's not really Ed's style to keep knocking when he's been sent packing. I'm assuming it was him, but didn't check. I still can't believe he's emptied our bank accounts. I've only got what's left in my current and savings account – I'm not going to get very far on that.

I've kept the boys off school today and have decided to drive over to my mother's. I don't feel safe here. Despite the wine I drank, I've been awake half the night, hearing noises. Plus Ed's texted me saying he wants to move back in. I thought I wanted him to, but now he's done what he's done with the money, I'm not so sure. Hopefully Mum will give me a hand with the kids. I love them to bits but I can't think straight right now.

"Why were you cross last night Mummy?"

"Why aren't we wearing our school uniforms Mummy?"

"I want Nutella on my toast."

"Right, boys. We've got a long drive so I want best behaviour." I've already packed our things. I just want to get away.

"But where are we going? What about school?"

"We're off to see Grandma." I drain my coffee and bustle around the kitchen, tidying away breakfast things.

"But that's not a long way."

"Your other Grandma." It makes me feel a little sad that they immediately think of Ed's mother at the word 'Grandma.' They hardly see my mother. I remember the first time I took Ed round to meet her. He stood, huge in her tiny lounge, his polished air making the surroundings feel even shabbier by comparison. I'd felt irked because she'd not bothered to tidy up, or make any sort of effort with her appearance. She'd known he was coming to meet her and that it was important to me.

The drive to North Wales consists of half of it spent with the boys bickering and the other half of it with them sleeping. They won't sleep tonight but I'm glad of the peace now. I've a lot to think about.

I miss my own space as soon as I walk up Mum's garden path towards the door of the home I grew up in. The garden is overgrown now. It used to be her pride and joy - I paid, a couple of years ago, for a bit of a makeover but she's not kept up with it. The house is a tip as well. She never used to be like this. When we were kids, she worked three jobs to look after us, and the house was impeccable. Her motto was that you should appreciate and look after what you've got, then something better is more likely to come along. But in her case, it never did. I hate coming back here. It reminds me of the years where I was too embarrassed to bring my friends round and was made to wear my cousin's hand-me-downs.

"So, to what do I owe this pleasure, Kerry?" Her voice oozes sarcasm.

The boys fold themselves into either side of me. It's a different ball game when we arrive at Marie's. They storm in and throw themselves at her. Still, it's partly my fault that they're shy of their other Grandma.

"Don't be like that Mum. We wanted to visit you."

"It's been over a year," she sniffs, clicking the TV off with the remote. "Since I've seen you, that is. In fact," she looks thoughtful, "I don't think we've even spoken on the telephone since Christmas!"

"I know. But we're here now."

"What's with the bag?" She eyes the large holdall I've placed on the worn arm of the sofa.

"I was hoping we could stay for a few days Mum." I can't look at her. My face will give me away.

"Why? Have you fallen out with wonderboy?"

"Something like that. Long story." I sink to the sofa and the boys sink with me, flanking me on either side. "Boys, give your Grandma a big hug."

They grip me tighter and I regret my words as soon as I've said them. "They just need time to acclimatise Mum. They've gone a bit shy."

"I'll put the kettle on." I watch as she rises from her chair and goes into the kitchen. She's put weight on and is wearing a frumpy knee-length skirt with an elasticated waist and a baggy t-shirt. Her steely-grey hair hangs down her back. I will never let myself get like that.

"Boys, shall I put something on the telly for you, whilst I'm talking to Grandma."

They nod. I reach over to Mum's armchair for the remote and find *Peppa Pig.* They're immediately transfixed.

I listen to Mum clattering about in the kitchen. "Do the boys want some juice?"

"Yes please," I call back, looking around at her framed photographs. I can hear in her voice that she's not really that annoyed with me. My eyes fall onto one, of the four of us. Adam and I were twelve and fourteen - it was just after they had diagnosed Dad. We were having a holiday that had been funded by a charity. Dad had finished work and Mum was working all the hours God sent.

There's one of us at four and six. I'm struck, by how much of the boys can be seen in me and my brother. I'd always thought George and Alex look like Ed. Then my gaze rests on a beautifully framed wedding photograph. At the time, I thought it was the happiest day of my life but now, looking at it, it feels like the saddest. I've never noticed it before but Ed's body language points away from me. At least I can admit that I buried what I'd long suspected. And I buried my suspicions to escape the life I had known here.

Mum returns, carrying a tray. She places a plate of biscuits and some juice for the boys on the coffee table.

"Ooh, you've made a teapot. I am honoured!"

"Well, so am I." She pours milk into the two mugs. "It's not often enough that *you* visit. Though I have to say, it will be a bit of a squeeze. Your old room is full of junk. You'll have to have Adam's old room and share a bed with the boys. How long are you thinking of staying? Just tonight?"

"I'm not sure. How is Adam? I've seen a couple of his posts on Facebook but we haven't spoken for ages."

"He's too busy with his girlfriends and his work." She looks down at her feet and I notice her overgrown toenails protruding from her slippers. I make a mental note to treat her to a pedicure for her next birthday. "I must have done something right," she goes on. "At least you've both been able to make yourselves some money as you've grown up. And work hard, as I had to. I just never suspected you'd forget where you came from. And me."

"We haven't Mum. I'm sorry." And I am. I think of the friends I've made at the gym and how they've bitched about me behind my back. At least Mum genuinely cares about me.

"So what's happened? At home, I mean?"

"We've separated." I stir my tea.

"I thought as much. I can see it in your eyes. Why?"

"Long story. Do you want another one, boys?" I point the remote at the TV and choose another episode of *Peppa Pig*.

"Have you left him at your house? Is that why you've come here?" She crams a biscuit into her mouth.

"No. He's moved out."

"I hope you've got yourself a good solicitor."

"Not yet." I sigh. "I need to though. He has. And I've got a lot to lose."

"That still doesn't explain why you've come here. And you seem really jumpy." She follows my gaze to the window.

"Do I?"

"You still haven't said what's happened." She puts her cup on the ring-marked coffee table.

"I've found out I'm the wrong gender for him to be married to." I lower my voice, not that George and Alex will understand what I'm on about.

She doesn't flinch. "Adam guessed that as soon as he met him."

"I know. I should have listened."

"That still doesn't explain why you've left your house and come here. Especially if he's not even there."

"There's a bit more to it. But honestly. Let's change the subject. Let's talk about you."

"Not much to say really. Same old. Same old."

It's not long before the boys come out of their shell a bit. It smells like home here. Chip oil and lavender. And at least I feel safe, albeit, a bit worried about my house and the business. I realise that I need to let Mandy know where I am. "I'm going to give my shop manager a ring Mum. I need to let her know that I'll be away for a few days."

"A few days! But I haven't got enough food in for you all."

"Don't worry. I'll buy some in. That is, when I get my bank accounts sorted. Ed seems to have done something with them."

"Perhaps you should ring a solicitor whilst you're at it."

"Yeah, you're right. Can you watch the boys whilst I make a couple of calls? I'll sit in the hallway. Just stick them another episode of Peppa Pig on."

"I'm coming with you Mummy." Alex stands with me, George remains where he is, his eyes glued to the TV screen.

"There's been a large withdrawal made from the account," Mandy says. "Cash. From the main branch in the centre. But there's no more information than that. What's going on?"

"Just keep everything ticking over." I try to keep my voice cheery. "I'm seeing a solicitor later in the week. Everything is going to be sorted out."

"Was it Ed? Is there a problem with finances or something? I know all about your…"

"Absolutely nothing for you to worry about," I say. "I really appreciate how you've stepped up in the last few weeks. I know I've had a lot going on. There'll be a pay increase coming your way as soon as I get things sorted."

I click onto my personal current account. There's enough in there to keep me going for a couple of months. Just. I might be applying for a credit card at this rate. I then type in Solicitors in Harrogate and start scrolling. The first one that comes up is MSB. Trust Ed to appoint himself a posh bloody solicitor.

I feel like Kerry Barnes again. I need some help. I click onto a Family Law specialist and book an online appointment to see Annette Waller in two days time. I'll have to go home. I know I have rights and can probably force Ed's hand with the household bills and school fees. I can hardly bear to imagine the school fees not being paid. I'd have to put the boys into a state school. Not only would I be unsettling them even further but I cannot begin to imagine what everyone would be saying about me.

As I lie in my brother's old room, staring at the ceiling, I can hardly believe my life has come to this. Having had no wine this evening, I'm wide awake, watching the minutes tick by. I've got George at one side and Alex at the other. It's a bit of a squeeze but I'm glad I've got them with me. They feel like the only positive thing in my life at the moment.

I hear what sounds like a branch snap in the back garden. I freeze. A few minutes later, I hear a stifled cough also coming from the garden. I slide down the centre of the bed, so as not to wake up the boys and peep through a crack in the curtains. Nothing. Then a knock. Shit. It's 1:40 am and someone is knocking at my mother's door. I slip from the bedroom and stand on the landing, trying to control my breathing. Tap. Tap. Tap. Softly on the lounge window now. I creep to the bottom of the stairs, hoping it's Ed but knowing this isn't really his style.

I look through the spyhole of the front door but can't see anyone. I'm too scared to go into the lounge – I don't think Mum drew the curtains. A car door bangs and an engine starts up. It doesn't sound like Ed's Audi. I should know. I've listened for it often enough when I've been waiting for him to come home.

"Kerry! What are you doing?"

I jump at Mum's voice and turn towards it. She's tying her dressing gown as she descends the stairs towards me.

"Sorry Mum. I couldn't sleep." I'm not going to tell her that I've been hearing noises. She doesn't need to know. However, I've decided that I might as well go back home tomorrow. I'm as safe here as I am there. The boys haven't taken too well to being dragged out of their routine either. I'll see the solicitor then everything will settle down.

Chapter 23

Ed

I wake once again in my old single bed. Instead of any fond memories of being back in my old room, memories of BF hover around me. And now he's back. His timing couldn't be any worse – as if things weren't bad enough.

Mum was on about selling up again last night. She's really rattled by his reappearance. I think he's just using her to get to me. Intimidation first and then he'll do whatever he's planning to do. That's how he used to operate when I was growing up. I remember once when I'd been truanting with some other kids at school. Mum had tried to keep it from him but there'd been a letter home confirming my punishment which he'd intercepted.

I thought he was leaving it at that when he walked from the room, but then he reappeared with his belt. He'd whack me with whatever was available as a kid. Said it had never done him any harm. Mum hates herself for staying with him. I couldn't understand it at the time either. It was only after he flipped and put me in hospital for a week, that she saw the light.

"Do you want a cuppa Ed?" Mum's outside the door. "It's nearly eight."

"If you're making one. Ta." I swing my legs over the side of the single bed and drag my suitcase towards me. I can't go on living like this. I'd got my hopes up last night that Kerry would let me back in, if only because of BF hanging about, but the solicitor letter has put paid to that. And my emptying the accounts. I realise she'll be entitled to something, but there was no way I was leaving all my money where it was for her to help herself to. It could have been Kerry emptying the accounts, and I wasn't risking that. I'll have to pay her a good whack of maintenance and she'll be entitled to stay in the house. She came into our relationship from her poxy council house – it was my graft and my success with Bitcoin that bought us the lifestyle and savings we have.

"Morning." I accept the coffee Mum passes me. "It feels weird waking up here. Especially in that room."

"I bet. However, what happened in there is all over and done with now." She's wearing her dressing gown. She looks tired.

"But he's back. I slept with an ear open, half expecting him to turn up again."

"Me too." Mum runs her fingers through her fringe. "Seriously though – what can he do? He's not a young man anymore – he's in his fifties for God's sake. We could probably knock him over with a feather."

I slot a piece of bread in the toaster. "The man is capable of anything Mum."

"I need a holiday." Mum sighs as she wipes the surfaces down. She looks deep in thought for a moment. "Then there's bloody Alistair."

"He's harmless enough," I say, grabbing a knife from the drawer. "He just wants you all to himself."

"He's even jealous of the boys."

I knew this, but it's the first time I've heard Mum say it out loud. She's normally defending him or making excuses for his behaviour. "We're a right pair, aren't we? With our dysfunctional relationships!"

"Life is short." Mum wipes her hands. "Too short to be wasted in relationships that can never make us happy."

"Are you talking about you, or me?"

"Both, I guess. Much as I'm gutted over your breakup with Kerry, you're my son and all that matters to me is that you're happy." We sit in silence for a moment and then Mum speaks again. "Anyway – what are your plans now? Are you going to stay here for a while?"

"For as long as I can face sleeping in that bedroom. Really, I should think about renting something so I can have the boys. I guess everything will be up in the air until the divorce goes through."

"And then what?"

"I suppose I'll be able to live as I was always meant to."

"There's just your father to contend with."

"Stop calling him that, Mum. Really if it carries on, I'll see about getting a restraining order. But I can't get the police involved, can I?"

"Why not?"

"I don't know where he's based, so they couldn't serve an order on him. I think I will have to face him, to get rid of him."

"I don't know about that." Mum passes me some toast. "In fact, that's not a very good idea at all." She falls silent again for a few seconds. "I'm going to look at getting this place valued today. The time is long overdue to move on."

"There were over forty messages on the answering service," Annie informs me as I scan the diary for my appointments. "But they were all silent."

"Get the line checked," I reply, even though my gut tells me it's BF ensuring I feel his presence at my workplace too. Great. The arsehole is definitely stalking me. I take my post from my pigeon-hole and walk along the corridor to my surgery. How life has changed in the last few weeks. This time three weeks ago, Russell was still alive. The thought almost winds me. I realise too that his funeral could take place at any point, but I wouldn't be made aware of it. I must keep checking the death notices.

I'm pleased Laura is late this morning. Normally it grates, but it gives me a few moments to check on things. I type Russell Lawson into Google. There are the usual news reports that they're looking for witnesses, in the search results, so I add death notice to his name. Sure enough, what I'm looking for appears. It was only posted yesterday.

Russell Lawson, age 36, beloved husband of Davina, father to Eloise and son of Joyce and Allan. Died tragically on Thursday March 19. Funeral to be held at Leeds Crematorium on Tuesday April 9th at 11:30 am. Family flowers only please, donations to be made to CRUSE.

It's in six days. They must have taken all the evidence they need from his body and released it. I have to attend. He meant more to me than everyone else in his life put together. I'll sit at the back, pay my respects, then leave. I'll hardly be noticed slipping in and out.

"Morning Ed!" Laura comes bounding into the room. "We've got a busy one today, according to the diary." She hangs her coat on the back of the door. "There's a last minute appointment come through at lunchtime as well. Annie asked if you'd take it? Apparently you've been asked for by name."

"Yes, that's fine. We never turn customers away!"

"It's probably just someone who wants their teeth whitening before a wedding or something." She tilts the blinds.

Laura continues prattling and doesn't really let up for the rest of the morning. Maybe she's a welcome distraction for the patients whilst they're in the chair, but I find her irritating. Even more so than normal today. Usually I deal with her by zoning out like I do with the twins. I can say *yes* and *really* in all the right places and act as though I'm hanging onto every word. It's a skill all parents need to master.

By one o'clock my stomach is growling. I'm thinking of asking Laura to call the sandwich shop and place an order for us both but remember that I've had the extra patient slotted in and their arrival is imminent.

"I'm just going to pay a call, Laura. If that patient arrives, just get them settled in. I'll be back in a moment."

"Right you are, Ed."

I dawdle in the loo, glad of the few minutes peace. I take a deep breath before returning to the surgery. My patient sits in the chair, grinning inanely as I let the door swing shut behind me.

"What the… How did *you* get in?" I stare at him.

"Ed!" Laura cries, looking at the person in the chair. "What's the matter?"

"Get out!" I march towards the chair and yank at his arm. He doesn't move.

"Do you two know each other?" She backs towards the window, looking from me to him and then back again.

"I've got an appointment." His voice hasn't changed one bit. It *still* sends fear through my spine. He grins again. "Edward. Is that really any way to welcome your father after all this time?"

"Your father!" Laura asks. "You said he was dead!"

"He is to me," I reply. "And he will be for real if he doesn't leave – now!" I grab at his arm again. "I said get out."

He jumps up then, no longer towering over me but able to instil the same chill of dread as he always did. "I'm going nowhere. We have unfinished business. Perhaps you could ask your assistant to give us a few minutes privacy."

She's already backing towards the door. "Do you want me to get someone Ed?"

"No. You take your lunch break now." I speak without taking my eyes off BF. There's sharps all over the place. I don't trust him one iota. "Sit over there," I say, pointing at the couch in the corner.

163

"I don't take orders off you," he replies, not moving. "I'm fine here."
I step away from him and lift the tray of surgical instruments from
the side table to the back ledge. "What do you want?"

"You know what I want. *You* ruined my life, and now you'll pay."

"You ruined your own life. And there's nothing more you can do to
hurt me."

"Oh, I think we both know that's not true, don't we?" He looks
exactly the same. His hair has receded a bit and his face is lined but
he's hardly aged. He looks as fit as a fiddle and I wonder how we'll
fare if we come to blows.

"I want you to clear off and stop stalking me. Or I'll go to the police."

He laughs now. "Now that wouldn't be a good idea, would it, son?"

"Don't call me that! I'm not your son!"

"Do you know how hard my life's been because of you? Do you
know how hard it is to find a relationship or a job after what you
brought on me?" He grabs me by the scruff of my neck, like he used to
when I was younger. The force of his grip snatches my breath away.

"Get off me!"

"I will when I get what I came for." He pats his top pocket with his
free hand. "You're not the only one with sharp instruments. What I've
got in here will ensure you never see the light of day again."

I swing my arm out, lunging for the anaesthetic injection, which I
plunge into him and squeeze down. I was aiming for the side of his
neck but get his shoulder instead.

"Aaargh." He yanks the syringe out. "What the fuck's that?"

Laura's back at the door with building security. Two burly men
flank BF and steer him towards the door.

"I can't feel my arm," he screams. "The bastard has stabbed me. You
should be dragging him out, not me!"

"Do we need the police?" one calls back.

"No police," I say. "It's bad for business – unless he comes back."

"You OK?" Laura asks, walking towards me.

I look up and see one of the senior partners, Justin, framed in the doorway. He nods at Laura. "Give us a minute, will you?"

She scuttles off again. I look at Justin, so self-assured, and with everything together in his life. Mine is an absolute mess.

"What happened?"

"That was my father."

"I don't understand." Justin walks into the surgery and the door falls softly closed behind him. In the distance I can still hear shouting and banging as BF is hopefully being escorted from the building. "Your father?"

"He beat me up when I was a teenager. Badly. He put me in hospital. And now he's back. He's stalking me."

"So why not call the police?" He looks unmoved. "Why stick a needle in him? We could lose our licence to practice."

"Of course we won't. Anyway, who's in charge here? This is my practice."

"As a senior partner, I've a right to intervene. We'll lose all our patients with a carry on like this."

"It's not that serious." I'm now starting to believe it is though.

"Ed, I know you've a ton of stuff going on. Why don't you take some time off? Get it all back together."

"I don't like being told what to do." My jaw throbs.

"I know. And I'm not telling you. I can't. As a work colleague, and as a friend, I'm advising you. We'll hold the fort, don't worry."

I know he's right. But I worry that I'll collapse without some semblance of routine and normality. Still, if I'm not here, it's one less place for BF to find me. Shame I was an inch or so too low when I got him with that anaesthetic. It should have hit his windpipe.

Chapter 24

Tony

W hen we arranged our 'transaction,' you assured me it would be a cut and dried process with no danger of repercussions. However, there's cameras where there shouldn't have been and people coming out of the woodwork with stories about why people might have wanted to kill Lawson. I want another thirty grand in full and final settlement.

I'm laying low for now but want to get far away from here. More money means that I can. If you refuse, I will take you down with me. Meet me at the same spot as before. Cash only, obviously. Nine pm tomorrow night.

That gives you twenty-four hours. Fail to show and I'll do to you what I did to him. Without the pleasurable bit, you understand. You've got more to lose than I have. A lot more.

See you tomorrow.

Chapter 25

Kerry

"You'll need to drop a note into the office," Mrs Richardson says, looking up from the register. "Were they both poorly at the same time?"

"Erm no," I begin.

"We went to see our Grandma," George explains as he joins the other class members on the carpet.

"Our other Grandma," adds Alex, flopping beside him. "She lives a long way away."

Thanks boys, I want to say. "We've got a lot going on at the moment, I..."

"You know the school takes a no tolerance view on term-time absences?"

"This is an extenuating circumstance." I'm not standing here, arguing with a jumped up teacher, over the heads of nine five-year-olds. She's just annoyed because I didn't come in to hear readers yesterday. "I'll see the head now."

"A note will suffice." Her voice is clipped. "The head is busy this morning."

"In view of the fact that I am paying nearly two and a half grand each month for my boys to be here," I snap, "I'm sure she can afford me five minutes of her precious time." As I say this, I'm acutely aware that if Ed doesn't pay next month's fees, I may have to pull them out of here and place them in the state school.

I walk along the opulent corridor of the school, festooned with trophies and accolades. The head *is* too busy to see me and I'm told curtly by the bursar to write a note which will be 'considered.'

"You might be looking at a fine though," she adds.

Bring it on, I think, as I walk towards the revolving doors. I wonder if they're as abrupt with all parents or just me. Perhaps they can see through to my 'Kerry Barnes' core. I'm desperate to follow my usual morning routine of going to the gym but know that duty calls today. My legal advice appointment with Annette Waller to start fighting back with Ed isn't for another two hours, which means I have time to call in at the shop.

The petrol gauge of the Range Rover is nearing empty. I sigh, knowing it costs around eighty pounds to fill up. The thought depresses me beyond measure. This sort of consideration is one that has not been necessary for a long time. Being skint Kerry Barnes again is something I don't want to contemplate. I feel absolutely exhausted this morning. The drive back from Mum's yesterday nearly finished me. The boys slept for lots of it in the car which meant they were little sods at bedtime.

Then, like at Mum's house, I heard knocking at the door through the night. However, I have wondered if my mind is playing tricks on me. Surely if someone was to come to our door, they would just ring the doorbell? But I heard a car engine – I'm certain it was the same car engine again. It sounded like a diesel. Anyway, it took me ages to get to sleep after that. Perhaps it was Ed checking up on me – I don't know. I'm accepting that our marriage is over – I've got to. Fighting for survival seems to be what I've got to concentrate on now.

Mandy is serving someone as I walk in. The lady smiles at me as she brushes past me, on her way out with a bulging carrier bag.

"How's it going?" I say brightly, glancing around my gorgeous boutique. I hope to God that I can hang onto all this.

"We can't grumble," Mandy replies. "People are shopping for holiday clothes now. We're getting to the point where we could do with buying in some more stock though."

"I know. It'll just have to wait a week or two."

"Did you find out about that large withdrawal?" Mandy sits on the stool behind the till and flicks back her hair. "And what's happening about the new shop?"

"All is a little up in the air at the moment Mandy. I'm sorry I can't give you more than that – I don't know myself."

"Is there going to be enough in the account to pay me this month's salary? I can't work for free, you know."

"I wouldn't expect you to." I'm snapping at her now. I'm prepared for the fact that I might have to take this over on my own and let Mandy go, the way things are looking. "I'm off to see a solicitor in an hour." I pause, then decide I might as well tell her. "If you must know, Ed has emptied *all* our accounts so I'm off to see what I can do about it. But don't worry, your salary will be prioritised."

"God, you must be so stressed." The edge has left her voice. "Surely you've got rights?"

"That's what I need to find out," I reply. "And I've told you that in confidence. Please don't repeat any of this to anyone else."

"Of course not." But my instruction must strike a nerve as she adds, "your friend, Alison, is it – was in here again yesterday, asking after you and wondering why you've not been at the gym." I notice her face is flushed as she speaks.

"Well, like I said before, tell her nothing. It's nobody else's business. Everything will be sorted. One way or another. I'll have a quick cuppa and then I'm going to see this solicitor in Harrogate."

"I'll put the kettle on." Mandy jumps up and I notice how great she looks in one of the dresses from our Spring range. She's got an amazing figure and customers will often ask for the same of whatever she is wearing. I can't even afford new clothes at the moment.

I put an hour on the parking meter in Harrogate town centre. I'm pretty sure my free consultation won't go over its allotted thirty minutes. I wander past the new shopping centre and the upmarket tea rooms, usually two of my favourite places when I'm here, towards the street where all the solicitors seem to bunch together. I'm told to sit whilst the impeccable receptionist announces my arrival through an intercom.

"Mrs Huntington Barnes," she announces a few moments later. I'm the only person in the waiting room so I don't know why I look around. "Mrs Waller will see you now."

As I stand, I feel woozy. I realise that I haven't eaten breakfast. In fact, I hardly ate last night either. I had wine, which took the edge off my appetite even more. I fish around in my handbag and find a Rice Crispies Square Bar. One of the perks of motherhood is that there's nearly always something in my handbag for every kind of emergency. I sink back to my chair. "I'm sorry. I came over faint. I think it's all the stress and because I haven't eaten."

"Can I get you some water?" The receptionist asks, rising from behind her desk. I feel miserable as I notice her impeccable pencil skirt and heels. I look down at my jeans and trainers. I should have made more of an effort. I'm just lurching from day to day at the moment – trying to survive.

"Yes, thank you. I'll be alright in a moment. When I get my blood sugar back up. I think I stood too quick."

"I'll let Mrs Waller know."

By the time I get in there, I've wasted over ten minutes of my appointment. "I'm sorry," I say to the sharply dressed woman behind the desk. "I came over funny."

"Are you alright now?" She stands and offers her handshake. "Anita Waller. Family Law Specialist. Have a seat."

"Yes, thanks. I'm Kerry Huntington-Barnes. Thanks for seeing me at such short notice." I sweep my gaze over her room where all her accolades stand in frames. I'd like to ask of her success rate in terms of swinging this the woman's way, but it seems rude somehow.

"Not a problem. You'll be aware this is just an initial consultation. Unfortunately, I've got another appointment in straight after you so we've only got until half past."

I curse myself. I can't believe I have messed up at such an important appointment. I had better talk quick.

"So how can I help you?"

"My husband. He's walked out on us. Me and my two boys. And now he's emptied all our joint accounts and taken a sizeable lump out of my business account."

"Hang on. Your business account? What sort of business are you in?"

"I have a clothing boutique. I'm supposed to be opening another one, but Ed - Edward, my husband, - is a silent partner. He put the majority of the money up, when I started out, I mean."

"And what does he do?" She's scribbling things down.

"He's got his own practice in cosmetic dentistry. Plus, he earned a fortune from Bitcoin a few years ago. He's very well off. I can't understand why he would empty our accounts."

"Can you prove what was in them before he did?" She has a stern face. I have faith that she will fight my corner. She looks to be in her early fifties and from the testimonials on her website, seems to have secured settlements for many a divorcing wife.

"I can get statements. He can't close the accounts, can he?"

"Not if they're joint. Your signature would have to be on an account closure form. What about your house?"

"It's all in his name. He bought it outright. And he turned up the other night, wanting to be let back in. His father's hanging around, you see. He beat him up when he was a teenager and went to prison. And now he's threatening him. It's all a mess."

"Why has he left you and your children?"

I swallow. "It's all such a mess. He's gay. He's been having an affair with someone."

"A man?"

"Yes." There. I've said it out loud. I've had wonderful friends over the years who've been gay but I still can't believe Ed ever married me. He must have known he'd do this to me one day.

She looks at me but her expression isn't giving anything away. I expect she's heard it all over the years.

"Does he have anyone acting for him?"

"Yes." I pull out my letter from MSB Solicitors and thrust it in front of her.

"Right, OK. I'll ask my PA to make a copy of this." She presses a button with a pristinely manicured finger. "Clare, could you take a copy of a letter from Ms Huntington-Barnes when she returns to reception in a few moments. And have her fill in a personal information form?" She pauses. "Thank you." She turns back to me, her face illuminated by the ornate desk lamp beside her. "We'll require a payment on account. In this case it will be £1000 for me to open your file and begin work on it. You can pay by direct transfer or drop a cheque into the office. We won't be able to draft your paperwork until it's cleared though. And my rate of engagement is £230 per hour."

"One thousand pounds! I've already told you that my husband has practically emptied our accounts. I've got two five-year-olds to look after. Can't I get Legal Aid or something?"

"I'm afraid Legal Aid is no longer available in family matters," she replies. "You could, of course, represent yourself, but I'd advise against that. It can be a complicated, drawn-out process, and you will need representation to ensure you get what you're entitled to." She looks at her watch.

She's probably trying to get rid of me but I carry on. "What do you mean? What I am entitled to?"

"Well, off the top of my head, at the least, you will be entitled to stay in the house until your youngest child reaches eighteen, and your husband will be required to pay maintenance for the children. There will need to be a settlement process, in relation to the monies he has removed from the joint accounts, and you will get a settlement of some sort with regards to his other assets. But like I say, I can't begin to act for you until I get your payment on account."

"I'll get it together." I can't believe I'm having to consider how I will scrape one thousand pounds together.

"The sooner the better. I will then write to your husband's solicitors and ask for an explanation around the money movement situation. Are either of you planning to file for divorce?"

"Possibly. Probably. Him. I don't know at the moment."

"Well, we can discuss it further at our next appointment. Fill in the form and make a sixty-minute appointment at the time of your account payment. I will then open a file for you and we can get the ball rolling." She looks at the door.

"Thanks for your time," I say, standing and offering my hand.

She looks at my jeans and trainers and I feel like a specimen under her microscope. "Take care," she says.

Tears are stabbing the back of my eyes as I leave her office to return to reception. As if things have come to this. I make mental calculations around paying Mandy, filling up the car, my gym membership, school fees, food. I want to cry. I must ask for help, but my list of potential people is shorter than short. I've never felt so alone.

I feed some more money into the parking meter then head into Wetherspoons. I need to eat something. And I want a glass of wine. One won't hurt. I need to get my head together a bit and work out what I am going to do. Normally I would lunch somewhere a bit more upmarket but I'm feeling more and more like Kerry Barnes again. I hate Ed. I can't believe what he's reduced me to.

I sit, staring into space, waiting for my lunch to arrive. The large glass of white doesn't touch the sides. There's a jovial atmosphere in here and I sit amongst the hum of animated conversation, seeing office people enjoy lunch and men drinking. I expect many of them are on their third or fourth of the day already. If I wasn't driving and having to pick the kids up, I would be doing the same. I log into online banking. £836 available and that's including my £200 overdraft. Shit.

Then I log into my business bank account. I can't believe there's only two and a half grand in there. I owe Mandy over four grand for this month's and next month's salary. I take my list of passwords from my purse and log into our joint current account and our joint savings account. I'm wondering if he's softened and replaced the money. He hasn't. I order a statement for both.

"Thanks," I say as a rushed-off-her-feet waitress plonks a plate in front of me. It's not the greatest salad I've ever seen, but I know I've got to get some food inside me. How am I going to get a grand together to pay this solicitor? I think of Mum, of Marie, of my friends at the gym and then Adam. Yes, I'll ask my brother. We've not been in touch for a while, but I'm hopeful he'll help me.

I can't believe you're asking me for money! You OK?

He's always quick at answering texts. I've laughed at him before that he's attached to his phone.

I've been better, I type. *Things are a bit rough at the moment.*

Mum said. I'll try to get over to see you soon.

I'd like that.

Send me your bank details and I'll sort a transfer.

Tears fill my eyes again. They're never far away. I'm so glad my brother has responded to me. I feel less alone, but utterly depressed. I chew on a piece of cucumber; I'm really struggling to get any of this salad down but have to soak this glass of wine up. I don't want to add drink driving to my list of catastrophes.

I stand alone, waiting at the edge of the playground for the boys to come out. Mrs Richardson has pulled the blind down again. I don't stand with the other mothers. I expect word has spread around everyone by now, that my marriage is breaking up. The playground ladies avoid me more than usual, perhaps because they don't know what to say and what can they say without sounding nosy?

Once again, I can't face going home. It's a pleasant afternoon and the kids' shrieks of excitement bring me the tiniest bit of warmth as we pull up in the car park at the edge of the park. I want to flop down on the grass and just watch them play, but they will not allow me that luxury.

"Push me Mummy."

"Watch what I can do Mummy!"

"Can you catch me at the bottom of the slide?"

"Can we have an ice-cream?"

That seems to keep them quiet for a few minutes. They sit, side-by-side in the younger swings, licking at their ice creams whilst I turn my attention to sending Adam my account details through. When I look up a few moments later, there's a man talking to them. I jump up and rush forward. I was only ten steps away. How could I have been so careless?

"Can I help you?" I say.

"I think you probably can," he replies, smiling at the boys, then at me. Something about him is familiar and I struggle to place him.

"Who are you?"

"Kerry," he laughs. Do I detect an undercurrent of menace in this laugh? "You know exactly who I am!"

Chapter 26

Ed

I haven't told Mum that I'm looking at a flat this evening. I think she enjoys having me around, especially with everything that's going on at the moment. The same cannot be said of Alistair though. He's always side-lined me, but now he's totally ignoring me. I can't stand the atmosphere and I don't really want to bring the boys into it either. Then there's the fact that I can't bear sleeping in my old bedroom. Every night I lay in that bed, I'm sixteen years old again. It is not doing me any favours.

I'm a thirty-two year old man of means. No way should I be sleeping in my childhood bedroom. So the flat I'm looking at today isn't too far from Kerry's. The boys will be delighted if I take it as it backs on to the park. Parkside Mews. The irony of the name isn't lost on me. I arrive before the letting agent and hang around the intercom area. It looks secure and with underground parking. Secure is what I need at the moment. I feel like I'm looking over my shoulder, checking for BF at every turn.

A woman finally pulls up in a Merc. I do a double take to begin with as she's the double of Kerry. Short strawberry blonde hair, not very tall; I can't see her eyes behind her sunglasses but I bet they're green too. She dresses completely differently though. As she stretches a leg out of the car, I see heels and a trouser suit. Kerry lives in jeans and Converse these days. I may not be attracted to women but I can appreciate when they've made an effort, or in Kerry's case, not.

"Penny Foster," announces the woman, offering her hand. "You must be Mr Huntington. I'm here to show you around."

"Thanks." I accept her handshake. "Yes. Great. Well, so far, so good. Is it an upstairs flat?"

She takes a bunch of keys from her handbag. "Erm yes, I believe it is. Will that be a problem?"

"No. It's what I'm after."

"And is it just for you?" She presses the number three inside the lift.

"Yes. Mainly. And maybe my two sons at the weekend."

"How old are they?"

"Five-year-old twins." I smile. They'll love coming up and down in the lift. I hope I like the flat. It all feels like a positive step forward.

The estate agent frowns. "We don't usually allow children below the age of ten. The other residents might complain, you see."

"They're very well behaved," My voice echoes around the lift's marble walls. "And we're literally talking one night a week. They would love being this close to the park."

"Well, if they were babies, it would be a definite no-go. I will have to run it by my manager – he will probably say yes, as he has little ones too, but that might change if other residents were to complain."

We arrive outside the door of flat fourteen. The first thing I look for as we go in is security. There's a five lever mortice lock, deadlocks on the inside and a spyhole.

"Is this the only entrance and exit?" I ask.

"That's right." She puts the key into the lock. "And all the flats are alarmed. You seem very security conscious."

"Yes." I'm already looking around and imagining George and Alex fighting over who will get which room. They'll both want the one that overlooks the park rather than the street and will have to fight quietly by the sounds of it. Parkside Hotel is just visible in the distance. Russell would have liked it here. He should have been here with me. I think it's where we would have ended up eventually – getting a place together.

"I'll take it," I say, after wandering around the rooms and asking questions about parking, deposit and references. "When can I move in?"

The intercom cuts into her reply. I watch as she lifts the receiver and speaks at the screen. "I'm sorry sir, this one's been let now," she says. "But I'll buzz you in so you can see the one we've got next door."

"No," I gasp, looking at the screen. "Don't let him in. He's dangerous. He's..."

She looks terrified as I grab at her hand to stop her pressing the button. Her hand immediately flies to her bag and pulls out her phone, whilst simultaneously starting towards the exit.

"Don't go out there." I fly at the door. "Lock it. I mean it!"

"You can't do this!" Her voice is shrill in the empty flat. "You can't keep me in here!"

"I'm not trying to keep you in here!" Shit. She thinks I'm trying to kidnap her. "I'm trying to stop you going out there! Trust me – that man out there – he really is dangerous."

"Police please. Quick."

I grab the phone from her ear. "There's no need to ring the police."

"Give it back. Help!" she shouts. "They'll trace my call! Please! Just let me out!"

"I'm not going to hurt you, you daft woman. That man outside. He's stalking me. He's my father. He's violent. I'm sorry you've been dragged into this."

"Oh," her shoulders sag. "Thank God for that. For a moment I thought I was in trouble."

"We still might be," I say, checking the lock on the door. "If someone lets him in."

I go to the window. There's no sign of him. There's a dark coloured car that wasn't there when I arrived. I can't see my car from this window. I hope to God he hasn't got into this block. That this woman is in here with me too, makes it so much worse. I hate that I've involved some innocent bystander in all this.

"I don't suppose you'll want to let this flat to me now? It's a shame. I rather like this place. Having said that, he'd know where to find me now." I jerk my head in the direction of the window. "How has he managed to book a viewing here at the same time as me anyway?"

She looks thoughtful for a moment. "Ah yes. I was struck by how you had the same surname. It's not exactly a common surname, is it? Anyway, he telephoned just after you'd left the shop yesterday."

"How would he have known which flat I was interested in? Did you tell him?"

"Of course not. Perhaps he saw you studying the boards outside. Like I said, only minutes had passed before he made the enquiry. And it made sense to book the viewings in at the same time."

"So what now?" I ask.

"I'd better call my office and let them know where I am. I think we need to ring the police back too. They might come anyway, but if this man, your father, is as dangerous as you say, then we need them here."

"I would prefer them not to be involved." I say. "Oh, what the hell. I can't fight him on my own anymore. Ring them."

"Hello. It's Penny. I thought I should let you know that I'm here, showing this flat at Parkside Mews, and there's an unsavoury man hanging around outside. I'm currently locked in a flat with his son." She pauses for a moment.

"Yeah. I know what it sounds like, but I'm OK. I think. I don't know if the police are on their way – I tried ringing them, but…"

We both jump to the sound of the thumping at the door. "Police!"

Penny jumps up and throws the door open. "It must have connected. Thank goodness. Was there anyone hanging around? Downstairs I mean?"

"No."

Both police officers have all sorts of paraphernalia attached to them. My eyes fall on the taser gun. Pity armed police hadn't come with real guns. Had BF still been here, they might have shot the bastard. I can't believe he's hanging around like this.

"Right. Do you want to tell us what's been going on and why the three nines call got cut off?"

"It was me who cut the call off." I feel stupid now. I should be using them to help me. "I was panicking with him trying to get in. He's my real father, you see. He's threatening me."

"All the more reason why you should have wanted us here," the other one says. "What's the story?"

"He beat me up pretty badly when I was sixteen. Put me in hospital. In fact he served time for it. And now he's back, after years of not bothering us, he's stalking me and making threats to my mother. I'm worried my five-year-old twins and ex-wife are at risk from him too. It's a mess."

"Well we'd better find him then by the sounds of it." He looks around. "Is there anywhere to sit whilst we take some details?"

Penny gestures to a built-in window seat overlooking the park. "I'm the letting agent. I was showing this gentleman around. Ah, my manager is here."

I follow her gaze to where a blue Golf is pulling up. The dark coloured car has gone. Damn – I wish I'd got the number from it! I've decided now that I will hand all this over to the police. I feel relieved and scared in equal measure.

An hour later, I drive away from what could have been my new home. I've made a statement and given the police what I can. I don't have an address for BF or his car reg but they've a bit to be going on. They've told me to keep a log of everything and to get his registration number next time I have the chance, so he can be dealt with. Surely what he did before will carry some weight now? I've decided I might hire someone to try to find out where he's staying. He's affected my life for long enough. And now he's even getting in the way of my being able to grieve for Russell.

Every time I think of Russell, it's like being battered around the head. His absence has left an indescribable hole inside me. I'm going to look for a different flat with a different letting agent. I can't buy anything at the moment. Not until all this money stuff is sorted out.

Without really planning to be, I find myself outside Kerry's house. I feel surprised at myself for thinking *Kerry's house*, after all, it was only weeks since it was my home. I want to see the boys.

Kerry looks startled as she opens the door. I can tell straight away that she has been drinking. She's lost a ton of weight and looks really miserable. For the first time since I've left, I feel guilty. I can't help who I am but I should never have dragged her into it.

"I'm sorry," I say, the words surprising me. I hadn't planned to say them.

"For what?" She leans against the door frame and folds her arms.

"Everything. I'll make it right."

"Well, you could start with sorting out the bank accounts. You don't know how much stress you've caused me this week."

"You're going to get a settlement, and maintenance, and to stay in the house." I look behind her to where the boys are running up the hallway towards us. "But I want it made official through the proper channels."

"Daddy!" George and Alex launch themselves at me. I scoop them into either side of me.

"It's a wonder they've remembered what you look like," Kerry sniffs. "I can't believe how you've behaved Ed."

"I know. But I've had a lot going on too. Look, I'm seeing the solicitor again tomorrow. I've been acting on his advice so far. We'll get some mediation sorted, work out a way forward. We've got the boys to think of, haven't we?"

"What about my second shop? You've pulled everything Ed. Emptied all the accounts. Why?"

"I'm not the only one who's been making big withdrawals, Kerry. You've been on a bit of a spree. Did you not think I'd notice? I moved the rest of the money before you did." I lower the boys to the floor where they stay, flanking me on either side.

"Daddy, are you coming home now?"

"Yeah, Daddy. I need you to fix my bike."

"Why don't I take them to my mum's?" I ruffle Alex's hair. I badly need to spend some time with them. Every time I encounter BF, it makes me want to be a better father. I haven't been a very good one lately.

"I need you to take them to school on Tuesday morning," Kerry says without answering me. "I've got an important meeting."

I think for a moment. What is happening on Tuesday morning? Then it hits me with a thud. Russell's funeral.

"I can't. I'm sorry."

"I've been looking after our boys twenty-four hours a day, day-in, day-out, and you can't even take them to school for just one morning. You own your own business, Ed – surely you can rearrange things?"

"I'm at a funeral." She doesn't know whose, at least, I hope she doesn't.

"Whose?" I can see the usual suspicion in her eyes as we stand still, facing each other across the threshold at the door.

"A friend's."

"I hate what you are Ed. I hate what you've done to us all. I hate…"

"Mummy. Stop it!"

Poor Alex. What are we doing to them? "Go and wait in the car boys," I say, stepping forward. "I'll get some stuff together for you. We can go and stay at Grandma's tonight."

"You're not stepping foot in this house." Kerry also steps forward, blocking my entry. "I trust you about as far as I could throw you."

"I'll wait here then whilst you pack up some PJs for them. Make sure you keep your door locked this evening." I decide I might as well tell her. "I was looking at a flat earlier and BF was hanging around."

I watch as the boys race to the car which beeps as I unlock it for them. "Seatbelts on and don't touch anything. I'll be there in a second."

"You were looking at a flat? So it's really over then?"

She's more interested in the fact I've been looking at a flat than BF stalking me. "You know it's over. I can never be what or who you want me to be."

"So you'd rather have been chasing after some slag of a man who couldn't have cared less about you. He was putting it about everywhere."

I glance around, hoping none of the neighbours are in their gardens. It's the first time she's been so direct about my relationship with Russell. "I don't want to discuss this with you."

"You could have put me at risk of God knows what." she continues.

"That side of our relationship wasn't happening though, was it Kerry?" That's as nicely as I can put it. I don't need her reminding me about Russell putting it about. Usually I could push it out of the forefront of my mind and tell myself that sooner or later, he would realise I was the only one who could fulfil everything for him. Sometimes, though, his promiscuity had eaten away at me like a cancer.

"Like I need reminding. Anyway, you'll be pleased to know that I've got a solicitor now."

"Yeah?" I look round. I'm going to have to sort the boys in a minute. They're bouncing all over the car. "Get them to get the ball rolling and then we can start sorting things out."

"I can't believe what you've done to us Ed. Leaving us. Emptying the accounts. And I want some maintenance and school fees by the end of the week. And there're some bills to be paid."

"I'm paying nothing until there's an agreement in place. Apparently we should go for mediation."

"And how long is that going to take? I've got your two sons to look after Ed!" She's thin and I've never seen her look so miserable. I can't feel bad though. If I hadn't cleaned the accounts out, I'm sure she would have done.

"I'll push for it to happen quickly. I don't want things dragged out either. I'm off to wait with the boys." I step backwards. "Bring their things to the car when you've sorted them. And don't forget what I said about keeping the door locked."

"I've already seen him," she replies. "He doesn't scare me."

Chapter 27

<u>Kerry</u>

The house feels so empty without George and Alex. Even when they're fast asleep, I can feel their presence here. It's hard to believe that we've gone from, on the face of it, being a happy family of four to this, in less than a month.

I sit, glass of wine in hand, staring at a programme on the TV I'm not even interested in. I've tried reading, sewing and listening to music for distraction but nothing is working. I reach for the wine bottle and start to refill my glass, slopping it as I hear a knock at the door. It's after nine and dark outside now. I look through the spyhole of the front door and I can't see a thing. Then there's a knock at the lounge window. I jump in response and hardly dare pull the curtains back for fear of who I'll find there.

I know I said I wasn't scared of BF, as Ed calls him, but I don't want Ed moving back in, just because he thinks we're scared. I want him back here because he wants to be. I'd be lying if I said his father hadn't unnerved me though. The way he looked at us all, worried me. And what he said to me left me in no doubt as to the dangerous, unpredictable individual I already suspected him to be.

I peep through the curtains and see nothing apart from my reflection staring back at me. Someone is trying the handle on the side door.

Another knock. "Who is it?" I call out, my voice shaking so much in the silence that I hardly recognise it. I hear footsteps walk away from the door and I follow their sound as they pace around the side of the house, knocking the bin over as they go. Shit. Shit. Shit.

"Who's there?" I call again as I notice a figure reflected in the conservatory's glass. I panic as I can't remember if the conservatory is even locked. I rush towards the glass door, my eyes immediately meeting the eyes of the person trying the handle at the other side. He's not on his own.

"Adam," I cry, throwing the door open and staring at his six foot frame in relief. "What are you doing here – you scared me to death."

"Is that any way to greet your little brother?" He steps towards me, enveloping me in a hug. "I came here to check that you're alright. You look bloody awful."

"Cheers bro." I fold myself into his shoulder, unable to recall the last hug I had received. It feels good. The woman beside him clears her throat.

"Sorry. This is Laura."

"Nice to meet you," she offers her hand.

I step away from Adam and immediately feel inadequate. She's tall and slim with long blonde hair and a peachy complexion which can be seen even in the dusky light. If I didn't feel dowdy enough before, I really do now. "Likewise," I say. "Come in. You like em young, don't you?" I whisper to Adam as we walk through the conservatory into the kitchen. "Coffee?" I offer.

"Haven't you got anything stronger?" Adam wraps his coat around the back of one of the breakfast bar chairs. "I was hoping we could stay over?" He pats the chair next to him. Laura obediently slides onto it and flicks her fringe from her eyes. She looks nervous.

"Yes, of course. The guest room is reasonably tidy, I think. Unless the boys have got in there. Wine? Beer? Gin?"

I pour three generous gin and tonics and perch on a stool, facing them at the other side of the breakfast bar. I wish Adam had come on his own. I could really have done with confiding in him at the moment, but can't with this girl here. She's irritating me already, pawing at him like she's frightened he'll run off. "So to what do I owe this pleasure?" I ask. "And why could you not just have rung the doorbell like an ordinary person?"

"I didn't want to wake the boys," Adam replies, squeezing Laura's hand as she places it on his denim-clad thigh. "And I wanted you to meet Laura."

Give over, put each other down. But the familiarity of Adam's presence comforts me. Even though he made me jump out of my skin, I'm glad he is here. "The boys are with Ed for the night. It's only the second time he's taken them since we've been split up."

"I've heard all about it off Mum." My brother's eyes, the same green as my own, emit a spark of sympathy. "I did try to warn you about him. Don't you remember?" His eyes narrow. "I saw straight through him."

"There's nothing worse than someone who says I told you so."

"He's on the other bus, isn't he?" Laura's voice is sickly sweet. "Isn't that what you said?"

Adam frowns at her. "Bit of a sensitive subject, sweetheart."

Sweetheart! "I don't really want to talk about it if you don't mind." Not to you, anyway.

"We're getting married," she squeaks, thrusting a diamond clad knuckle at me. "Adam proposed last week. That's the main reason we've come over." Her outstretched hand lingers. She obviously wants me to inspect her bejewelled finger more closely but I've absolutely no desire to. "We wanted to ask if the boys would like to be pageboys. I've no younger family, you see. I've seen them in the albums at Adam's mum's. They'd look cute in the wedding photos. What size do you think they'll be next June? I want to get the suits ordered."

I stare at her, gobsmacked at the fact that she's barely drawn breath. "Congratulations," I say through gritted teeth. "Forgive me if I'm not in wedding mode. I'm in the process of getting divorced."

"I told you not to blurt it out straight away," Adam laughs. "She's turning into bridezilla. I can't stop her talking about it!"

"Have you eaten?" I want to change the subject. "I can't be arsed cooking, but I'll make you both a sandwich." I get up and pull the fridge door open. "I don't want to be up too late, to be honest. I've got a mad day tomorrow. Meetings and all that." I would have stayed up late if it had just been Adam. He and I have had many a late night, staying up talking into the small hours, putting the world to rights. We'd say we were talking booze infused shite, but we covered a lot of ground in those chats, going back over old childhood stuff and making sense of the people we had become. I miss how close we once were and how much life has got in the way.

"Did you get the money through OK sis?"

"What money?" Laura swivels round and looks at Adam.

I bristle. Why the hell does he have to discuss this in front of her?

"Kerry needed some help with the solicitor's fees. Ed's cut her off."

"But we've a wedding to pay for now." Her voice is a whine. I hate her already. She avoids my gaze and I resist the urge to tell her to grow up.

"I'll pay you back Adam. Every penny. Don't worry." I continue to glare at Laura.

"I don't want it back. And if you need any more, just say."

I'm not sure what's got into him. Maybe it's guilt, because so much time has elapsed since we last spent time together. And since he last saw the boys. If I'd have asked him for a loan when we were kids, he would have charged me interest. Still, I'm grateful for his help. I've been able to appoint a solicitor and can start putting the pieces of my life back together.

I put up with Laura for another hour and thirty seven minutes exactly before making an escape. I hear all about the marriage proposal, her parent's reaction, the champagne, the roses, the horse drawn carriage, the bridal fair she's going to, the fact that she wants me to do a reading and be a witness, I'm going to be her sister-in-law after all. Her high-pitched voice still rings in my ears as I climb the stairs up to my bedroom, hoping that they will only stay for one night.

I'm wired as I lie on my bed, trying to read. I have drunk enough not to be sober, but not enough to be sleepy. I haven't had chance to process what was discussed earlier with Ed. He still couldn't admit to whose funeral he's about to attend. He must know that I know. One thing is obvious – he's never coming back. And it looks like it will need a court order for any money to start coming through. None of it is right. I'm glad I'm seeing the solicitor again in the morning and can start getting some answers. I feel sure he will be made to help with school fees and other bills in the meantime. I don't know how he can live with himself.

I listen as Adam and Laura make their way up the first staircase, Laura giggling inanely as Adam closes the door to the spare room on the floor below mine. I sigh in the darkness and pick up my Kindle to try to tire my eyes out. I can't bear reading anything to do with relationships at the moment, so am trying to read crime thrillers. However, I struggle to concentrate on anything for more than a few minutes.

I've just about managed to retain a whole paragraph when I hear the bedsprings in the room below mine start to creak rhythmically. I thrust a pillow over my head as they become louder, faster and accompanied by moans and shrieks. I want to walk in and chuck a bucket of cold water over them both. How dare they come here, carrying on like this, with what I'm going though? And they don't know the half of it either. If she hadn't been here, perhaps I would have been able to actually talk to my brother.

Monday morning arrives, bright and large as life. I've slept terribly as always, seeing the edge of every hour as the night has ticked by. Eventually, around five am, I seemed to have slumped into a heavier sleep. I feel groggy and hungover. I glance at the clock. 8:55 am. For a moment I panic, then remember. Ed will be taking the boys to school. I luxuriate in bed for a few more moments. I'm too late to go to my usual gym class and couldn't go even if I wanted to, not with Adam and Laura here. I just wish once again that he'd been on his own. I walk across the bedroom and flick the shower switch in the en-suite. I linger longer than normal, trying to scrub away my envious response to my brother's nocturnal activity. Why couldn't I have found a normal relationship as well?

By the time I've made it downstairs, I'm surprised to find the house in silence. There's a note propped up against the kettle. *Sorry sis – we had to dash. We had a few more people to tell our news to. Chin up and let Laura know about sizes for the twins. X*

Another day. Another week. How am I going to get through this one?

Chapter 28

<u>Tony</u>

S o you ignored my last letter.

You've pissed me off no end. I've decided it's not just you at risk now. I've been watching you. And not only you. By ignoring me you've signed the death warrants of those who you reckon to care about.

The only way you can stop this is to pay what you owe. By way of compensation I've upped the stake by ten grand.

You have until close of business on Tuesday to get forty grand to me or gay boy's funeral wont be the only one happening this week. Usual place. 6pm.

No more chances.

Chapter 29

Ed

After all the shit with BF at the surgery last week, I've relented and taken a month off. As the senior partner, it's not as though I'm losing any money. Granted, our overall profits will be a little down but they're taking a salaried locum on to cover the next month, so our income should be maintained. We'll just have to take the hit of the locum salary.

The confrontation with BF was played down amongst the surgery staff and patients. That kind of thing can be terrible for business. I mean, who enjoys going for dental treatment anyway? But when there's a crazed maniac hanging around, especially one who has no qualms about inflicting injury, so the dentist has to stab him with a syringe – well it was no wonder that the other senior shareholders pulled ranks and persuaded me to have at least a month off. I'm not used to not being at work. The routine and responsibility have always defined me. A month stretches in front of me like an exhausted yawn.

I love taking the boys to school. It's ages since I have. But I feel their teacher's eyes boring into me as I help them put their indoor shoes on.

"We encourage them to do that sort of thing themselves," she says with a sniff. "Good morning boys. Did you have an enjoyable weekend?" There's no warmth in her voice and there's a chill in her eyes as she continues to observe me. I wonder what Kerry has told her, and how much she's given them to gossip about in the staff room.

"Oh, whilst I think on," she says. "There was a note in Friday's register saying that Mrs Wilkes would like to speak with either you or Mrs Huntington-Barnes."

"Mrs Wilkes?"

"Our bursar. You can use the main classroom entrance and make your way along the corridor."

"I haven't really got time. I've got an appointment." It's true. I'm apprehensive about it but I've arranged to see a private investigator this morning. He came recommended by Phillip at work. He apparently hired him to prove what his wife was up to. It saved him a fortune in the long run when she tried to take him to the cleaners. "I'll get my wife to speak to her." I know what it's about anyway. It'll be the bloody school fees. I suppose I'd better sort them out. They're my sons too, after all. But as for backing the next leg of her business, she can go whistle.

The private investigator operates from a log cabin in his garden. I park a couple of streets away near Valley Gardens park. I thought our house was large but many of the houses on this estate in Harrogate, dwarf it into looking like a two-up, two-down. I slip into the park, alongside the lake and check the road up and down before venturing onto it.

I walk up the pebbled driveway towards the log cabin. If this house and the landscaped garden is anything to go by, he must be charging some serious fees. According to Phillip, his fees are in the same league as what I'm paying the solicitor. Still, it will all be worth it in the end. I knock.

"Mr Fitzpatrick?" I say as he swings open the wooden door. "Edward

Huntington."

"Mr Huntington. Good to meet you. Come in."

"Call me Ed," I say as I follow him in. It's an impressive set up. Completely different to my pristinely organised consulting room. A comfy looking leather couch nestles in the corner and his desk is piled high with files. His walls are covered with certificates and press cuttings.

"Call me Trevor. Sorry about the mess." He gestures to a seat in front of his desk as he picks up a pile of files and places them on a table beside him. He stoops beneath a beam. I stare at his enormous feet as he wanders towards a coffee machine in the corner. "Can I tempt you?" he says.

I know what Russ would say to that. I try to quell these thoughts as I reply. "A coffee would be good please. Great place you've got here."

"Thanks. It's nicely tucked out of the way. It needs to be. Milk? Sugar?"

"Neither. Thank you."

I watch the back of him as he pours coffee. He obviously works out. I guess he must need to keep in shape if he gets into any scrapes. What an exciting job, I think. Better than making a fortune out of straightening, bleaching and veneering people's teeth. He returns to his desk and places a mug in front of me.

"So how can I help you Ed, and can I ask where you heard about me?"

"You were recommended to me by a work colleague. What it is - I need to find out the residential details of a man who is causing me problems. As well as information about his activities, and his car registration number."

"OK. Well before we proceed and I take more information, I need to tell you that I charge five hundred per hour. On top of that would be expenses for such as travel tickets, entrance fees and fees accrued for certificates or internet searches, where applicable. I don't charge for any food or drink on the job."

"That's fine," I say, meeting his eye so he knows I'm good for it. He's about the same age as me, maybe older, as his hair is showing signs of grey around his ears. He's clean shaven and isn't really what I imagined a private investigator to look like, although I'm not really sure what my preconceptions were. Just not someone clean shaven.

"Because of the preliminary research that would be required, I would be asking for payment on account, equivalent to four hours."

"That's fine." I hold his gaze. "I can sort a transfer whilst I'm here. Do you want me to do it now?"

"Fabulous. Here's the sort code and account number. I'll just find the forms we need to complete whilst you're taking care of that."

I log into the new account I've had to open. It's good to know that only I can get at it now. All the monies from my own account, mine and Kerry's savings account and our current account are in there. It's looking pretty healthy. Two grand is pocket change. "All done," I say, a couple of minutes later and thrust my phone in front of him so he can see a summary of the transaction.

"Good stuff. Right, let's proceed."

I tell him everything I can. The history with BF and everything I know about him. Appearance, name, date of birth. It makes me nauseous to think about him in a detailed way, but I must give Trevor all I can. I tell him everything I know about his recent visits to me and Mum. I remember that Kerry has had some sort of dealing with him though she hasn't said exactly what he said – just that their paths had crossed in the park. Like I tell Trevor now, it's my sons that I am most concerned about. BF would want to hit me where it hurts and must be stopped.

"It is stalking, from what you're telling me," Trevor says, "which is a criminal offence. Have you had any police involvement?"

"A little. Though, with no location details, they can't ask the courts to serve an injunction or anything. They've asked me to keep a log of everything and to try to find out more about his whereabouts. They said his car reg would be useful."

"As long as he's not using false plates." Trevor's making notes as he speaks. "What can you tell me about his car?"

"Not a lot. Dark. Perhaps a Volvo. Be warned though. He's a nasty piece of work. I wouldn't get too close."

"Don't worry. You've no idea the types I've encountered in my time."

"How long do you think it will take you to get what I need?"

"I'll start by doing a bit of digging around on-line. Then I'll need to get a mugshot of him - check with you that we're dealing with the right man. In the meantime, if you have any dealings with him, let me know straightaway. That way, I can hopefully get across and tail him."

"It sounds like it'll be fairly quick."

"It's what I do, Ed." Trevor takes a big sip of his coffee then his eyes meet mine. "I'm paid to get results and believe me, I will."

"I just want him stopped."

The meeting lasts forty-five minutes. In contrast, the solicitor's meeting after that, goes on for nearly two hours. I have to give a financial disclosure ahead of any mediation process. I make a mental note to speak with my accountant and see if anything can be somehow moved out of Kerry's reach.

"I feel a bit of a shit to be honest," I say. "My ex has our sons to look after and I've moved all the money in our joint accounts, out of her reach."

"Well, whilst I understand why you've done this, I should inform you that you are obligated to preserve all of this money you've moved, until the divorce is finalised." He flicks through the statements I've brought in. "However, it looks as though she had a bit of a spree before you moved the money. Do you know what she was spending on?"

"Probably the new shop, but I don't know for sure. What does it say on the statements? I don't think there were any details apart from *withdrawal*."

"Cash," he replies, running his finger down the sheet of paper. "To me, it looks like she was trying to hide which account she was moving money into. It would definitely be helpful for us to know the purposes behind her transactions, if you can find anything out."

She's hardly likely to tell me anything. I think of Trevor Fitzpatrick. However, I then decide that I don't need to engage his services to dish any dirt on Kerry. She's not as smart as she thinks she is. She never was.

"Whatever happens, I'll get you the best outcome," Mark assures me. "Her solicitor is pushing for this mediation meeting. We might as well get it out of the way. Along with the Statement of Arrangements for your children. Have you had any thoughts yet about when and where you would like access to them?"

"I'm just looking for somewhere to stay. I've been staying with my mother and at a couple of hotels. I've taken a month off work now so I can get sorted."

Before I return to my car, I buy a black tie, and a shirt from a department store. Russ always fancied me in a suit whilst we were seeing each other. I'm dreading tomorrow but nothing could stop me from being there, even if I do have to just slip in at the back.

I should be following his coffin down the church and I should be sat at the front. It is me who should place a rose on his coffin and have chosen the music. I loved him. More than anyone. Especially Davina.

Chapter 30

Tony

I should relax now nancy boy is to be incinerated. Only I can't. I have a feeling in the pit of my gut, that's never been there after other jobs. This one was always going to be a challenge. I only accepted it because of the thirty grand price tag. It all seemed cut and dry. Only it wasn't.

The sordid details of Russell Lawson's death have ended in a load of social media shit and far more than it deserved press coverage. I've listened to his hard-faced wife rave on about how he was not gay. She seems more bothered about that, than him dying.

I've watched Russell's gay boyfriend as he's left his home and family. I was an unknown in that area, so the entrance lobby shots didn't worry me. However, what I hadn't bargained on was a hidden internal camera. Now it was known Russell Lawson might not have been alone.

I've burned the holdall I'd taken the ligature in. I've kept a low profile. But a trace of Russell's spunk was found on the corridor carpet.

It's no longer looking like suicide. And as they suspect he wasn't alone, there are doubts about it being an accident too. The police might find where I threw up, or trace the ligature back to me. Neither of these things would have mattered before. There's also the risk that connections from this job could lead them to me, for other contracts I've taken care of. I need to lie low for a bit. Get away. Take stock.

This job's rattled me. I need more money to really get away. And I'm not the only person with everything to lose.

Chapter 31

<u>Kerry</u>

I can hardly believe Ed and I have reached the fourth week since separating. An entire month. As it's gone on, the hours have crawled by, yet when I look back now, it seems to have gone fast. My biggest stress is money. I'm thinking I may have to borrow from Adam to pay Mandy her wages. The mediation can't happen quick enough. Though my solicitor has said that she might be able to put an order on Ed even before then.

The boys are still sleeping in my bed with me and somehow, I'm limping through each day. I'm going to try and have as normal a day as possible today. Try and forget about the wretched funeral that is taking place. I hate him.

"Mrs Huntington-Barnes." I barely get into the cloakroom before Mrs Richardson has pounced on me. "Mrs Wilkes needs to see you urgently. We asked your husband yesterday to deal with things, but we were referred to you."

Sounds about right, I think to myself. Then looking around for Alex's pump, I say, "Is it about the school fees?"

"I believe so."

"I can't do anything right now. My husband has emptied our

accounts."

"Oh." She looks taken aback at the directness of my answer. "Can I ask that you discuss this with Mrs Wilkes? There might be something she can do."

"I haven't got time this morning. Tell her to ring the boys' father. He's the only one who can pay their fees."

"But he's already referred her to you."

"He knows, full well, that he's got control of our money." I look inside Alex's book bag as I speak, unsure whether I've remembered his reading book. "There's no point speaking to me about this. If that changes, then I'll let you know."

"I should warn you," continues Mrs Richardson, shooing George and Alex into the classroom, "more than three months fee arrears, results in a removal from the school letter."

"Tell your colleague to ring my husband," I repeat, looking her straight in the eye. "And if you think I'm coming to help in your poxy classroom tomorrow morning, when you're issuing threats about a removal from school letter, then you've got another think coming."

I flounce back across the playground towards the car park, determined, if necessary, to give the same short shrift to anyone who crosses me at the gym too.

"I haven't seen her. Is she OK?" I hear Jo's voice as soon as I enter the changing room.

"You talking about me?" I don't look at any of them. At least it's nothing derogatory for a change.

"Don't be like this Kerry." Alison slides her belongings along the bench so I can put my bag down. I am honoured. She usually occupies the entire area of bench that is meant for two or three people, and wouldn't dream of moving her things for anyone. "I've said I'm sorry. I even called into the shop on Friday to speak to you, but you weren't there."

"I know you did. You were asking Mandy about my husband's involvement with the Parkside man, weren't you?" I don't give a monkeys what they think of me anymore. I've spent my whole life trying to fit in with people and I am sick of it.

"It's his funeral today." Alison seems to be trying to steer the subject away from the altercation between me and Jo. "My Robert's gone. A few of them from his work have – wanting to support Davina."

"I expect he'll see my husband there then," I say, brightly. All goes quiet as if they're waiting for me to say more. I enjoy the momentary power for a few seconds.

"Come on girls." Claire holds the door open. "We'll be late for our class if we don't get a move on.

Tuesday is legs, bums and tums. I'm last in line, as we queue into the studio cupboard for a mat. Abruptly, a woman pushes in front of me and takes the last one. "I'll have that," she says to Jo, who is holding it towards me.

"That's alright," I say to the woman. "You are, of course, far more important than anyone else. I'll just use the hard floor to lie on." I decide then that I can't be arsed with the class today, walk back to the studio door and leave. No one comes after me. They won't want to miss a moment of legs, bums and tums.

I find myself at Leeds Crematorium and can just about see the entrance from the main road. Ed's lurking at the back. It takes me a few moments to find him, but after several years of marriage, I'd recognise him anywhere. There's so many people there that I find myself wondering how they will all fit in. There are a few police officers, which I'm taken aback by. If they're laying the man to rest, why are they still looking for answers?

The hearse pulls around the corner, the word husband spelt out at the side of the coffin. It's a sorry sight, even though it contains the man who has inadvertently wrecked my life.

Davina is in the car behind, surrounded by several other people. She dabs at her eyes and I wonder how she can mourn so publicly, given the circumstances. For a minute she seems to look straight at me then turns the corner into the crematorium. I feel more alone than ever, sat in my car, not knowing what to do next. I'm avoiding the shop because I have no answers to give Mandy about money. To keep busy, I go to the supermarket instead.

Normally it's a regular high-end supermarket delivery, but I've cancelled it this month. With less than a grand in my account and no way of knowing when Ed will be forced to release some money back to me, I head for the budget supermarket. The women at the gym would be laughing about it. I'm very much Kerry Barnes today, thinking twice about everything I chuck into the trolley. I'm fuming with Ed. *See what you've reduced me to.* I want to drag his sorry arse out of that funeral and shake some sense back into him. This is probably the worst day I've had since he left. I want to feel normal but don't know if I ever will again. Just as I'm pushing the trolley down the first aisle, my phone beeps.

I need to see you.

Chapter 32

Ed

I'm not doing myself any favours by being here, but I couldn't be anywhere else today. When I see the coffin containing the man I love, it is all I could do to stop myself breaking down and inviting attention.

Davina has chosen *With or Without You* as the song Russell arrives to. I sit at the back, listening to the life story he was gradually telling me over beer, in the gym and in the hotel we spent time in. I cry silently as I listen to his sister's eulogy. In it, she describes the gentle, funny, caring brother she had grown up with, and adds her hopes that speculation will soon pass and that his memory will be properly laid to rest.

When Davina gets up at the end of the service to lay a rose on the coffin, I want to take the chance to leave. However, we are asked to remain seated until the family has left the room. The exit is a different door to the one we came in.

I sit a bit longer, deciding to wait until last and slip out in the crowd. In doing so, I endure the agony of watching the velvet curtains wrap around the coffin as I walk towards the exit. I slip a note onto the collection plate and then walk straight into DC Burnley and DI Milner, who spoke to me when I went to the police station.

"Edward," Milner says. "I'm surprised to see you here. I thought you and Russell were just gym acquaintances."

"We are." I wish he would keep his voice down. "I'm just paying my respects like everyone else."

"Quite. Now you know that he's passed away."

"What are you doing here? You've got a nerve." I am horrified to see Davina tunnelling through the crowd towards me.

"You should be taking him in again." She looks from me to DC Burnley. "He knows more than he's letting on."

"I know you're upset," I reply, "but you don't know what you're talking about."

"If I see you again after today," she continues, "I'll be reporting you for stalking, and before you think you can come, no, you're not invited to the wake."

DC Burnley shrugs his shoulders as Davina walks away. "Seems like Russell was a popular man," he says, looking around.

If it wasn't for Davina, I would have wanted to go to the wake and taking another look at the photos which were displayed on a screen throughout the service. I would have liked to have listened to stories from Russ's younger days, and found out who everyone here is. I'd only known him for a few years, though that had been enough. Lots of the rumours that are being bandied about on social media don't tally with the man I had come to know.

I return to my car, lay my head on top of my arms, almost hugging the steering wheel. I stay like that for a few moments. I watch the now-solo family funeral car leave the crematorium's driveway. Davina is laughing with the people she is travelling with. Bitch. How can she laugh? I certainly can't remember the last time I was able to laugh. Many more cars follow her out. It's over – it's all over.

I don't know what to do next. I can't go into work and don't feel like going back to mum's. I decide to walk the route by the lake near the gym where Russ and I ran the triathlon together. We went there with a flask of coffee too, not daring to walk hand in hand but having an enjoyable afternoon anyway. It was down here that I first told him how I felt about him. That he made me happier and feel more alive than any other human being ever had or could.

Apart from the odd dog walker, it's quiet down here. I guess it would be early on a Tuesday afternoon. My thoughts clear with every step as I stare at the lake beside me. I take cleansing breaths of the fresh air and begin to relax, my feet crunching the gravel path. Russ has been cremated and I must move forward. One positive thing has emerged – I am finally being honest about who I really am. I have lots of things to sort out before I can truly move forward with my life. Though, at last, I am no longer forced to live a lie. However, meeting another man in the future is unthinkable right now.

By the time I return to the car, I'm glad I decided on a walk. I feel slightly better. I rummage in the glove box for my phone. It's been busy whilst I've been inside the crematorium and at the lake. There's the usual from Kerry, ranting about money and the boys. I can't face it, or her. She's right, to a point, but I want to sort things out officially. I've got a lot to lose if I don't box clever. Speaking of which, there's an appointment from mediation for next week – that will be a barrel of laughs.

Then there's one from Trevor, the PI. *Is this him?*

Lo and behold, as clear as a bell, he's captured BF across the bar in a pub. I can hardly bear to look at his face. It still wears the sneer he had, towards every aspect of his life. And now he thinks he can come back, threatening my mother and my sons.

Yes, that's him. Excellent work.

Trevor replies instantly. *Great. In touch soon with movements, address and car details.*

Thanks. I'll wait to hear from you.

Chapter 33

Kerry

I'd hoped the funeral might bring about a change of heart in Ed. But I've not heard from him. He won't answer his phone or reply to my texts. I want to tell him about the noises I hear and the fear that snakes up and down my spine every night. I desperately want to sort myself out and return to some sort of normality. I'm scared. I can barely afford a weekly shop. All last month's profits from the shop have been used to pay Mandy. At least the solicitor is applying for an interim order to release some of our money to me.

The boys are playing rowdily in the garden, repeatedly coming in to tell on the other. They keep me going. I can't fall apart whilst I've got my sons to take care of. I'm working through some paperwork I've been sent ahead of the mediation appointment, counting the minutes until it's wine o'clock and I can put the boys to bed. I hate drinking wine each night, but it's the only way I can get any sleep. Although I am wondering if the knocks and noises I hear throughout the night are in my imagination because I'm so anxious all the time.

Like now. I slop my tea as the doorbell goes. Maybe it's Ed, but more likely it's someone selling something. I nearly drop my cup as I swing the door open, cursing myself for not looking through the spyhole first. I'm not at all on the ball today – I've relaxed my vigilance a bit too much.

"What are you doing here?" I stare at Davina, who steps towards me, holding the hand of a little girl. "Has anyone seen you come to the door? You shouldn't be here."

"This has all gone tits up," she says as I shut the door after her. "Look what was waiting for me yesterday when I got back from the funeral." I scan the letter she thrusts into my hand.

You'll be rolling in it now, it says. Life insurance, pension, investments. In hindsight, an extra thirty grand was too generous. Let's make the whole thing a nice round figure of £100,000. Cash.

You should know that I'm getting severely pissed off with your lack of contact. This is your final warning. Noon tomorrow. Usual place. Or your kid will be my next hit.

"He was sitting outside my house," she says. "I can't risk him hurting Eloise. We're in this up to our necks."

"We?"

"Can I have a biscuit Mummy?" Alex runs into the house, spots Eloise and looks at her shyly.

"Take the tin into the garden." I turn to Eloise. "Would you like to play in the garden with the boys?"

She curls into her mother for a moment but George comes in and tempts her outside with a chocolate biscuit.

"Thanks," Davina says, grim-faced. "This isn't something we should discuss in front of a five-year-old."

"I want to know what you meant by *we*." I walk towards the lounge and Davina follows me. She's lost weight as well. Who needs WeightWatchers when a bit of misery will work just as well?

"Do you mind if I sit down," she says.

"Suit yourself." I walk to the window, checking there's no one hanging around. There isn't. I fiddle with the fabric of the curtain. I can barely think straight.

210

"We're in this together Kerry? Don't think you can step away now."
I spin around to face her. "My involvement stopped with the money
I gave you. You'd have to prove what it was for. It could have just been
a loan."

"Don't you think I covered that?" Her face twists into an expression
that I really don't like. "I recorded that conversation we had back in
March. You're just as involved as I am."

As if my life isn't awful enough. Why the hell did I ever get caught
up in this hit man stuff?

As if reading my mind, Davina says, "Come on Kerry. You wanted
him dealt with as much as I did. You put ten grand in. And now I need
your help."

"I wasn't thinking straight. Your husband was threatening my whole
world." It's true. My life is unrecognisable from what it was. Though
thinking back, I was hiding from the truth. "You should never have
come to me."

Davina laughs and flicks her hair behind her shoulder. I sit then,
facing her; the severity of what we've done, juxtaposed with the
children's carefree laughter echoing from the back garden. I wasn't
thinking straight at the time. Though I know that won't hold up as a
defence.

"You're the one who hired him. Made all the enquiries. Paid him all
the money."

"Ten grand Kerry, which you put in, is a lot of money. Don't get me
wrong, I appreciated it. How was I to know he would up his fee?"

"I still don't know why he did."

"When he found out *how* we wanted him to kill Russ."

"You're using the *we* word again. It was all your idea, Davina.
Especially the bit about how you wanted him taken out."

"You knew what was happening and went along with it. I can't sort
this on my own. That's why I'm here."

211

I walk to the fireplace, looking at the photograph of my innocent boys. "What do you want from me?"

"We need to raise the rest of this money. Get him off our backs."

"You've got to be kidding." I laugh. "I can barely afford the gas bill. Ed's emptied all our accounts."

"You've got a business. A house. Look, Kerry, he's not going away. This is the third threatening letter. We know what he's capable of. Look at his track record. And he's threatened to hurt Eloise. I've got to do something." Panic is rising in her voice.

"Surely you've got more chance of being able to release funds than me. Your husband must have made provision for you?"

"Nothing's come through yet. Remember, there's a police inquiry going on. The life insurance probably won't touch us if there's any hint of suicide." She looks down at her feet. "It was supposed to look like an accident. I'd told him to use a ligature which had a safety mechanism on it, and he didn't. That way the insurance would pay out."

"But thirty grand was agreed. Why's he come after more?" This conversation is surreal. To an outsider looking in, we could be two friends having a chat whilst our children play in the garden.

"Because he can. I can't exactly take him to court for breach of contract, can I? And things haven't been as straightforward as they should have been, have they? As I said, it wasn't supposed to look anything like a suicide. Even with the police investigation pointing towards someone else being involved, because he didn't use the right ligature, the insurance company are investigating more into it now. But that's the least of my worries."

Davina and I are united in something terrible. Maybe once, in another life, under a different set of circumstances, we'd have been friends. From initially feeling like throwing her out when she arrived, I now feel a small amount of affinity. What we've done is wrong, but we've both been shat on from a great height.

"Can you get in touch with this man? Get him to compromise? Ask for more time? I'm seeing a mediator next week and I should…"

She laughs. "God, you're green, Kerry. It doesn't work like that. He wants to disappear. He wants more money like, yesterday. We're risking our lives and more importantly, our kids' lives if we don't pay him off and get rid of him. He's a maniac. Here, look at the other notes he's sent me." She reaches into her bag and passes me some tatty bits of paper.

As I'm scanning them, Davina gasps. "The kids. They've gone quiet. They can't get out of the garden, can they?"

My chest palpitates as I realise we've not heard them for a minute or two. How could I have been so stupid? I tear from the lounge and through the house towards the conservatory. The back garden gate is swinging in the breeze. Kerry darts through it and up the drive.

"Eloise!"

"Alex! George!" I'm turning in circles at the end of the drive. No, no no! Why the hell did we leave them?

"They've gone. Oh my God." Davina bends forward, grabbing her fringe in her fist. "He's taken our kids. What if he hurts them?"

"We're going to have to ring the police." A myriad of possibilities are rotating around my head.

"And tell them what? *A hitman we hired has kidnapped our children.*"

"Right. Let's stay calm." I steady myself on the garden wall. "They might have just wandered off. They might be hiding somewhere. George! Alex!"

"Eloise," Davina also calls. "Eloise!"

"Can you get hold of him? Have you got a number?"

"It's at home."

"You're joking right. Is it not on one of those notes?"

"He could have hurt them by then. I can hardly ring him from my phone anyway."

"I don't care about any of that right now. All I care about is finding our children." I start along the street at a run. "George! Alex!"

"Is everything alright?" Joan from over the road rushes towards us. "Is it the kids?"

"They've been taken," I gasp, stopping in my tracks.

"What! By who?"

"A man, we think. I don't really know. Were you looking out? Did you see anything?"

"I noticed a new car a little while ago at the bottom of your drive. I thought your husband must have bought a new one. I know he likes his cars."

"Did you see anybody? A man? Did you hear the kids? He can't have just taken them. Surely one of them would have screamed or something."

"The car drove off again quite quickly. I noticed that. It could have just been turning round. But to be honest, I was busy gardening and had the radio on." She glances back at her house as she speaks. "They won't have been taken. They won't be far away, I promise. There will be an explanation."

Ring the police, every fibre of my being is shrieking. Call it mother's instinct but I know they haven't just wandered off. That monster has taken them because we haven't paid him what he wanted.

Joan pulls a phone from her pinny. "If you think the kids have been taken, you must ring the police."

"No. Not yet," Davina darts from the end of the drive to where we're stood on the street. "Let's look for them first. Eloise," she calls again.

"Ring them." I say to Joan. "I'm not taking any chances here."

I listen as she's connected. "Police please. I need to report three children who've gone missing. How old are they?" she mouths at me. "Hang on. I'll pass you to their mother."

I can't tell them much. Just that they were playing in the garden one minute and gone the next. I give them our address. "What was the car like?" I hiss at Joan. "They're apparently going to get some units straight out."

"Oh, Kerry. I'm sorry. I'm honestly not sure. Dark, I think. And big. I'm no good with cars. Never have been."

"Could they have just wandered off?" asks the operator. "especially if there's three of them?"

"My twins would never do that." I'm struggling to breathe. "Besides, the gate was bolted at the top. It always is. The kids can't reach it."

"They could have stood on something?"

"No, it's too stiff."

"Is it possible to open it from the other side?"

Yes, it is. I've now just got to pray that this monster, who kills people for a living, doesn't hurt them. It's money he wants. I just can't lay my hands on any. But Ed can. No matter how useless he's been lately, he'll do anything for them.

"I've got to let the children's dad know," I say to the operator. "Will the police be long?"

Davina is slumped on the garden wall.

"We need you to stay on the line until one of our response units gets there. They're on the way."

"OK. I'm on my neighbour's phone. I dash back into the house and grab mine from the breakfast bar.

I can hear a siren; it's getting louder. Blimey, they're on this. I suppose they would be with three five-year-olds missing. "They're here," I say. "Thanks for your help. I'm going to hang up."

"Hopefully they're just hiding somewhere," she says.

"God I hope you're right." I punch a line into my phone to Ed and pray he'll see it straightaway.

THE KIDS HAVE BEEN TAKEN FROM THE GARDEN – GET OVER HERE NOW!

Davina runs to meet the police from their car. Another one is right behind it. They all assemble on my driveway. If George and Alex are hiding and come out to see this, they'll find it very exciting. George would probably have the brass neck to ask for a ride in one of the police cars. Jesus, I hope so. I'd be so relieved to see them, I couldn't even tell them off.

"I'm DC Burnley, West Yorkshire Police. We've received a report that three children have been taken. Is that right?"

"From the back garden," Davina replies. She's crying now. I'm not. I feel numb, like I'm on some sort of autopilot.

Joan darts to Davina's side and puts an arm around her. She's nice is Joan and has always been good to me and the boys.

"What makes you think they've been taken, rather than having just wandered off somewhere?" He's a short man, somewhere in his fifties. I'm relieved we've rung the police – they'll find them. They'll be back with us soon – I can feel it.

"They wouldn't. The gate was bolted, and there was a dark car on the drive earlier."

"How long have they been missing?"

"About twenty minutes now." Twenty minutes! No way would they have hidden for this long. "Look we're wasting time here. We need to be finding them."

"Of course. We're getting to that. So, we've three five-year-olds. Two boys and a girl. Do you have a recent photograph?"

"It was over half an hour since I saw the car," says Joan.

"Half an hour?" I look at Davina. "We didn't take our eyes off them for long."

With urgency in his voice now, DC Burnley commands us. "Please, we need those photographs."

Davina pulls her phone from her pocket and I run back into the house to grab George and Alex's latest school photo, taken just after they started at Harlow last September. I race back outside and wait, becoming impatient as the six officers pass the photo and the phone around. Surely three small children won't be that hard to find.

"Right." DC Burnley stands in front of his colleagues. He immediately has their attention and instructs them in turn. "You two are to cover the right-hand side of the street, one taking charge of door to door; the other covering gardens and sheds. Then can you both…" he gestures to the next two officers, "take the left-hand side of the street. And you last two…" He points at the two officers stood expectantly, furthest away from him. "If you could drive around the surrounding streets by car. Hopefully, the children will have stuck together. You all know what they look like now. I think we'll find they're not *too* far away."

"That's what I said," Joan adds. "They'll be back before you know it." She places a reassuring hand on my shoulder.

I wish I could tell him the truth. That some crazed hitman wanting more money has probably taken them. They'd probably step up their game then. My only crumb of comfort is that his need of the money should stop him from hurting them. He'll know he's got leverage to get us to pay up.

They'll be absolutely terrified though. Panic suddenly rises as the enormity of what is happening hits me like a truck. "Please find them," I say as the police personnel disperse. I turn to DC Burnley. "What should we be doing?" Davina rushes towards us from the gateway where she's been watching down the street. Her thumbnail is bleeding from where she's been chewing it. Joan is heading back to her house.

"You need to be here when they come back," he says. "I'll wait with you." The word *when* reassures me. "Besides, I need to get some more information from you both. Shall we go inside?"

I hesitate, looking after the officers who have just left. "I feel like I should be doing something."

"You are," he replies. "Don't worry. They'll find them. Let's just stay calm and let them do their job."

I need to get Davina on her own. Send her home to get that number. But right now DC Burnley doesn't seem to be taking his eyes off us.

I lead the three of us inside and towards the bay window of the lounge so I can keep an eye on the gate to the driveway. "My husband's here."

Ed abandons his car on the street and comes hurtling in, wearing an expression I've never seen before. Finally, I let the tears slide down my face.

Chapter 34

Ed

"What's going on?" I burst into the lounge. "I got your message?"

"Edward?" DC Burnley says, raising an eyebrow at me.

"You two know each other?" Kerry looks from me to him.

"We've met," I say to her, then I turn to him. "I'm the boys' father." Then I clock Davina. I want to say, *what the fuck is she doing here? Why is this woman, who totally hates my guts, stood in my front room?* It's not going to be a social call, she probably came around to dish some dirt on me. I guess there'll be time to ask those questions soon.

"We've got a number of officers out looking for the three of them. I'm sure they'll be found soon. In nearly all cases, little ones are hiding, or lost – there will be a simple explanation."

"The three of them?"

"My daughter Eloise is with them," Davina replies flatly, not taking her eyes off the window.

"I didn't realise the two of you knew each other?" It's a question rather than a statement but neither of them reply. I'm aware that Kerry knows the link that exists between Davina and I – the fact that we both loved the same man. It still doesn't explain how Davina has come to be here. Never mind all that right now though. I still have a million questions to ask. "How long have they been gone?"

"About half an hour," Davina replies.

"Half an hour! But that's ages for three five-year-olds. What's being done?" I'm baffled. George has probably got it in him to wander off, but not Alex. He's always been so sensible.

"We've four officers doing house-to-house, searching gardens and outbuildings." DC Burnley like everyone else is watching the window. "Another two are searching the local area by car."

"Shouldn't you have a helicopter up or something?" Fear mingled with anger is coiling around my spine as I realise what might have happened here. BF would do anything to hurt me. "My boys are five, for God's sake."

"We've no reason to believe yet, that anything has happened, other than them wandering off. If we don't find them soon, we'll escalate things."

"BF," I say, quietly at first.

"What?" DC Burnley turns to face me.

"My father. We're estranged, but he's returned to the area." I feel sick. "He's been making threats."

"What sort of threats? Against your children?"

"All of us really. He will have taken them to get to me."

"OK, I need to get some details from you sir."

"We haven't got time for that. The man's a nasty piece of work. He beat me to a pulp when I was a teenager. Put me in hospital."

"He's not going to do that to the boys, surely?" Kerry's face is pinched and white. "He's their grandfather when all said and done. That must count for something."

"That doesn't mean much. He was my father and look what he did to me." I push the memory out of my mind. I need to focus on finding my sons.

"But you were older, not a defenceless five-year-old." She tugs a tissue from the box.

I feel guilty. I can't believe that because of my maniac of a father, we're all in this predicament.

"I don't understand. Why would he have taken my daughter too?" Davina asks. "Your dad doesn't know her." She looks at me directly for the first time.

"Don't call him my dad."

"Never mind all that." Davina stands with her hands on her hips, her lip curling slightly. "Whoever he is, he's a stranger to Eloise. Why would he take her?"

"Because she was there?" I reply. "Maybe he thought she'd say something if he left her behind. Raise the alarm. I don't know. I couldn't begin to fathom a mind as warped as his."

"Right." DC Burnley presses a button on his radio. "I will check with my control on progress, and then I'll get all the information I need from you."

I'm pacing the room whilst Kerry and Davina stand still. How all this has come about, with them all being together, still needs to be got to the bottom of. They can't possibly be friends.

"DC Burnley here. I'm at the property now - number eight Hawthorn Close, Farndale – can you check with the units as to whether the three missing children have been located yet? Or if we've any information?"

"Give me a minute or two. I'll be right back to you."

As we wait, DC Burnley scribbles our names and addresses down. Then the full names, schools and dates of birth of the children. I'm getting impatient at the triviality of this. I need to get out there, looking for my boys. If that bastard hurts them, I will...

"Control here."

"Go ahead."

"I've been in touch with everyone. Nothing yet, I'm afraid."

"It's been about forty minutes now. And I've just had information from the father to suggest it could be an abduction. Someone known to the children though."

"No he's not known to them," I shout. "They've never even spoken to him."

"Eloise doesn't know him either," Davina shrieks in echo. "She'll be terrified."

"Right Sarge," begins DC Burnley. "We need to activate a Missing Children Alert. Straightaway. And get the helicopter up. I'll get some photographs and descriptions organised for the media. Can you alert the forensic team too? I'll seal off the driveway and the garden." He turns to me. "I'll be back in a moment," he says.

On the surface, I possibly appear the most level-headed of the three of us. Kerry has slumped to the sofa, her head in her hands and Davina has tears rolling down her cheeks.

"My husband has just died. I can't take any more."

My heart bleeds, I want to say. It's not so long since I saw you laughing in the funeral car. I absolutely can't believe she's stood, large as life in my front room and we're united in this terrible situation.

"OK, you must try and stay calm," says DC Burnley striding back into the room. "We're doing everything we can – and we will find them, I promise. I'm going to make copies of these photos and I will need a description of what the children are wearing."

"I don't know," I reply. I lower my eyes to the carpet, then raise them to look at Kerry. How could I not know what my own sons were wearing?

"Alex is wearing blue jeans and a Batman t-shirt," she says. I detect a note of smugness in her voice. "George hasn't got changed. He never does as he's told." Her voice wobbles. "He's still wearing his school uniform. He goes to Harlow Boys."

"Can you describe his uniform?"

"Grey trousers. Navy blue jumper and light blue polo shirt. But he'd put his red wellies on to play in the garden. Oh, and Alex will have been wearing his light up trainers."

"They weren't even wearing coats," Davina sobs. "They'll get cold."

"It's April," I say. "And they'll be back soon. We'll find them." I say this with a conviction I don't feel. Having not seen BF for fifteen or so years, I have no idea what he's after, or where he might have taken them. Neither have I any way of getting hold of him. Yet.

"What was Eloise wearing?" DC Burnley asks Davina.

"A pink Disney princess t-shirt with frills at the bottom and dark blue leggings. She always feels the cold – I don't even think she put her cardigan on before we left the house."

"What about shoes? And her hair? We will be putting a description out through the media soon. Just local to start with – hopefully we won't have to go any wider than that."

"She still had her plaits in from school. And blue ankle boots." Fresh tears fall down her face. Though I hate this woman because Russ always went home to her, part of me feels for her. She has been through a fair bit. And so have I. I dig my nails into the fleshy parts of my palms. They must be found soon. They have to be.

I nip to the loo and by the time I return, a big police van has arrived. Four people get out - three men and a woman. Neighbours are agog, looking to see what's happening from their gardens. By now they all should know what's going on – at least I hope so, if the police are doing their jobs properly. DC Burnley is back out there stretching *do not enter* tape across the driveway and a uniformed policeman is guarding it. Kerry and Davina are talking in low voices as I re-enter the lounge. Just as I'm about to start asking questions, I notice two policemen returning to the van, whilst the woman follows DC Burnley back into the house.

"This is PC Coates - Polly." he announces. "She'll be your family liaison officer."

"What does that mean?" Kerry stands up as they enter the room. "Shouldn't everyone be out there, finding them?"

"Polly will be the link between everything we're doing and yourselves." DC Burnley gestures towards Polly as he speaks. "She's here to support you and answer any procedural questions until your children are found. She'll stay with you, to take as much information as you can possibly give her, that may help us find them quicker."

Shouldn't we be doing something," I ask. "I can't just sit here. I need to be doing something to find my sons." I should have been here in the first place – protecting them.

"I'm going to get out there," DC Burnley replies. "It's all being escalated as we speak. And Polly will advise you how you can best help with the situation. Don't worry, you'll be able to do your bit."

"Is it alright if I sit down?" Polly asks.

I nod. "Please do."

"Right. I gather you think your father might have abducted the children. I need as much information as possible around this. Who he is, where he is and what events might have led him to it?" She poises a pen over a notepad.

"I've actually got a private investigator on him at the moment," I say.

"A private investigator?" Kerry looks at me as though she would like to punch me. "Why? And why haven't you told me?"

"I mentioned he was hanging around," I reply. Then turning back to Polly, I say, "my father, who I haven't seen for many years, has been following me around and has turned up at my mother's house too. I suspected he meant business. But I didn't think he would just take my children."

"And mine," Davina says. "God, I just hope they find them soon. Isn't there a statistic that says there's a certain time frame where they should be found or –?"

"Twenty-four hours," says Polly. "Though the first sixty minutes are often called 'golden minutes,' as an abductor can get a long way in that time.

"But we're already past that," Kerry wails. "You should have told me you'd hired someone Ed. I'd never have let them play in the garden if I'd known they were at this much risk. I had a right to know."

"I told you not to..." I start to reply.

"No, you didn't," she snaps back. "Your bloody mother said something but still didn't let me know the full extent of it. You've just about cut off communication with me, haven't you?"

"Look," says Polly. "I know emotions are running high, but we'll get your kids back here quicker if we work together." She tears some pages out of her book and hands one to each of us. She then hands pens around, her bracelets rattling with the movement. "I want you to make a list," she says, "of everyone known to the children. Friends, other family members, places they love, where they might be heading for or hiding, that sort of thing. Even though we have a potential suspect, we have to keep all the other possibilities in mind." Then turning to me, "Mr Huntington," she begins...

"Call me Ed," I reply.

"I want you to add to your list, anyone on your dad's side of the family, friends he might have or anywhere you think he could have taken the children."

"I don't call him my dad," I say. "Not since he put me in hospital and went to prison when I was sixteen. I could give my investigator a call though, see how he's getting on with finding his address and car reg. I think he'd have let me know if he'd have found anything yet, so I'll speed him up on it."

"I think you should probably contact your mother too. See if she's had any contact with him in the last couple of hours."

"She'll go nuts when she finds out what's happened." God. Mum's reaction doesn't bear thinking about. She'll be straight over. Though, to be honest, I could do with her here right now. She'll keep us sane.

"I'll let you all get on with those lists. Then I suggest you ring round where you can." Polly stands. "Whilst you're doing that, if you could point me in the direction of the kitchen, I'll make us all a drink."

I lead her to the kitchen and show her where everything is. I'm shocked that Davina hasn't tried to tear me apart, given the situation. My blood runs cold as I spot figures in white suits, head to toe, walk past the side window. Please, please let them be alright.

Chapter 35

Nearly two hours has passed and they still haven't been found. Marie has just arrived. I literally fall into her arms as she enters the lounge. "They've been taken," I wail into her shoulder. "What if he hurts them?"

As she hugs me, I can't tell her that secretly I'm relieved that it seems to be BF who has got them. The alternative, the man Davina hired, and his demands for more money, does not bear thinking about. The fact that BF is the boys' grandfather has to count for something. He's done this to get back at Ed. Simple. And when he thinks he's rattled him enough, he'll let them go. They're going to be traumatised but I'll get them through it. I'll get them counsellors, therapy, whatever. Everything will be fine.

"I've just been on the phone to the investigator," Ed announces, returning to the lounge. "You OK Mum?"

"I can't believe what he's…"

"What did he say?" I step away from Marie.

"He hasn't got what I've asked him for yet? But he says he's getting close. He has an assistant who is talking to people, and it seems like he's staying around here somewhere."

"Well, that's helpful, he's staying around here somewhere! What are you paying this man? Oh, don't answer that. The boys' school fees, probably."

"Give it a rest Kerry. I'm doing my best."

"Pack it in you two." Marie walks over to Davina. "I'm Marie, Ed's mum."

"Davina." She offers a limp hand which Marie grasps. "He's taken my girl too. She was playing with the boys in the garden."

"Are you a friend of Kerry's?"

"Sort of."

I don't look at them. I don't want to offer any sort of explanation.

"They'll find them," Marie says, keeping hold of Davina's hand. "You'll see."

"Do you know anyone in his family Mum, where he could have taken the kids?"

"Not anymore," Marie steps back from Davina and sits with me on the sofa. "It's been fifteen years since I saw him, apart from when he turned up the other week. He had a brother but he was a heavy smoker and a drinker. I don't even know if he's still alive."

"I've asked the investigator to get me his car registration and his address. He's turned up at my work, a flat I was looking at and the hotel I was staying in."

I notice that Polly is writing as Ed speaks.

"I ended up stabbing him with anaesthetic at the surgery. That's why I'm off work. They asked me to take some time off."

"You never said anything to me," Marie says.

"Nor me." My body tenses with anger. "Not only have you dumped your boys, you've also put them at severe risk."

"You're the one that wasn't keeping an eye on them."

"They were playing in the garden!"

"After you'd been told not to let them."

"Don't you come the caring parent now, Ed," I begin. "After…"

"How are we getting on with those lists?" Polly lays a tray on the coffee table. Then spotting Marie, says. "I'm Polly, the Family Liaison Officer."

"Marie. The boys' grandma. I'm here to help."

"I'll get you a cup. Then we'll go through these lists."

"A bloody cup of tea," I think to myself. My boys are God knows where with God knows who and we're sat here making lists and drinking tea.

The evening is spent making phone calls, pacing the floor and bursting into tears. I could murder a glass of wine but I've got to keep a clear head. I can't believe they haven't been found yet. They will be cold by now. It's half past nine and pitch-black outside. I'm convinced they're with BF though, rather than the hitman, clearly the better option of the two. But they've definitely been taken. There's no way they'd have wandered off for this long.

"What if they haven't eaten? Why haven't they been found yet?"

Polly puts a hand on my arm. "There's lots of the neighbours involved in the search now. We'll be working overnight on it, obviously."

"Oh God. All night. What if they're gone all night?" I couldn't bear it.

Davina's Mum arrives now - a thinner, older version of Davina. They talk together in low voices for a few moments then her mother retreats to one of the sofas where she sits, wringing her hands and sighing.

I've let my mum know too. She lives in the house she's always lived in so there's always a slim chance the boys could end up being taken to her. Adam asked if I wanted him to come over. Even though I do, I said, "Everyone's looking for them. It's even going on the news soon. If they don't turn up tonight, then maybe come tomorrow."

As I end the call with Adam, I notice a BBC van pull up outside. Polly goes outside to meet them. Alistair pulls up behind them and Marie rushes out too.

"I can do without him," Ed says. "He doesn't give a shit about anyone apart from himself."

"Who is he?" says Davina.

"My mum's boyfriend. He's irritated by anyone who takes my mother's attention away from him. Even the boys."

"Could he be anything to do with…"

Davina's mum stops talking as two men in BBC overalls follow Polly into my very crowded living room. "This is Mike and Steve," she announces. "They're going to brief you now about what to say in front of the news cameras."

"Right," one of them says, "the purpose of this is to get images and information about the children as far and wide as possible."

"Am I right in thinking they've been missing for nearly five hours?" asks the other.

Like I need reminding. "Yes." I reply. It's like a bad dream. I don't think the enormity of what's going on has really sunk in. And somehow, in my gut, I feel like they're alive and safe. I would know if anything had happened.

"The three of you will be filmed on the drive," says Steve, or Mike. I don't know which. It doesn't matter really. All that matters is getting my darling boys back. A sob catches in my throat. "Will this work? Us going on the news?"

"You'll be the first item," he replies. "You're going out on the BBC Ten O'Clock News, which is obviously national. Usually other news channels will pick up the story then too."

"The story." Davina swings around to face the men. "My daughter being kidnapped isn't some sort of entertainment fodder."

"We're not suggesting it is." The man's voice is gentle. "There'll be the pictures of your children flashed onto the screen, the newsreader will give out the details and the specifics and it will be your job to appeal to the public, for their help and vigilance."

"And to whoever has taken them," Polly adds.

"God, I'm dreading this," I say. I know I've got to do it but national television? I look at Ed. "They will be alright, won't they?" I whisper. He squeezes my arm, the first time he's touched me in weeks. "I bloody hope so Kerry," his voice cracks. "I don't know how I'd go on if anything happened to them. If that bastard father of mine has harmed a hair on their heads, I'll kill him with my own bare hands."

"Do you really think it's your father?" Davina says to Ed. I see hope in her eyes. We both know it's the best scenario compared to the other possibility. The prospect of our children being held by a renowned hitman, who is fearing repercussions from the police and now wants seventy grand for the children's safe return, doesn't bear thinking about.

"We need to be making our way outside," says one of the news team. "We're on in five minutes."

"What do we say?" gasps Davina.

"Just speak from the heart," says Polly. "Say what you feel, how worried you are, how you need them back. "You don't have to give any actual information, the newsreader will do that."

We're stood in front of the porch with Ed in the middle; Davina and I are at either side of him.

"Who's going to speak first?" Momentarily, my fear and nerves are directed more at the fact we're about to be on News at Ten, rather than on the fact my children have been abducted.

I can just about see a screen at the back of the van. Two people from the news team are watching it. I see the smiling faces of George and Alex, then Eloise flashed up, then a newsreader speaking. The sight of their smiles brings tears rushing to my eyes. I just want them back.

Mike, or Steve, is speaking into the camera.

"And whilst the search intensifies for the three missing five-year-olds, here their parents are waiting, desperate for news. Kerry, mother to the boys, would like to speak to our viewers." The camera swings round to me first, probably because I am the one nearest the microphone.

My voice falters but I must find the words. I have to do it for my boys. I swallow, then clear my throat. "More than five hours ago, my beautiful twin boys were taken from our garden. They're not wearing coats, I don't know if they'll have eaten and by now, they should be tucked up in their beds." My voice wobbles as I picture Alex with his arms around his sheep. "Someone out there has taken them or knows who has. Please, please if you've seen anything or know anything, please call the police." Tears are running down my cheeks. Ed puts his arm around me. It feels nice. I can't believe it's taken something like this to get a caring gesture from him. "I just need them back. Please help us."

The camera moves to Ed. "I'm the boys' father and can only echo what my wife says. I'd like to speak directly to the person who has taken our children. We can end this right now. There needn't be any repercussions. Please just take them to a safe place and let us know where they are. We are desperate for them to come home safely. That's all that matters."

I feel a warmth that he referred to me as his wife. The camera moves to Davina.

"My daughter Eloise is a gorgeous, bubbly five-year-old who will be absolutely terrified, wherever she is. I can only pray she, along with the boys, are safe and will come home soon. Please, everyone, take a good look at their photographs and keep an eye out for them. We need the public's help to bring them home safely." She's crying again too. "My husband died last month. My little girl is my world. Please help us. If anyone has any information, anything at all, you are urged to contact the police."

The news returns to the studio and I see the children's photographs flashed up again, before it moves onto something else. I feel absolutely wrung out.

"I don't know about you," I say to Davina, "but I need a glass of wine."

Chapter 36

Ed

"You should try to get some sleep," Polly says. "You won't be any good to anyone, least of all your children when they get back, if you don't."

"Sleep!" I know there's an incredulous tone in my voice. "I don't think I could. I need to be doing something. Out there, looking for them."

"We can get something together in the morning," Polly suggests. "Some posters perhaps, a team of locals. But we can't do anything until then. You need some sleep, even just a few hours. Honestly, you need to keep your strength up."

We've all forced a sandwich down, so that's something at least. Davina looks like she's dropping off in the armchair. I still don't know how she came to be here with Kerry, but that will keep until our children are back safely.

"The spare room is made up." Kerry nudges her. "Go and get your head down for a bit."

"Thanks." She gets to her feet. "You will wake me if there's any news, won't you?"

"Of course. Straight away." Polly touches her arm. "You two need to go too."

234

I'm not sure she knows that Kerry and I are separated. Surely she must have guessed. There's no way I'm getting in bed at her side anyway. Not under any circumstances. "I'll have a lie down on the conservatory sofa," I say. "I can't imagine sleeping though – I'll just have a rest."

Kerry looks too done in to argue but says, "why don't you just come up with me Ed? I don't want to be on my own."

"I'd rather be on hand down here," I say quickly. "One of us should be."

Polly watches us all. "Just go and get some rest, all of you. Even if you don't sleep, go and close your eyes. I'll come and get you, the moment I hear any news, I promise."

"What about you?" I notice that Polly looks tired too.

"I'm off duty at seven," she says. "Another colleague will take over from me to support you. Then I'll be back on at seven tonight."

"God I can't imagine them still being missing then." I'm too tired to think straight as I leave the room and head into the darkness of the conservatory, tripping over their toys and shoes as I go. Normally this would annoy me – right now I would give my right arm to be able to tick them off for it.

I lay on the sofa, watching the clouds roam around the sky, imagining my children and Eloise, out there somewhere. It's agony. Where I'm laid is where they usually sit to watch TV. I can't believe they're not back yet. The door-to-door and ground search has been called off until the morning but patrol cars are keeping a look out and blocks have been put in place at ports and airports. I'm glad it's going to get light early. I'm going to get myself out there. No way can I sit around here all day whilst my boys are God knows where. I can't believe how low BF has stooped to get at me.

I see each corner of each hour, yet when I haul myself back up at

6:15 am, I feel slightly more rested than I did. There's been the odd occasion I've dozed off. I put my head around the lounge door to offer Polly a coffee. She's already got one, and informs me there is no news of the children yet. The curtains are undrawn and I see the police tape flapping around in the early morning breeze with a uniformed officer standing guard. I wonder if he's been there all night. What a boring job. The forensic people concluded their investigations after a couple of hours last night. They didn't get any fingerprints but took some fresh imprints of shoes and car tyres. There was no sign of any struggle – the gate had been unbolted and somehow the children had been taken unheard and unseen. A different car had been noted by one neighbour, but she hadn't taken much notice of it.

I take my coffee to the office and fire up the desktop. I have to do something. *What to do?* Then it dawns on me. Social media. I post onto my own Facebook page first.

Last night my five-year-old twin boys, George and Alex were taken from our garden on Hawthorn Close in Farndale, along with their friend Eloise, also five. They have so far been missing for thirteen hours. Please, please look out for them.

I go onto the BBC news page and copy the photographs of them and Eloise. We *are holding a local search which will begin at 9 am. If you're free, we are desperate for some help to find them. Please meet at All Saints Church Hall. If you know or see anything, please get in touch with the Police or call me directly on 07700 900369.*

I feel better for doing something. I tag Kerry in. Davina and I are not friends so I can't put it on her page. Then I share it onto the Our Town page, the Leedspage, the Churches Together page – they're bound to want to help and the local Mumbler group thing. Hopefully there's a few mums on there who aren't at work today and will want to help look for them. Maybe the investigator will turn something up on BF today as well. I'm paying him enough. I then set about making posters, using the same photographs and leave the printer running them off whilst I head downstairs.

Polly is putting her coat on. "This is Helen, she'll be taking over from me for the day shift and I'll be back later. Even if they're found, there'll obviously be an investigation that you'll all need to be supported with."

I don't like her use of 'if' they're found. Last night it was 'when.'

"You must be Ed. I saw you on the news last night." Helen, a young blonde lady, stretches her hand out. "I've got twins too. Three-year-old girls."

"Thanks for being here." I smile through the stab of envy that her twins are probably still tucked up in bed, where they belong, being looked after by their daddy. In the cold light of a new day, the situation we are in seems even more unbelievable than it did last night.

"Has there been anything?" I look at them both in turn.

"Nothing," says Polly. "I'm sorry."

"Often, in cases like this," Helen says, "an abductor will make contact. Give some clue as to their reasons for what they've done or what they want to happen next."

"That's one of the reasons my mother went back home last night. In case he shows up there."

"I'm going to get off," Polly says. "I hope there's some news really soon. You take care."

"Thanks."

"Your mum isn't on her own at home, is she?" asks Helen.

"No, her partner's with her. She'd have been in touch if there was anything to report. I haven't really slept but I've had my phone with me the whole time she's been gone. I'll text her shortly."

"How certain are you it's your father who's taken them?"

"I can't imagine who else would have. Have you seen the statement I gave?"

"No, not yet." Helen walks to the window.

I look to see what she's looking at. "God look at that lot." There's already several reporters behind the police cordon.

"Should I talk to them? We already spoke on the TV last night."

"It won't hurt to go out and say something about the fact that they've now been gone overnight." She touches my arm. "But don't mention your father. It may dilute the intensity of the search if the public think your children are with someone they know."

"Should I get Davina and Kerry?" The shower's running in the en-suite and I've heard movement from the spare room.

"If you want to. Or you can just go out alone if you're OK with that. I'll come with you, obviously."

"I'll do it. I'll let them get themselves sorted." I take a deep breath and then follow Helen's small frame onto the driveway.

"Helen Gouldsborough," she announces to the small crowd. "West Yorkshire CID. Family Liaison Officer. Would you like a few words from the father of the twin boys who've been taken?"

They all push closer. "Is it true your father has abducted them?" One of the crowd calls out. God knows how they've heard that.

"Why were they left unsupervised?" calls another. I glare at her and ignore that question as well.

"I'll speak to you." I gesture to a man wearing a Sky News jacket. At least it's a reputable news company. They'll hopefully be happy with facts rather than speculation.

Within moments there's a camera and a microphone on me. Davina and Kerry watch from the doorway. "I've got this," I shout over to them. "I'll be back inside in a few minutes."

Helen places a hand on my arm before stepping back.

"Late yesterday afternoon," begins the reporter in the jacket, "three five-year-old children were taken from the garden behind me as they played. No one heard anything and all that was seen was a large, dark-coloured car. We have no witnesses who recall seeing *who* was driving or the children being taken.

They have now been missing for fifteen hours and police resumed their search this morning at first light. After we have heard from the father of the twin boys, George and Alex Huntington-Barnes, we will show the photograph of them all. He turns to me. "Mr Huntington-Barnes. What would you like to say?"

"Three very small children have been out all night." Tears spring to my eyes. I think the enormity of the situation is only just starting to hit home. I've been on autopilot so far. "They are not even wearing coats. We do not know where they are, if they are safe, and we are obviously going out of our minds with worry." I'm crying on national TV. "We can only say to the person who has them to leave them in a safe place and let the police know where they are. Whatever your reason for hurting us, the children do not deserve this – they are innocent five-year-olds who have done nothing wrong. I can only pray they are safe and will come home, where they belong, today. I will be out, joining the organised search today. If anyone in the locality can help us, we will be setting off from St James's Church Hall in Farndale at nine am. Thank you.

It feels better to be doing something constructive. I will print off a map with a ten-mile radius centred on home so we can divide areas amongst anyone who comes to help. Once I have got that underway, I'll give the private investigator another call.

"Well done." Kerry smiles through her tears as I walk towards them.

"Thanks," says Davina. "Do you mind if I get some tea and toast before we get this search started?" If anyone had told me twenty-four hours ago that I would be sharing breakfast with Davina, I would have said they were deranged.

"I'll sort some for all of us," says Kerry. "I don't feel like anything, but we've got to keep going until we find them."

"This is Helen." I gesture towards her. "She's taken over from Polly until this evening. Helen, Kerry. Davina." They all shake hands in a business-like fashion.

Messages are coming through thick and fast on social media.

Praying for the safe return of your little ones.

I can't imagine what you're going through.

Thoughts and prayers.

I hope you find them soon.

Family, friends, neighbours, colleagues, strangers; all offering hope and support for our children. I show them to the others.

"I'm hoping Adam and Mum will get over later," Kerry says, as she butters toast.

"What for?" That's all I need after everything that's happened lately.

"They're Alex and George's Grandma and Uncle. Why shouldn't they be here?"

I snatch my phone up as it rings. It's Trevor.

"Have you found anything?" I say, without even saying hello.

"I've got an address for you. And a registration number."

"That's great. Fire away." I grab a pen from the windowsill and a post it note that I find on the breakfast bar.

"Twenty one, Carlton Street, Burley," he says. "It's a through terrace, belonging to a Graham Warvis, who's currently away long term in South Africa. We've seen your man coming and going from the house. Though there's been no sign of him last night or this morning."

"Good work. I'll get over there with the police after I've got this search going. What about the reg?" I write everything down as he gives me it.

"OK, it belongs to a VW Passat. Dark grey. It's, Yankee. Delta.

240

Twelve. Echo. Tango. Sierra. I've had my assistant tailing it but again, it's not been seen since yesterday afternoon."

"Yesterday afternoon?" I feel like I'm hearing things.

"Yes."

"You're joking! RIGHT?"

"Unfortunately not Ed. I'm sorry."

"So why are you only letting me know this *now?*"

"I've only just this minute got the information from my assistant. He says his phone must have been out of signal, when he emailed it to me, and it went into drafts."

"I needed this yesterday Trevor - you know he's taken my children." The line goes silent. I'm so mad I can't verbalise it. "Are you still there?"

"Ed! I'm sorry. Of course I'll reimburse you and…"

"I don't bloody care about the money. I only care about getting my boys back, and hiring someone competent enough to do their job properly."

"I can't start to know what you're going through Ed, but we are onto him now. I'm taking sole charge at no cost to you. I've already passed the information we have to the police and I'll be in touch as soon as I find him. I promise we will find him."

I've heard enough and hang up. I haven't the energy to keep arguing and drag myself upstairs to get changed, grateful that I've left some of my clothes here.

Chapter 37

I t's looking like it is Ed's father that has taken the children. It's the dark coloured, large car thing, and the fact that it, and he, hasn't been seen since yesterday afternoon. Under normal circumstances I would be beside myself but there's a small feeling of relief within me. I keep telling myself he's their flesh and blood, and therefore, far less likely to hurt them. He's taken them to get back at Ed, to teach him a lesson, to get revenge. I feel it in my gut that we'll get them back today. My precious babies.

God, if it had been the other man who'd taken them, I don't know how I'd be coping. It can't be though. He wanted money. We'd have heard something, if it had been him. Besides, it's Davina who's dealt with him. He knows nothing about me. I don't think he even knows that someone else put ten grand in for Russell Lawson to be taken out.

I've got a message from Adam. *Do you want me to get across sis? I'd have to bring Laura with me though. You know what she's like.*

Do I? No thanks. *I'm OK. We think we might know who's taken them and the police have got more info now so hopefully it's just a matter of time.*

Who do you think's taken them?

Ed's Dad.

You're kidding! Why?

To get back at Ed. For the past. For being gay. I can't believe I've just said that. It's a huge step forward though. Over the last sixteen hours, Ed and I have pulled closer than we have been in the last sixteen months. There's been the odd moment when I forget we've even split up. Then it slaps me around the face again. As does the fact that my kids have been taken. I think I've faced up now to the truth that my husband is gay. I've no choice.

Do I regret what I've got involved with? Yes. I do. Big time. I got swept along by Davina's assurances that we'd both get our lives back with Russell out of the picture. I kind of trusted her. She seemed to have it all mapped out. The man who'd been recommended to carry out 'the job,' was supposed do it efficiently and professionally. When I think about it now, I can't believe such terms are attributed to the role of a contract killer.

Since Ed left, I've changed. I've had to. I've had to find a strength and a fight within me and look to a future as a divorced woman. I realise I'm no longer as obsessed with fitting in with the women from the gym, I couldn't give a rat's arse about what I look like or having the best of everything, so long as I can look after my boys. I take a deep breath. My boys. Finding them is all that matters.

"Are you coming to the church hall?" Davina says. "Or should one of us wait here?"

"I think one of us should wait," I reply. In case they get brought back." Davina and I haven't had a chance to speak without someone there apart from when we went up to bed last night, but I think we were both beyond any coherent conversation. I am sure I can sense in her face the same 'almost relief' I feel, that it doesn't seem to be the hitman that's got our children.

"I'll be stopping here." Helen says, wrapping her fingers around her mug. "With whoever is staying."

Davina and I look at each other. "It's your house," she says. "It makes sense for you to wait here. I'll help with the search. I can't sit here any longer."

"OK." God I hope they find them soon. A day at home, waiting, pacing around and tearing my hair out stretches before me like an abyss.

"Is there anything I can be doing?" I say to Ed as he slides his feet into his trainers. He's clutching a huge wad of posters. "I can't just sit here. Shall I put some of those out?"

"No, you need to stay here. He could bring them back anytime or they could find their way back." He pats the phone in his pocket. "We'll keep in touch. Ring me if there's any news and I'll do the same. Maybe get on social media a bit. Keep spreading information about the search and make sure people are keeping their eyes open. That would help."

"Do you think anyone will help with the search?" Davina asks, then without waiting for an answer, says, "who's going to do the talking to everyone who turns up?"

"I can do that," Ed replies. "The police will probably be around too. I'm sure there'll be a bit of a turn out." He tugs his jacket from the peg in the hallway. "There's been tons of comments on Facebook. They're three five-year-olds when all is said and done. Everyone is waiting for a happy ending. Come on, let's go and find them." He turns to Davina.

I'm not sure if Ed knows that I'm aware of the connection that exists between him and Davina. He sure as hell isn't aware of the allegiance she and I have. We've done a sterling job of disguising it. When all this is over, we've still got that to face.

The house is eerily silent after they have left, apart from Helen's tapping on her laptop. "It's all over the news," she informs me. "Local and national. I'm sure something will emerge today."

"We're only seven hours away from the twenty-four hour point." I fold washing and stack it on the arm of a chair. Alex's jeans. George's jumpers. Batman socks. Dinosaur pyjamas. Though they're twins, I've never dressed them the same. Even at five, they both have very definite ideas of what they want to wear anyway. The beautiful day streams through the window, taunting me. "I should be getting them ready for school now. At least with it being sunny outside, I know that wherever they are, they won't be cold. I can't get out of my head that after twenty-four hours, the likelihood of them being found is significantly reduced." Found alive is what I've read but I can't bring myself to say it.

"It's a slightly different situation." Helen closes her laptop. "That's if a complete stranger had abducted them. But in this case, we're suspecting that they've been taken by your father-in-law."

"I've never met the man." I point the remote at the TV to catch the nine 'o'clock morning news. "Neither have the twins. So yes, I agree, he's a little less likely to hurt them than a total stranger – at least they're his flesh and blood. It still doesn't explain why he'd take Eloise as well though." I'm glad Helen is here. It's helping me keep myself together a bit, just having someone to talk to. I kind of feel like falling apart but I have to stay strong. If anyone had asked me how I'd cope in this situation, I'd have answered, 'a jabbering wreck.' It's amazing how strong you can be when you *have* to be.

As I flick from BBC to ITV to Sky, they're all over the place. I catch snippets of what's being said. "Concern is growing …" "Missing for sixteen hours." "Out overnight." "Three vulnerable children." "Prayers are going to be said at school." They've put out a photograph of BF now. I study it, searching for Ed or my boys in his face and find nothing. They cite him as the possible abductor before flashing up a picture of his home. It's cordoned off, with a police constable guarding it. They flash up a picture of what must be his car. It's been caught on CCTV about thirty miles away at 6:42 am. According to reports, he's been alone in the car. What does that mean?

I've sunk onto the sofa by now. *6:42* am. I drop my head into my hands. This is an utter nightmare.

Helen touches my shoulder. "Shall I go and make us a cup of tea."

"I could do with gin." I smile weakly, then jump as a voice calls from the hallway. "It's my mother-in-law. Come in Marie."

"I need to talk to you," she says, mainly to Helen. "I've had him on the phone."

"Ed's dad?"

Helen pulls a notebook and pen from her laptop case and sits. "When did he ring you?"

"At about seven o'clock this morning."

"And you've only just come around?" I stare at her.

"I didn't know what to do." She dabs at her eyes with a hanky. "What I'm about to say puts me in a very bad light."

"Go on." I've got little sympathy for her. She's been sat on information, that could find the children, for nearly two hours!

"He's got them. And he's been planning it. Like we suspected, he's been wanting to get back at Ed for a long time, for putting him in prison and ruining his life. That's how he sees it anyway."

"Did he say why he'd taken Eloise as well?"

"No. They were apparently all asleep. He'd left them alone when he rang me."

"I still can't believe why you've only just let us know. I've been awake half the night. You should have rung me. We could have been out there, looking."

"I'm sorry. I knew they were safe."

"But we didn't."

"So where are they?" Helen hasn't written anything yet.

"I don't know." Marie wrings her hands in her lap. "All he wanted to talk about was the genetic testing kit he had bought. He had a right go at me."

"Genetic testing kit?" What is she on about?

"He says the boys aren't his grandsons." She glances at the photograph on the mantlepiece as she speaks. "He said he was relieved to be finally disproved as Ed's father. He reckons he knew he could never be the father of a queer."

"I don't understand." And I really don't.

She doesn't look at me, or Helen. Instead she stares at her hands as she continues. "I always knew there was a slight chance he wasn't Ed's dad. But I was so scared of him that I could never have said anything."

"Is this why he took the children?" Helen says quietly, her pen still poised over her notebook. "So he could run a genetic test?"

"That seems to be part of it. But hurting Ed was the other part."

"So why hasn't he brought them back? Now that he knows he isn't their grandfather?" Grandfather doesn't sound right. "Surely he's punished Ed enough?"

"They were still OK when I spoke to him in the night. But then apparently his car has been picked up on CCTV since, hasn't it?"

A coldness creeps over me. "When he took them, no matter what his suspicions were, they were his grandkids. Do you suppose they're at more risk from him now he's saying they're nothing to do with him?" I look at Helen.

"I'm afraid I can't possibly answer that. We've just got to find them." She looks at Marie. "I'm baffled though. Genetic testing kits usually have to be sent away to a lab."

"He's used an express service and a courier."

"He's an absolute nutter. How's he taken DNA from my sons." Suddenly I have visions of him with syringes or something.

"It's normally hair or a cheek scrape," Helen replies.

"Have you told Ed any of this?" I ask Marie, who is fiddling with her necklace. "He needs to know. And if he isn't his dad, who is?" I don't even know why I'm asking this. Really, we need to be acting. Finding the children.

"I was eighteen when I got pregnant with Edward. The man responsible was married at the time. It only happened once. I didn't know what to do."

"So what did you do?"

"I got married to the other one. I didn't tell him my doubts that there was a slim chance the baby might not be his. And I didn't tell the married one either."

"Don't you think Ed had a right to know?"

"The longer it went on, the harder it was to tell the truth. I can't believe it's come out like this."

"Ed will be relieved. But he'll want to know about his real dad?"

"Well that's just it. He doesn't get on with him either."

The realisation immediately hits me. "Alistair," I say.

"Yes. Like I said, he was married at the time."

"Does he know?"

"Not yet. I thought I should speak to Edward first. What an utter mess."

I can't take it in. Alistair is Ed's Dad! That means he is grandad to George and Alex. He can't stand being around them! And my kids and Davina's daughter are being carted around by some homophobic weirdo who's just found out he's not related to them after all. Right on cue, I get a text from Ed.

Seventy people have turned up to help look for them. The police have given them all areas to look and I've given them posters. It's going well but no news yet. Anything there?

It's the first time I've had a text off him in weeks. "Marie, can you stay with Helen in case they get brought back here? I'm off to find Ed.

And we need to let DC Burnley know about the fact that he's definitely got them."

"I should be the one to speak to…" Marie begins but her voice trails off as I stride from the room.

Seconds later, I'm backing the Range Rover from the drive, waiting for the PC to move the cordon.

As I head towards the church hall. I get another text from Ed. I pull over to read it.

His car's been picked up again. The police are after him. He's got the kids in the car and he's on the M62.

My heart hammers harder within me. I ring him. "Where exactly?" I gasp.

"Just before the Huddersfield exit. They'll get him Kerry. Any time at all. We're going to get our boys back."

"Thank God." I clutch the phone like it's lifesaving debris. "I'm going to head over there. I need to be there for them. Where's Davina?"

"She's out with one of the search teams. She's given me her number, so I'm just about to let her know. God, I hope they're alright. If he's hurt a hair on their…"

"I need to go, Ed. It's going to take me a while to get to the motorway. I'll ring you." Telling him about what Marie's told me can wait. Getting there quickly is the only thing that matters.

The boys have always loved the motorway. They're both car mad and pretend the three lanes are having a race. At five, I can already see the young men they'll be. I reckon I'll have to get saving for driving lessons and first cars when their seventeenth birthday comes into sight. I'm told it comes around quicker than we can possibly imagine. Occasionally I've complained about the hard work, early mornings and lack of freedom. But from now on I'll never wish our time away. I'll make the most of every moment with them. I just can't believe that this man would put my babies through this.

I tap the steering wheel. The lights are taking ages. To my left, I watch the activity around McDonalds. Families in the drive through queue. Kids coming out and reaching for the hands of a mum or dad. I usually say no to McDonalds with my two but when I get them back, they can have anything they want.

I thump the button on my radio to see if anything is coming through on the news about his car. They've probably stopped him by now. They'll have maybe closed the motorway. The boys and Eloise are hopefully, by now, sat in the back of a police car; my two will be excited about that. They'll be arresting that monster of a man. If I get my hands on him. Bloody adverts on the radio. I'm on the slip road now. No one is letting me in. Pillocks. The motorway is rammed. I've always felt nervous driving on them. It's all the big wagons. I feel nervous beside them. My dad once told me that the bars along their base are to stop people being decapitated if their car ends up under them. The weather comes on. Surely travel will be next and they might mention something about the motorway. No. A song. *Despisito.* George loves this! It was played at Ben Strachan's birthday party last year. He came home singing it and asking 'Alexa' to play it repeatedly. It's 10:55 am. The news will be on in a minute. I'm just a couple of exits away from Huddersfield. I should have asked Ed which direction the car was travelling in. What an idiot. I've just assumed, they're travelling away from Yorkshire, when they could have been returning. They could be going the other way, towards Hull. But I remind myself that no matter where they were going, the police will have them now. The children will be safe and will be being checked over. They'll probably have to go to hospital for medical assessment.

This is the eleven o'clock news. Good morning. We first bring you some breaking news regarding three missing Yorkshire five-year-olds, taken from their garden in Farndale, just before four pm yesterday.

Police are currently dealing with a second sighting of a vehicle which is believed to be involved in the abduction of George and Alex Huntington-Barnes and Eloise Lawson. They are thought to have been abducted by their estranged paternal grandfather. The M62 has been closed between junction 33 and 35 Westbound. We will bring you more news as we get it.

I'm going the right way! I've just passed junction 32 so I'm not far away. Within a few minutes, I'll be back with my boys. I'll do anything it takes to help them forget what they've just been through. Decorate their rooms, take them on holiday. I can't believe it's taken something like this happening for me to realise that absolutely nothing else matters – they are my world. Sod Ed. He can go off with as many men as he wants. How on earth could I have been so blinkered and stupid that I got involved with Davina? How I thought, sinking ten grand into the killing of that man would bring my husband back, I'll never know. If my boys are safe, I will do anything to put things right. Probably starting by moving well away from the man we hired and starting again.

M62 Closed.
Leave at next exit.

Everyone is indicating and moving into the left-hand lane. As I approach the exit, a queue is building. I go straight past it. Other drivers are probably wondering what I'm doing. After half a mile there's no going any further, the carriageway is blocked by police cars. In the distance I can see a helicopter. My heart is pumping out of my chest as I abandon my car on the hard shoulder. I would have expected to see someone in one of the police cars but there's no one around.

I run through the inside of the blockade and start up the hard shoulder. I gasp at sudden sirens behind me. A police car, then an ambulance squeeze through a previously unseen gap and hurtle forwards, presumably towards the spot where the helicopter is circling. What is going on? Why an ambulance? I keep running. I hate running, normally. I tried taking it up after the twins were born, and on a whim, I spent over a grand on a double running buggy. I think I took it out twice. But as I lurch forwards, I can't run fast enough. I'm scared of what I won't find as much as what I will. Another police car and ambulance, this time with two fire engines, screech past me. Fire engines. If they've just stopped his car and rescued the children, why are fire engines here? My phone's ringing in my pocket. There's no point me answering it – I've no breath left. I've just got to get to my kids. I keep going. After a few moments, I see it all in the distance. An Aldi lorry is laid on its side and a white car has smashed into the central reservation. I stop. Take it in. It's nothing to do with my two. It must be a different incident. So where are they? Ed said the M62. The news said the M62. Where are my sons? Someone is running towards me. A policewoman.

"Get back. You're not allowed here." She gestures in a sweeping away movement. "What are you playing at? We've closed this road."

"I'm..." My gaze travels to some movement to the left of the carriageway. Fire crew and paramedics are skidding down the embankment. I take a few more steps forwards, gulping back bile as I see how the fencing at the side of the motorway has been smashed through.

There, on its roof, is another car. "My children..." I begin as I fall into the policewoman's arms.

Chapter 38

Ed

She's not answering. I've lost count of how many missed calls she'll have. No one's telling me what's going on. Reports on the media are just promising 'more when we have it.' DC Burnley has called the search teams back. I pace the parquet floor of the community centre, recalling when I've been here with the boys, dropping them off for playgroups or birthday parties.

My gaze travels to the poster I've pinned onto the notice board. My smiling twins, displaying perfect rows of baby teeth, one a butter-wouldn't-melt smile, the other, a cheeky impish grin.

Below them, a photograph of Eloise. The sole reason that Russell had said he must stay with Davina. He didn't want to be a weekend dad. She's got his soulful eyes and the same shaped nose. In her, Russell will live on. God, I miss him so much. Bloody hell Ed. What the hell are you thinking about him for? Your sons are still out there, and you're thinking about Russell.

"Edward." DC Burnley's voice sounds hollow in the large room.

I look at him expectantly, waiting for him to tell me that the boys are shaken, or tired, and a bit hungry, but that they're OK. And Eloise of course. Russell loved her so much. Once I felt a stab of resentment at his devotion to her and this has rumbled back up a little, especially since I walked out on my own boys. But Davina has been quite reserved in the face of all this. All that matters is getting our kids back. What's gone before has gone before.

"Edward. I will drive you to the hospital." His voice is grave.

I search his face for answers. "Are they OK?"

"Let's talk in the car. We need to get going. They're on their way to the hospital."

"Who?" A cold hand of fear clutches at my heart.

"All of them. There's been an accident."

I tug my seatbelt across myself, mentally calculating how long it will take to get to the hospital. Twenty minutes if the roads are quiet.

"Davina," I say. "Does she know?"

"She's being taken over by one of my colleagues," he replies. "Your wife is with the children."

I let a jagged breath of relief out. They're with Kerry. For him to say that must mean they're OK. Alive anyway.

"What happened?"

"I don't know too much at this stage. We'll find out more when we get there."

My eyes are fixed on the road ahead. I need to get there. "What do you know?"

"Only that the car they were travelling in left the carriageway. They've had to be airlifted. There's a lorry and another car involved as well."

"What about *him*?" I spit the last word out. I hope he's dead.

"I don't know, Edward. Let's just get there."

I tug my phone from my pocket and try Kerry again. She still doesn't answer. I fire off a text.

What's going on? I'm on my way to the hospital.

Mum's phone's switched off. I try her landline.

"Hello."

"Alistair, it's Ed. Is my mum there?"

"Nope."

Knobhead. His is the last voice I want to hear right now. "Where is she?"

"Out."

"Look. I know you can't stand me, or my family, but this is urgent."

"I don't know where she is. Ring her mobile."

"I've tried. It's off."

"Then I can't help you."

I begin asking him to get her to ring me the minute she turns up, but quickly realise I'm talking to a dead line. I feel like punching something.

DC Burnley taps his fingers against the steering wheel as we wait at the third red light in a row. I try Kerry again. It rings out. Dread pools in the pit of my stomach. I see the air ambulance in the distance as it lowers to the roof of the infirmary. "My boys," I say in the silence of the car. DC Burnley stays quiet. I get a sense he knows something but can't, or won't tell me. "Come on, come on," I say to the next red light. I want to get there, and don't want to get there. "Please," I turn to him. "If you know something, please tell me. I need to prepare myself." I glance at his silhouette; he seems deep in concentration.

He sighs. "I can't tell you anything with any certainty right now. Apart from one of the passengers in the car that crashed into the central reservation has died."

"What about the children?"

I watch as he briefly closes his eyes then says. "All I know is that it is touch and go for one of them. But I don't know which one. I'm sorry I can't tell you any more than that."

"Oh my God." I find myself hoping it's Eloise. Evil bastard, I say of myself. How could I think such a thing? A sob catches in my chest.

Oh my God. An innocent child. The daughter of the man I absolutely adored. And it's my father who's done it.

The roof of the hospital is too high for me to make out any activity up there as we pull into the entrance of the hospital. I guess one good thing about arriving in a police car is that it can just be abandoned near the doors. I tear in, ahead of PC Burnley, past an ocean of people I don't really see and up to a sign saying reception. "My sons have been brought in by helicopter," I gasp to the woman. "Where are they?"

"Excuse me," says a woman, clutching a compress to her head. "Do you mind? I'm getting booked in."

"My five-year-olds have been in a road accident. Don't you think that's more urgent than your…"

DC Burnley takes my arm and steers me to the other side of the counter whilst gesturing for someone on a computer for attention.

"I was listening," she says. "Just give me a minute." After what feels like an eternity, she says, "I'm looking at the admissions and we've just had a sizeable one. They've all been taken to Resus."

"Where is it?"

"I'm afraid you can't just go in there. I'll have to find out what's going on first."

"But two of them are my sons." I scan the overhead signs for a clue of where to go.

"Take a seat sir. I'll double check the identities of who we've brought in and I'll get someone to take you through. I promise I'll not be long."

I can't sit. I pace the floor for several moments, then I turn to DC Burnley. "Do you know where it is? Resus? They can't stop me from going in. I'm their father."

"It's that way." He gestures his head to the right. "But I didn't tell you. I'll wait here until the woman comes back."

I head towards where he's indicated, scanning the signs for more information. "Where's Resus?" I gasp at a passing porter, who is wheeling someone in a chair.

"Just there," he replies. "You'll need to ring the intercom." And then, as though he senses my impatience, he adds, "and they don't always answer straightaway."

I press it repeatedly. Just when I think no one is going to come, the door opens and Kerry falls through it.

I grab her shoulders. "What's going on?" I say as she raises her eyes to mine. "I've been ringing. And texting."

"Alex," she gulps. "I think we're going to lose him." She steps away from me and slides down the wall.

"No!" I tug at the door which has closed after her. "We can't."

"He's going into theatre. He's got massive internal bleeding. I feel sick. She rocks herself forwards and backwards against the wall.

I stare at her. This isn't happening. My. Little. Boy. Can't. Die.

"George?"

"Concussion. Broken bones. He should be OK." She's still rocking against the wall, on her heels. "I can't believe it. I can't fucking believe it."

"Where is he? We should be with them. With both of them."

"He's going for x-ray. I had to get out of there. Alex has already gone down."

"Gone where?"

"To theatre."

"Eloise?"

"I don't know. She didn't look too good in the ambulance. Davina's just got here." She stands, anger blazing from her eyes. "That man. That fucking man. When I find out where he is…"

"I know. But for now all that matters, Kerry, is our boys." I reach for her hand. "Let's get in there."

After a minute of pressing the intercom, still no one has come. I can hear muffled sounds and bleeps coming from the other side of the door. "Come on, come on," I say as I notice DC Burnley striding down the shiny white corridor.

"Your little one is being prepped in theatre," he says as he gets to us. "I've just spoken to the A&E sister. He puts a hand on my shoulder. "Your father is also on his way there too. He's suffered massive brain trauma."

"He's not my father." My voice is a snarl. "And if he survives his operation, I'll be turning his machines off. If my son dies because…"

"He's under armed guard," says DC Burnley, pulling on the Resus door as it finally bleeps.

We dash in behind him. "Where's my son? George?" Kerry demands of the nurse.

"He's been taken to X-ray."

"Why didn't you wait for me?"

"With all respect," the nurse replies, "getting him looked at is our priority. A porter has taken him and a nurse has gone down with them."

"And Alex?"

"The on-call surgeon has just arrived. If you want to wait in the relatives' room down the corridor, we'll keep you posted."

I don't know where to go or what to do. I feel too stressed to make any sort of decision. Eventually I say, "I'll go to George. You go and wait for Alex." I touch Kerry's arm. "They'll be fine. I promise. They're made of tough stuff. They take after you."

Chapter 39

Kerry

My boys would have been really excited to travel by helicopter. But as it happened, George was given an injection to knock him out as he was in so much pain. Alex was already unconscious. Outwardly, he looked perfect, as though he hadn't sustained any injuries. George, however, was covered in blood and with his leg stuck out at an awful angle.

Eloise also came in the helicopter. She was strapped to a backboard. I held her hand, listening to words like paralysis, morphene, stand-by and transfusion as we made the fifteen-minute helicopter ride. I don't know what happened to the bastard who did this to them. They should have left him there to rot. At least they didn't try putting him in the helicopter with my boys and Eloise.

I listen peripherally as DC Burnley makes enquiries as to his where-abouts. He might be badly injured and under armed guard, but I don't feel safe knowing he's in our vicinity. However, I can't think about that. The twins need me. I head towards the family room, catching a nurse as she heads towards the theatre door.

"My son. Alex Huntington-Barnes," I begin. "He's..."

"I'm just going in," she says. "I'm part of the support team. Go and get yourself a cup of tea and I promise we will keep you posted."

I step inside the family room, a simple space with two small mushroom-coloured sofas facing each other. There's a coffee table and a box of tissues in between them. I sink onto a sofa and drop my head into my hands. I'm too numb to even cry. I've never been religious but I guess this is as good a time as any to start praying.

I don't know how long I stay in that position before footsteps walking up and down outside the room begin to irritate me. There's a pile of magazines and a hot drinks machine on another table. I make some tea to distract myself. I keep saying over and over in my head. *Please God, let him be alright. Please God, let him be alright.* I'll do anything for him to get through this. I poke my head through the door in case anything is going on that I need to know about. The person responsible for the pacing is Davina.

"Come and sit down." I catch her arm as she passes me. "I'll make you a drink."

She does as I say but can't sit still. Her gaze flits from the door, to the tea machine, to the table, to the wall, then the blinds then back to the door. "She might never walk again." She gets up again as quickly as she sits down. She walks to the window. "Eloise."

"My son might not even survive." I thought I'd be in bits, facing something like this. It's as though part of me has shut down. I sink back to the hard sofa, my hands wrapped around the warmth of the paper cup.

"It's all our fault." Davina sits opposite me again. "It's like karma or something."

"What are you on about?"

"What's happened. What do you think I'm on about? If we'd paid up. If I'd responded to that note earlier. I just didn't know what to do. That's why I came to see you. Then look what happened."

I stare at her. She's clearly rattled. "I don't follow you. I thought it was Ed's father driving."

"I got a look at him as they were wheeling him into theatre." Davina leans forwards and lowers her voice. "It's him. Tony. The man we hired."

"You're kidding." We've unknowingly hired Ed's so-called father as our hitman. You couldn't make it up.

"If he survives and talks, we're screwed," she says. "Or if he survives and does something worse than..."

"How could he do anything *worse* than what he's already done? My son's in theatre, fighting for his life."

"How did he know where to come?" Davina stands up again. "He came to your house. He must have been watching us."

"It's like a terrible dream." I wrap my arms around myself. "I should never have got involved."

"You wanted my husband dead as much as I did. You said it yourself."

"I was an idiot. I should have just let Ed go. You should have left Russell. Neither of them have been worth it in the scheme of things."

"I've stood by him for years. Put up with how he treated me." She lifts the paper cup to her lips but doesn't drink. "He made it very clear he'd fight me for Eloise. He had stuff on me too. Stuff about my past. He'd have probably won."

"Suppose all three of our kids are OK?" Something in me lifts, then falls again. "What if he survives? Will he come after us again? I haven't got any money. I can't pay him what he wants."

"Seeing him earlier on the trolley – it will be a miracle if he does. He looked pretty fucked up." It's the first time I have ever heard Davina swear.

"It's my son I'm more bothered about. I'll blame myself for ever if anything happens to him."

"I think we're going through enough." Davina puts her cup down.

"What's done is done. We paid thirty grand between us. Russell is dead and what matters now is getting our children through this. We might even get away with no one ever finding out about our part in this."

I close my eyes. "Somehow we've got to stop Ed finding out who that man is. He knows it's his father in there, and that's all he needs to know."

Davina and I jump as Ed bursts in. "The police let me look at him. I've just seen BF, before he went into theatre."

"How long have you been stood there?" I stare into his face, trying to read his expression.

"Long enough." He crouches in front of me.

"Where's George?" I lower my gaze to the floor. "Is he alright?"

"He's asking for you. That's why I came to get you. But first, I think you'd better tell me what's going on?"

Maybe Davina made a mistake. "The man," I say. "Was it definitely BF? Did you get a proper look at him?"

"One hundred percent. So perhaps you need to be explaining to me what thirty grand has to do with Russell's death."

I look over at Davina, still clinging to some hope that perhaps she made a mistake and maybe the man we hired for Russell is hopefully long gone by now. If this is the case, I've already decided I will be moving away with the boys and starting again.

Ed stands. "It's alright Kerry. Like I said, I've been listening. I heard every word you said. I knew Russ would never kill himself. Nor would he have taken the risk he'd been made to look like he had. You two arranged it." He points at us in turn. "He said you were selfish, Davina – he never mentioned psychopath. And you, Kerry – you…"

"I'm sorry." What else can I say? "I wanted him gone. I wanted you back. When Davina needed to put more money in, I kind of got swept along with it all."

"You got swept along with arranging for the only person I've ever properly loved to be taken out. You evil bitch. Like you're so arrogant, you just thought, getting him out of the way would make me come running back to you."

"The only person you've ever loved," Davina sneers. "Have you heard yourself? He was having it away with anything that moved. You didn't even know him. Not really. He deserved everything he got after the way he treated me."

"What, he deserved to have thirty grand spent on ensuring his death. Like that. So who did it? Who killed him?"

"His name's Tony. He was recommended to me."

"BF's name is Anthony. It can't be the same person. Surely." He falls silent. I can literally hear the brain cogs whirring around. "It can't be BF who took Russell out. He hates gay people. He wouldn't have got involved with the way he died."

"He wouldn't have needed to," Davina says. "He just needed to pretend." The room falls silent.

"So what happens now?" I eventually say.

"I'm going to tell the police," Ed says. "That Russ's wife, and my wife paid extortionate amounts of money to have an innocent man killed. By my so-called father."

"We didn't know he was your father."

"Mum!" We all look up as Marie bursts in.

"Where are they? I came as soon as I heard what was going on. Are they all OK?" She rushes towards me and takes my hand.

"George seems like he'll be alright, but we're not so sure about Alex." My voice cracks. This is all my fault. What a jealous, stupid woman I have been. "He's in theatre. They're letting us know."

"Oh my God!" Her hand flies to her mouth. "He's going to come through it, isn't he?"

"We don't know, Mum," Ed says.

"What about Eloise?" Marie shifts her attention to Davina.

"Not good. She might be paralysed."

"Who did this to them?"

"Who's the one person in the world who would stop at nothing to get back at me?"

Marie sits beside me on the sofa. "No," she says. "He wouldn't hurt his own flesh and blood." I look at her, aware I have a trump card if I decide to play it.

"It seems BF will stop at nothing to earn a bit of extra money as well." Ed looks at me and then back to his mother. "He kills people for money, doesn't he, Kerry?"

She glances at me then back at the floor. "What are you on about?"

I'm startled by a loud knock at the door. "I'm Professor Fleetwood," announces a man as he enters the room. "Can I check who you all are in relation to Alex Huntington-Barnes?"

"I'm his mother." I can hardly get my words out.

"I'm his father," says Ed, offering a hand that isn't accepted.

"I'm his grandma," says Marie. "How is he?"

"I'm sorry to have to tell you," Mr Fleetwood says, sitting on the sofa beside me, "that Alex has passed away. He lost too much blood. I'm so sorry for your loss – we did everything we could."

I hear a scream echoing along the corridor, followed by a wailing sound. Then I realise it is coming from me.

Chapter 40

Ed

In silence, Kerry and I follow a mortuary technician along a corridor. I've barely spoken since the consultant broke the news. I don't think I believe it yet. That's why I need to see him. We've had to wait for them to get him 'ready.'

My gorgeous, full of life, funny, clever baby boy is dead. Until I see him with my own eyes, I can't possibly believe it. We haven't told George yet. He's been sick three times with the concussion he's got, his arm and leg are in temporary casts and he's covered in cuts and bruises. We've left him laid on a trolley in A&E with my mum. She also seemed too shocked to cry. I think she'll need to see Alex too, to believe it.

As we approach the sign saying *mortuary. Please ring for attention,* I've zoned out. I imagine people in white coats, fridges lining the walls and bodies wheeled out on metal slabs.

A woman with sympathy in her eyes, wearing ordinary clothes, answers the bell. "You must be Mr and Mrs Huntington-Barnes," she says. "We had a call when you were on your way up. Come in. I'll take over." She nods at the man who escorted us here. She leads us into a little room, just like the relatives' room we sat in a couple of hours ago.

It's softly lit with a large painting of a candle hung on the wall. There's a box of tissues on the table, along with leaflets about bereavement, counselling and how to arrange a funeral. A funeral. How do you ever go about arranging a funeral for a five-year-old?

"I can't tell you how sorry I am," she begins. "To lose someone at any age is just dreadful, but to lose…"

Her words are cut into by Kerry's sobs. The woman looks at me as though she expects me to approach and comfort her. This isn't the time for an explanation. She sits down beside Kerry and passes her a tissue. "Let me know when you're ready to continue," she says in a quiet moment. "There's absolutely no rush."

"Is he ready to be seen?" I ask, closing my eyes. There's not many men, I hope, that will ever have to see their dead child laid out on a trolley in the mortuary. I cannot believe that is what I am about to see.

"I will go through with you what you can expect to see in there," she begins. "In a few moments, when you feel you are able, you can go through that door. There's another door opposite it, which opens into the room where Alex is. You can either stay inside the entrance of that door and look at him through the glass, or you can go around to the other side and sit with him." She gives Kerry's hand a squeeze. "Feel free to move the chairs around. Alex has a sheet up to his neck, but his face is visible. You've already seen his head and facial injuries, so hopefully you already know what to expect there."

"Can I touch him?" She pulls her hand away from the lady to wipe the snot that's dripping from her nose into her lap.

"Yes. He looks peaceful. He looks like he could be sleeping."

Kerry breaks into a fresh wave of tears. I haven't cried yet. I can't.

"Spend as much time as you want with him," says the lady. "And for as long as he's here, you can make an appointment to come in as often as you need to. Have you any questions?"

I shake my head. Kerry doesn't move. She's rocking backwards and forwards again, her face smeared in strings of snot.

"I'll leave you to go in when you're ready. Like I said, take as much time as you need. If you need me for anything, or when you're ready to leave, just ring this bell." She points to a button next to the door.

"Thank you," I say, like a robot. This isn't happening. It can't be. I stand at the same time as the woman. I watch her leave by the door we all came in. I reach for the door handle which will lead me to my son.

Kerry stands.

"You wait there if you don't mind," I say. "I want a few minutes on my own with him."

She sinks back down as I leave the room. I can almost hear the silence as I stand in the corridor between the two rooms. Bile burns the back of my throat. I see a room saying WC and rush into it. I've not really eaten anything so just lean over the toilet, retching. My eyes water with the force of it but they're still not tears. What's wrong with me? My beautiful boy is dead and I can't even cry.

Kerry will no doubt have heard me in the toilet but hopefully has stayed where she is. I've got to do this on my own. Taking a deep breath, I press down the handle and push the door open. There he is, on the other side of the glass; my angel. The colour of the lighting in here makes him look as though he still has colour in his face. All that's visible is his head and like we were told, he looks as though he's sleeping, apart from his eyes being slightly open.

As the woman said, there is a door to the left of the glass. I need to be next to him. I'm not sure how long I stand gazing at his face. He has a few facial injuries from the accident. Anger rises again. BF. The bastard. I'll deal with him shortly. I swallow it. He's not going to take away these moments with my son. I'm never going to see him laugh again, or get to kick a ball around the park with him. I'd never even taught him how to ride a bike. I touch his wisp of a blond curl at the front of his head. He'd have had all the girls chasing him. He'd have done so well at school. I'm never going to be able to give him driving lessons, fatherly advice or buy him his first pint. His future, his whole life, has been so cruelly snuffed out. That fucking man is going to pay for this.

I sink to a chair beside him, momentarily looking around the room we are in, which is painted in peach. A curtain is pulled over another door at the end of the room. It's different from the stark metal and white I was expecting. My attention returns to Alex. My darling boy. This time yesterday he would have been running around, full of energy, laughing, just being Alex.

"Wake up son." My voice sounds odd in the silence. "Please wake up." I press my nails into my other hand just in case I'm dreaming this. I want to wake up too. "Daddy's here," I continue. "And I love you so much. I-I just can't believe this has happened." I still can't cry. I drop my head into my hands. I want to know where he is now. Whether he can hear me. Whether there is such a thing as heaven. I need to know that he isn't totally and completely just dead.

I sense Kerry's presence. I look up, see her looking at her son through the glass. She carried him and his brother inside her. She must be in agony. For a moment, my instinct is to comfort her, but then the truth hits me like a truck. It's her fault. I don't know the ins and outs of her jealous actions towards Russ. However, without her arrangement with Davina, whatever it was, he would still be here. And so would our boy.

I rise from the chair and walk to the exit of the room without looking at her. I sink to the sofa, back in the family room, and read the words on the picture in front of me. *Those we love don't go away. They walk beside us every day.* I feel grief wrack through my whole body, bringing sobs from deep within, my shoulders aching with their force. I make a sound I didn't know I was capable of. My innocent, beautiful little boy is dead.

I'm curled in a foetal position when mum walks into the room. I don't know how long I've been there. I sit up and she sits beside me. I turn into her and sob into her shoulder. "I know. I know," she says over and over. "I can't believe it either. It's not sunk in yet."

"How's George?" I pull away from her.

"He's going to be fine." As she looks at me, I see her age. I never noticed it before, but Alex had her eyes. Had. I've just thought of him in the past tense. The pain throbs through me again.

"Who's with him?"

"One of the nurses. I've come to check on you."

"Do you want to see Alex?"

She pulls a tissue from her sleeve and blows her nose. "I don't know if I can, Edward. I think I need to remember him as he was." She rakes her fingers through the front of her hair. "Seeing him like that will destroy me."

We sit in the quiet for a few moments. I want to go back into Alex. Spend every moment available with him. Before long, he will be in a funeral home, then he'll be taken away from us forever. Burnt or buried. Fresh sobs erupt. I just can't believe it.

"How's Eloise?" To be honest, I don't really care. I just want my boy back.

"She's in theatre." Davina's sat outside, waiting for news.

"BF?" I spit his name out. I hope he's dead. It'll save me going in there and doing the job myself.

"He's..." She stops. "He's in intensive care in an induced coma. But they've said he'll probably pull through."

"I want to see him." I speak through gritted teeth. "And I'll be unplugging him whilst I'm at it. Or smothering his evil face." I feel sick again. Sick with rage. Sick with grief. I feel like I want to climb to the top of this hospital building where my boys were brought and hurl myself from it. I want to be with Alex. But then I remember that

George needs me too.

"He's under armed guard," she says gently. "And I don't think it would do you any good to see him."

"He has to pull through." Suddenly, I swing from wanting him dead to wanting him to pay. In fact, I want them all to pay. Russell is dead. Alex is dead. "There are a few things you should know, Mum," I begin. I'm interrupted by a soft knock at the door.

Mum gets up and opens it. "Can you just give us a few minutes?" She says to DC Burnley. "Edward was just going to tell me something."

"No, come in." My voice finds a momentary strength. "What I'm about to say, you need to hear it too."

Chapter 41

Parkside Victim and Tragic Twin - Justice

Sentencing took place earlier today in the case of Anthony Huntington, Davina Lawson and Kerry Huntington-Barnes at Leeds Crown Court.

The trials were held earlier last month when Huntington was found guilty of multiple charges in relation to the abduction of three local five-year-olds back in April; one of whom died as a result of his actions.

Five-year-old Alex Huntington-Barnes was involved in an accident caused by his estranged grandfather, Anthony Huntington, which left him with fatal injuries. His twin brother George was left with less serious physical injuries but with a life of emotional scarring. Eloise Lawson, also five, has been left with permanent paralysis and may never walk again.

The trials and sentencing also dealt with the death of father-of-one Russell Lawson, 36 of Kirby Brompton, who was discovered in a ground floor room of the Parkside Hotel in the early hours of Saturday March 19th by a member of hotel staff.

The cause of death had been recorded as sexual asphyxiation. Initially, the death was thought to be accidental, but CCTV, coupled with minute traces of Lawson's semen, trodden into carpet outside the hotel room, suggested the involvement of a second party.

Whilst police mounted a detailed investigation, Russell was finally laid to rest in April and the search intensified for the truth behind his death.

It transpired that his widow, Davina Lawson, had hired a man for the sum of £20,000 to carry out her husband's murder. This had been in collaboration with a local woman Kerry Huntington-Barnes, who admitted having paid £10,000 to Mrs Lawson.

Leeds Crown Court heard how Davina Lawson had 'snapped' after years of tolerating her husband's affairs with a string of men, to satisfy what she described as a 'serious sex addiction.'

Judge Clive Thornton-Hughes, when summarising the cases, did not dispute how sickened Mrs Lawson might have been by her husband's lifestyle, but asserted that she had laid immediate claim to his life insurance and other assets. She had then continued her life in a way not expected of a person regretting their actions. He added that she could have simply ended their marriage instead of taking her revenge and had been punished dreadfully, with the permanent paralysis her daughter now has to suffer.

Co-accused, Kerry Huntington-Barnes, he said, had already received the ultimate punishment too, the death of her five-year-old son. He acknowledged that although not directly involved in the 'contract killing' process, her actions had led to the three children being put in grave danger and the death of an innocent man.

She had admitted to being complicit in the process of 'eliminating' Russell Lawson in the belief that she would somehow save her marriage. This was after months of living in the knowledge that her husband was engaged in a sexual affair with him.

Both wept as the Judge slammed the actions of the two women, and what they had inflicted on their children, and stated that marital problems are not solved by arranging the brutal killing of a love rival. He reiterated his shock and dismay, at what they had indirectly inflicted on three innocent children.

In a further twist, and unbeknown initially to all parties, the hitman they had recruited at a total cost of £30,000, to lure Lawson to the sexual act that would result in his death, was in fact Anthony Huntington, father-in-law, of Kerry Huntington-Barnes, though estranged from the family for many years.

It was only when media attention began to mount around the case and, Huntington started demanding more money, and issuing threats to his estranged family members, that his identity was eventually uncovered.

Although he initially denied all charges, the presence of his vomit in the vicinity of the crime scene increased the strength of the case against him. From being placed in the vicinity, he could be compared to the CCTV footage obtained from the Parkside Hotel.

Anthony Huntington, described as a professional hitman, was sentenced to life imprisonment, and to serve a minimum of ten years in a high security prison, for the murder of Russell Lawson. He is now also, being investigated for other possible contract killings in the locality.

Huntington was sentenced to a further five years for causing death by dangerous driving and another three years for child abduction, after pleading guilty to the charge of unlawfully abducting and imprisoning the three children. His sentences are to run consecutively.

Judge Thornton-Hughes described him as a man without conscience or empathy, and therefore of maximum danger to civilised society. On sentencing, Judge Thornton-Hughes said he might have passed only a total of twelve years, but the fact that Huntington had attempted to blackmail and threaten his two accomplices into parting with more money, compelled him to pass a more severe sentence.

Davina Lawson, led from the court in tears, was found guilty of conspiracy to murder and sentenced to six years imprisonment. The judge described her as a callous woman who used her husband's sexual orientation and behaviour as an excuse to gain control of the wealth and freedom his death could offer her.

Kerry Huntington Barnes received a sentence of four years imprisonment after pleading guilty to conspiracy to murder. It was acknowledged that she had joined the collusion at a later point, but no grounds for diminished responsibility were accepted.

Judge Thornton-Hughes concluded his summing up by recognising that the biggest victims in the situation were the three children, caught in the crossfire of this dreadful situation.

Because of vengeful, jealousy-driven conduct, displayed by so-called adults who are meant to put their children first, one child has lost his life and the entire futures of the other two children have now been affected.

He added that the homophobic bigotry displayed by Huntington was something that must be stamped out of society and he was pleased to be taking a person, whose views could inflict such damage, out of the community where he could perpetrate more. The judge ended his summing up by saying he would be watching the subsequent investigation into unsolved local murders with interest and that Huntington will be dealt with using the severest penalties, should he be linked to any of those cases. We will bring more to you on this in due course.

Epilogue

Three years later

"So, how was she?"

Mum slides onto the breakfast bar stool next to me and stirs her coffee.

"OK. Looking forward to getting out." I blink away images of the awful visiting area. "She's a shell of who she used to be though. I almost felt sorry for her."

"Well, she's certainly been punished. Three years of not seeing your son is a long time." She takes a sip of her coffee.

"Forever of not seeing your other son is even longer."

We both sit in silence for a few moments. Alex would be eight now with the same gap-toothed mouth and core flick of his brother. We try to talk about him with George as much as possible. Keep him alive whenever we can.

Although George is oblivious to all around him right now. I can hear the whirr of whatever racing game he is glued to, through the surround sound in the lounge.

We live with Mum for the time being. I thought of staying in the house with George, but couldn't face it after losing Alex. Then Kerry's trial. We scuppered Alistair's plans of moving in. And that's another story.

I'd tried to get in to see BF in intensive care. Really, I'd been planning to rip all the plugs out of the wall. Kerry had screamed at me, "He's not even your dad. Tell him Marie. I'm not the only person who's hurt you."

It had been an awful way to discover the truth. Mum had crumpled. We'd only just seen Alex in the mortuary and after what I had told DC Burnley, Kerry was being allowed to see George before being taken to the station with Davina.

I couldn't believe it. The man who'd I'd thought was my father had hated me so much, that part of his reason for taking my sons was to disprove his parentage to me with some ridiculous genetic test. I wouldn't be surprised if he had run them off the road on purpose, once he found out they weren't his grandsons.

After all, killing people wasn't a problem for him. His involvement in another fifteen cases has come out since he was sent down. It seems he had a lot of enemies who were only too pleased to tell the police what they knew. He'll rot in there. I've thought of visiting him, but that wouldn't do me any good. He's nothing to me.

"So, have you discussed what will happen when she's released?"

Mum's hair's a lot greyer than it was and there's a permanent sadness around her. She partly blames herself for what happened, and has often said that if she'd told the truth earlier, she could have prevented things. And I've lost count of the amount of times she's mentioned that she would have died in Alex's place. She's had eighteen months in counselling, but misery still hangs over her.

"She's going to get a two bedroomed place. Somewhere close to school," I reply. "I'll have to reintroduce George to her slowly. I guess eventually we will share looking after him. So long as he's OK with that."

"Are you sure that's a good idea?" Mum sniffs. "George is settled with us now."

"Kerry's still his mother. And she's not a bad one. Not really. She's made some awful judgement calls, but in not forgiving her, I would have been hurting myself more."

"You're a kind man, Edward." Mum's eyes fill with tears and she puts her hand over mine. "You're not going anywhere, are you?"

"Maybe one day Mum. But not in the foreseeable."

Getting into another relationship is still unthinkable. My life now is George and work. And Mum. Yes, I'm in my thirties, but we've had to pull together to get through all this. George is settled here. Seeing Kerry again will no doubt throw him off kilter, so I've got to keep the continuity here for him. He's still at the same school with the same friends. They had an assembly for Alex a month after he died. I sat at the back with Mum and mostly we held it together. They flashed pictures of Alex onto the big screen, sang songs and the members of his class each offered a different memory of him.

I miss him beyond words. I can barely remember his funeral but will never forget the small white coffin that no parent should ever have to see. Kerry had been remanded by this time. Although she didn't pose a danger to society, she had been advised that she would be looking at a definite custodial sentence, so she might as well start serving it sooner rather than later.

According to her barrister, she had received a stiff sentence for her involvement in Russ's death. The judge had taken a dimmer view because she had continued to withhold the information even after the children were abducted.

I haven't been in touch with Davina since she was jailed. She went to a different prison to Kerry; Eloise went to live with her Grandma. I don't know how badly paralysed she was left by the accident. I never knew Eloise, but I think of her from time to time. After all, she was Russ's daughter.

All sorts of rubbish came out about him at the trial: sex addiction, debt and fraud to name but a few. Davina tried to throw it all out there. But I knew who he really was, and no amount of mud-slinging could ever change that.

Mum's on her own now too. The entire thing was too much for Alistair. It was an immense shock for both of us, discovering after years of only just tolerating one another that we are father and son. We're in touch though. We've been for a beer a time or two and it's becoming less strained.

We've taken George out together too. Alistair's started asking questions about Mum again. Who knows how things will pan out in the future? We've all been through a hell of a lot.

"Let's get out of here for a bit," Mum gets up and rinses her cup in the sink. "We could have a drive out to the coast. It's too nice a day for George to be sat on that blinking X-Box."

I smile at her sudden enthusiasm and remember her taking me, just the two of us, to the coast when I was around George's age. We have *to* start to live again. Losing Alex and Russ has shown me how short and precious life is. George is my priority and I am now living a life that is peaceful, and being true to myself.

"Come on George," I call. "Turn that thing off. How do you fancy an ice-cream at the seaside?"

He's in front of me within three seconds, smiling his big toothy grin, and I pull him towards me.

Before you go...

Join my 'keep in touch' list to receive a free book, and to be kept posted of other freebies, special offers and new releases. Being in touch with you, my reader, is one of the best things about being an author.

If you want to read another of my psychological thrillers, follow this link to find out more about The Yorkshire Dipper.

Book Discussion Group Questions

1. 'Living a lie' is a common theme in this book. Discuss.
2. To what extent have the characters received their comeuppance?
3. Explore the reasons Ed married, though confused about his sexuality.
4. In the early chapters, to what lengths would Kerry go to, to fit in?
5. Discuss how homophobia manifests itself in this story. How have attitudes to homosexuality changed over the years.
6. What was Russell's 'hold' over Ed?
7. Talk about the short and long-term effects adult behaviour has on the children.
8. To what extent can 'BF's' background offer any explanation for the person he became?
9. What might become of each character next?
10. Do you think Kerry deserved a custodial sentence?
11. Have any of the characters changed for 'the better' over the course of the story?
12. Discuss Marie's 'taste' in men.
13. Can a marriage be revived once it is dead?
14. Discuss how Davina's situation might have led her into the course of action she took.
15. To what extent does mental health play a part in this novel?

The Yorkshire Dipper - Prologue

My next psychological thriller...

The cold is like a million knives slicing into me. I've never felt anything like it. I try to shout, but I can't even breathe. How did I end up here? One minute I was cosy in the pub, knowing I'd had one too many, the next I was coming outside for some air, stumbling at the side of the river. Then, well, I don't know if I will ever see the light of day again.

I see the faces of my family in my mind. Again, I try to scream. Not a whimper. I'm going to die. *No, I am not.* I'm going to fight. I try to kick, to tread the water. Pretend I'm a girl again, doing my level one at the local baths. One minute in the deep end. But I can't move my limbs. I'm being frozen alive.

Something is sucking me under. A force is pulling me down. My foot lodges within something hard. I hold my breath. Try to kick again. All is silent apart from the terror inside me. I really am going to die. Here, in this river where people dispose of shoes and shopping trollies. I can't move. All around me is inky black.

I see a faint moonlight filtering through the surface of the water. Thoughts won't come anymore. My body is going to explode. I try, one last time, to return to the surface. To get another breath.

Instead, I choke as freezing liquid engulfs me from the outside in. It fills my stomach, my lungs. I'm sinking further. This is it.

Available at Amazon

By the Same Author

Psychological Thrillers
Left Hanging
The Man Behind Closed Doors
The Yorkshire Dipper
Hit and Run
The Hen Party
Last Christmas
Drowned Voices

Memoir
Don't Call me Mum

Poetry
Poetry for the Newly Married 40 Something

How-to Books for Writers
Write your Life Story in a Year
Write a Novel in a Year
Write a Collection of Poetry in a Year
Write a Collection of Short Stories in a Year

Acknowledgements

Firstly, a huge thank you to my wonderful husband, Michael, for all his help and the faith he has in my work. He acts as first reader for my early drafts and is an amazing support.

Thanks also to my book cover designer, Darran Holmes, who always manages to capture exactly how I wanted my book covers to look, and to photographer, Sue Coates, who took my author photo.

A special acknowledgement must go to my two beta readers, Edwin Stockdale and Vicky Sykes for early feedback on the story, and also to my amazing Advance Reader Team for the time and trouble they always take to give me feedback on my later stage manuscripts. Thanks also to my friends and family for continuing to support and believe in me.

The experiences I've personally known over the years have indirectly offered much of the emotion and material for my writing. Although difficult at the time, I can now be grateful for the empathy and personal growth they offered.

Lastly, and importantly, to you, the reader. Thank you for taking the time to read this. I hope you enjoyed it.

About the Author

The domestic thrillers I write shine a light into the darkness that can exist within marital and family relationships. I have been no stranger to turbulent times myself, and this has provided some of the raw material for my novels.

I am a born 'n' bred Yorkshirewoman, and a mum of two grown up sons. In my forties, I have been able to pursue a long-held ambition of gaining an MA in Creative Writing and make writing my full time occupation. Recently I have married for the second time and have found my 'happy ever after.'

This is not something you will find in my novels though! I think that we thriller writers are amongst the nicest people you could meet because we pour all our darkness into our books – it's the romance writers you've got to watch…

I plan to release four novels per year and if you'd like to be kept in the loop about new books and special offers, join my 'keep in touch list' or visit www.autonomypress.co.uk. You will receive a free book as a thank you for joining!

Printed in Great Britain
by Amazon